RAW

BRUTALITY AS ART

EDITED BY ADAM HUBER

SNUFF BOOKS
PHILADELPHIA, PA
SNUFFBOOKS.COM

For Joseph McGee…

A wonderful friend and writer.

You'll be missed.

CONTENTS

1
Introduction
By Adam Huber

2
Violin Concerto No. 9 in A Minor
By Inanna Gabriel

12
Painted in Red
By Brandon Ford

23
The City of the Dancing Lights
By Frank Roger

31
Pretty Face on Genocide
By Steven L. Shrewsbury

44
Scavenger Hunt
By R.J. Cavender

49
Still Life with Soul Juice
By L.L. Soares

63
A Willing Donor
By Kevin Lucia

79
Onyx Noir
By Jessica Lynne Gardner

92
One Headlight
By Eric Enck

110
The Exhibition
By James Roy Daley

130
Cry Little Sister
By John Edward Lawson

144
Squeezing Out Sparks
By Stephen Couch

161
You Come When I Call
By Trever Palmer

172
Chef of the Gods
By Andrew Wolter

184
The Maker of Fine Instruments
By Brendan Connell

INTRODUCTION

If nothing else, "Raw" has been a learning experience.

What started out as a themed anthology based around a single story (which ultimately didn't even make the final cut) turned into an incredible slush pile, months of editing, and new relationships with more than a dozen writers. As Snuff Books' first anthology, "Raw" has provided more than a few bumps in the road along the way, but when all was said and done, came together as a book we're incredibly proud to see go to print.

From newcomers to horror and bizarro genre veterans, what you'll find in the following pages are extremely varied takes on artistic expression and brutality.

The collection begins and ends with lyrical screams, and in between is everything from skewed body sculpting and painting with blood to "soul juice" slurping muses and perverse performance art.

"Raw" is nothing if not eclectic, and hopefully you can find the beauty in the brutal and bizarre the same way the talented group of contributors have.

-Adam Huber, Editor

VIOLIN CONCERTO NO. 9 IN A MINOR

BY INANNA GABRIEL

"Five minutes, Mr. Gaston," the girl calls into my dressing room door. I nod, and she leaves again. I've held my tongue with her, but I do wonder how anyone who works in the field of concert music, even in a clerical position such as hers, could suspect I wouldn't be aware of how long it is until I'm due onstage. The orchestra is clearly audible from my dressing room; the woodwinds have just completed the first repetition of their theme and are beginning to crescendo. I know, as would anyone familiar with the piece, that this is approximately two minutes into the movement, which is just over eight minutes long.

I slide my bow along a block of rosin and pass it across the strings one final time, making certain my violin is in tune and everything is perfect. I look into the mirror by the door, making sure my dark brown hair is neat and in place. A few curls at the nape of my neck defy the rigid style, but this is all right; this little bit of nonconformity is perfectly in line with my composition style. I go ahead and leave my dressing room even though six, not five, minutes still remain.

I wait in the wings until the overture is complete. From the audience comes the sound of conservative applause, followed by a shuffling of paper that tells me they are consulting their programs and reading my name. It's unlikely it comes as a surprise to any of them; they have paid dearly for the privilege of hearing the premiere performance of my newest concerto. I perform each of my compositions myself only once. After that, the orchestras must use other soloists and I return to my primary work of composing.

As I step out onto the stage, there is again applause, more robust this time. I give a polite bow to the conductor, lift my violin and begin to play.

* * *

Her name was Catherine.

The tentative opening notes of the piece are the story of the first time I saw her. I notice her in the parking lot of a shopping mall, her long, chestnut hair glowing in the bright afternoon sun. It moves with her as she places several shopping bags, most of them shades of red, pink, and black, into her small, silver car. Like her sleek hair, her body is also long and slender, and she moves with exceptional poise and confidence. She exudes an air of elegance, even while performing such a mundane task.

Long, smooth strokes of my bow describe her graceful movements.

I remain inside my own vehicle, drinking in her beauty. A subtle quickening in the tempo signifies how my interest is piqued, how I feel drawn to her in this moment. After a few measures, the tempo increases even further and grows somewhat dissonant. This is my desire to know her, my need to get closer.

The orchestra comes in now, as I follow along behind her, driving through the city streets. She turns into the gated lot of an apartment building and a tense, *pizzicato* melody depicts my caution. I don't dare to follow her through the gates, but remain outside, watching, as she gathers up her bags and enters the building through a side door.

The exterior of the building is covered with rough, off-white stucco, dotted with patches of exposed brick and tile accents, giving the impression of a Spanish villa. The music of the orchestra takes on a momentary flamenco-like lilt as indication. The door she enters, set inside an arched recess, is wooden, stained a rich red, its top rounded to fit the alcove. It appears to be an entrance to an interior hallway rather than directly into her apartment. I look along the three stories of windows, their frames stained the same color as the doors, and wonder which iron-railed terrace might be hers.

Once she is well away, my violin takes up the fore of the music again as I step out of my car and approach the gates on foot. They're locked. The design, however, is flawed; the gates would certainly disallow cars and other vehicles, but there is space enough on either side for a pedestrian to walk through.

I had noticed, watching from a distance, that there were markings on the ground inside the parking spaces. Upon entering the lot, I'm happy to have my suspicions confirmed; they are numbers and letters, clearly corresponding to units inside the building. My fingers flutter over the strings, an excited trill showing my delight at this discovery.

There are no empty spaces along her row, so I am unable to count in order to figure out which number is concealed underneath her tiny, sporty vehicle. The music slows now, as I peer around, confirming I'm alone. A *pianissimo* strike of the tam-tam tells of my dropping to the pavement, and pushing forward on my belly, crawling under the car until I can see, by the thin band of fading daylight that stretches across the quiet, dark space, the number. *Her* number, written on the asphalt in fading, oil-stained, yellow paint: 3C. I'm elated, and my own instrument joins the violins in the orchestra in a joyful crescendo.

The expectant series of notes from the beginning of the piece, where I first saw her and followed her home after her shopping, repeats here. She emerges from her apartment the next morning, a Saturday, and I follow as she drives. I play a light, patient tune as she sips coffee and munches a toasted bagel at a sidewalk café, as she pets a tiny dog trotting past her on a leash and smiles. That smile earns a pause in the music; the orchestra drops away, and after one small note on my violin, so do I.

All the world stops for Catherine's smile.

Of course, I don't know yet, at this point in the piece, that her name is Catherine. I know only that the music must continue, and so it does.

The orchestra and I follow her through her day. After her coffee, she goes to a salon, where she treats herself to a manicure and pedicure, and then to a park where the piccolos describe the birds she watches from a bench beside a fountain. She smiles again, and the music smiles with her, the same as before.

A variation on the theme, then, for Monday. She returns to work, and I am left free to explore her surroundings. That bright passage as she drank her coffee becomes a journey of discovery, as I see her kitchen and living room for the first time, see the dining room that sits between the two, decorated in a unifying palette, combining the warm, dark tones of the sitting area and the bright, sunny colors of the kitchen. The frivolous music of her visit to the nail salon darkens as I step into her bedroom. As I brush long, slender fingers across silky cool fabrics secreted away in sachet-scented drawers, the music pauses, but only for half a measure; the world doesn't completely stop for *my* smile.

I rarely follow standard formats in my composition. So although it's common for the second movement of a concerto to be slower than the first and the third, the second movement of this piece is *andante*, as I take the first steps of our mutual dance. I know her name now, have seen it on her mail and in her diary, have heard it spoken on her answering machine and in her voicemail with the love of a mother, with the anger of a jilted lover, and with the casual indifference of salesmen and secretaries. I now know what she does for a living; the natural grace I noticed the first time I saw her is explained by her work as a dance instructor. I am fully a part of her life now, as the richness of the orchestra illustrates. The melody of my own violin stays one beat ahead of the orchestra throughout this section, signaling my readiness, my eagerness, to make contact with her for the first time.

There is a short clamor of percussion as I bump into her on the street, just outside the café where she eats breakfast on Saturday mornings. It's no accident, of course, but my violin speaks my feigned apology for my clumsiness, and the world, once again, ceases to spin for a brief period.

As I walk past her table several minutes later carrying a cappuccino, she suggests I join her instead of rushing off. It's not quite time for this yet, however, and I decline, an almost imperceptible murmur of the bassoons belying my façade of disinterest.

This section repeats, as we meet again the following Saturday. There are, of course, slight variations in the music; we don't collide on this occasion, for example. I make light of that initial meeting, joking that I promise not to knock her down this time. The pause in the music here is the longest thus far, as a world that stops for her smile all but ends entirely for her laughter.

The tempo picks up even more at this point, an allegro minuet that tells of a developing romance. My violin converses with that of Concertmaster, the first violinist. The orchestra provides the background for our delicate *pas de deux*.

We dance through several weeks of courtship. I continue to visit her home when she isn't there, and later she welcomes me in. On many nights, I slip out of the bed that we now frequently share, continuing to learn more of her secrets after she has drifted off.

A new variation on the melody begins as we sit together on her sofa, before a glowing fire. The room is intimate and warm, decorated in shades of red and plum and dark wood. The remains of the plate of fruit and cheese we have been sharing sits on the

5

coffee table in front of us, an almost empty bottle of wine beside it. We hold our glasses, talking softly. The fire reflects in her brown eyes and casts shadows across her fair skin. I've been playing for her, and my violin lies next to the plate, the bow neatly beside it.

A dissonant note, so harsh and sudden the audience, upon first hearing it, may believe it to have been a technical error on my part, indicates my fatal mistake. I use the name of one of her friends, someone I've heard speaking to her in voicemail messages but whom she's never mentioned to me.

The First Violin asks me how I know this name. I respond with a lie, told in stuttering notes. She repeats the question, a bit more *forte*. I respond with the same lie, altered slightly, *pianissimo*. Her third inquiry is *fortissimo*, demanding a valid response.

My reply is the cadenza of the movement, a whirl of pleading notes and invention. In the past, the tradition was for the soloist to improvise his cadenzas on the spot in order to demonstrate his skill. While I do not invent this segment onstage as was once done, the music is composed with the tone of improvisation, just as I improvise my excuses and feints to Catherine.

Her responses to my lies are implied in my continued fabrications as the cadenza continues, increasing in tempo and intensity. At last, near the end, I falter. My music darkens, but it doesn't diminish in any other way. The orchestra joins me once again as I stand.

She is frightened as I tower over her, dangerous in my cornered state. She sees the threat in my eyes, and she cowers with the string section as my confession storms down upon her. "Yes," I say to her. "I know your friend's name. I know the names of all of your friends, your family, and of everyone else in your life. I know where you go, and when, and what you do when you get there. I know your every intimate detail, down to the smallest."

The First Violin asks me how I know these things.

I reply, with a shaking note, confessing all, revisiting the themes from the first movement in succession, all darker and stronger than before.

It turns out that the world stops for her cry as well.

As the third movement begins, she is still crying, still afraid. The First Violin demonstrates this as my own instrument continues to express my frustration, which is escalating into anger. I take a menacing step towards her, announced by the timpani, and then another. She stands as well, and with each step forward, she takes one back. The theme of our dance replays, but slower this time, and darker. This is the real dance, the one that I knew, deep down, we would reach. This third movement always comes in the end, must come, and it is each time, at its core, the same.

A rattling in the percussion section foreshadows the danger, the double bass and bassoon alternate, measuring out the beats of her pounding heart. She backs through the arched doorway, moving from the living room into the dining room. After several more steps of our tango she comes into contact with the table, and can back away no further. Another line comes from the First Violin, a confusion of accusation and pleading that enrages me.

With a wail of my violin I am upon her. I press her back across the table, pushing and bending her until her feet leave the floor. As I continue to hold her down, her screams pass through first the cellos, then the violas, and then finally the violins as the cries grow in pitch and intensity. She kicks and spits and curses me, the orchestra in a frenzy as my violin continues on with its singular purpose.

A concerto must, after all, have its climax.

I often forget that in the beginning, sometimes allowing myself to believe that the beauty and simplicity might go on. But at some point I always remember, as I do now in this powerful crescendo, that for the composition to be right, for the inspiration to be worthy, there must be a conflict, there must be some finalizing drama.

The Concertmaster begins the dialogue between her violin and mine again, her music a mélange of the harsh dissonance of screaming, the short, choppy notes of pleading, and the gentle melody of coaxing. My violin demonstrates my response to the confusion of music, remaining consistent for the majority of the tussle. As she struggles against me, I hold her down. As she begs me, I ignore. But when she slathers me with false flattery I, and my music, pause.

I step back from the table, and look down at her. I know her kind words are a lie, an attempt to win over a man she believes has gone insane, to convince him—*me*—to awaken to what he is doing and to stop. I recognize the falsehood, and though I do stop momentarily, it is not, as she has hoped, because I have become aware of some madness that my actions have betrayed. Her words have inspired in me a fury beyond any I have felt towards her thus far.

I take a few deep breaths, savoring my anger, while the orchestra carries us along for a moment. Catherine sits up and slides down from the table onto her feet; the First Violin is silent throughout this process, as she says nothing further, afraid that she might reignite a fury she believes she has abated.

I allow her to stand, allow her to step away from the table. She smiles, but this time the music does not stop, as I know the smile is insincere. She continues with her flattering words, her apologies for expressing suspicion.

With a long, powerful note, I step forward once again. She immediately sees she has misinterpreted my calm. She steps away from me again, one awkward step backward after another, until, just as she was stopped by the table before, this time she reaches the kitchen counter and can go no further. Her eyes widen as the First Violin depicts her gasping attempt to hold back her screams in short, unsteady notes. As the double bass and bassoon resume the pounding of the rhythm of her racing heart, she reaches out beside her towards the knife block on the countertop.

I see what she is doing, but make no effort to stop her. My violin describes my slow, steady progress as I approach her.

She removes the largest knife from the block and holds it in a trembling hand, but it's not until we're almost touching that she makes any threatening gesture with it. She makes one awkward swipe, the blade passing across my cheek. It cuts me, but the wound is shallow. I scarcely feel it, and I smile.

Calmly, I reach out and take the knife from her hand; she doesn't even try to stop me, which disappoints me somewhat, as her passivity could well ruin the passion of the music. She's giving up far too easily; I had believed there was more determination and fight in her. I realize that I need to renew her terror if I am to save the piece.

The First Violin, as well as the rest of the orchestra, has quieted to match Catherine's resigned calm. A sudden burst from my violin describes how I seize her by the throat and pull her forward. I have only one hand available with which to grab her, the other still holding the knife. But my hands are long-fingered and strong, trained by my art, and I have no great difficulty clasping tight to her slender neck with just one of them.

I drag her, sputtering and gagging, through the kitchen and dining room and back into the living room. I drop her onto the rug before the fire, where she lands in a heap, gasping for breath. As I drop to my knees astride her, she thrashes about, kicking the leg of the coffee table and upsetting the wine bottle. It falls towards her, spilling its remaining contents. The rich red liquid splashes across her face and she inhales some of it, choking as she continues to struggle against me. The heavy bottle rolls off the table and hits her. It opens a gash in her forehead, but she isn't knocked unconscious, for which I am grateful; I need her to be awake and aware for the sake of the music.

I'm delighted to see not only is she conscious, but that her terror has returned. A few drops of blood from the cut on my cheek drip down onto her face as I lean over her, and they mingle with the blood running from the wound on her head. The choking, both from my hand as well as from the aspirated wine, has robbed her of most of her voice, but I can see the screams in her eyes. The First Violin voices these screams for her, as my own instrument begins a dark variation of a theme from the second movement, the minuet of our courtship. This melody builds into the final cadenza, the finale towards which our dance has always been building, towards which *all* of the dances inevitably build.

I maintain my position, straddling her prone form, still holding her down. I don't slick my hair back other than for performances, and it falls into my face now, requiring me to brush it out of the way. I see my own eyes reflected back at me in the blade of the knife, my own blood streaked across the image.

As the cadenza begins in earnest, I draw the bow across my violin as I draw the knife across her throat. I continue to pass the knife back and forth, applying minimal pressure, playing her as I would play my instrument, its movements mimicked in the strokes of my bow.

After several passes, the knife makes its way through to the artery. The blood sprays hard, and it has drenched the violin and bow on the coffee table nearby before I notice it. Alarmed by this, I throw the knife aside. I can't allow any more of her blood to damage my violin; I must end this now.

I pull her up by her long, dark hair. She is still conscious and opens her mouth yet again, but if she had little voice with which to scream before, she now has less than none. Even the effort of trying to cry out seems to weaken her further, blood still fountaining from the severed artery. She is all but gone already as I twist her body around and force her head into the fireplace.

She thrashes, and the choppy, anxious strokes of my bow describe her convulsions. I hold her by the shoulders until, after about a minute, she is still. I pick up my violin from the table.

It is wet and sticky with the spilled blood already cooling on the delicate, varnished wood. The instrument is centuries old, and all but priceless. Every detail, down to the tiniest, can affect the sound of a violin; I wonder whether this blood bath will enhance or diminish the quality of my music. I pick up the bow, position the violin under my chin, and begin to play. Tiny droplets of blood spray from the bow hairs, spattering the carpet, the wall, and the painting that hangs above the hearth. The fine spray dusts the ivory marble of the mantelpiece, and I can feel the same mist on my face and hair as I continue to play. The music I play over her body matches that of this final segment of my cadenza.

Soon, however, smoke begins to back up into the room, and the alarm on the wall in the kitchen begins to scream. This is where the orchestra comes back in to finish the piece, heralded by the piccolo sounding for the alarm. I hurry through the small apartment and into the kitchen to deactivate the alarm. I then return to the living room and remove Catherine's body from the fire.

As I begin to clean up, the music comes to an end.

* * *

After a last repetition of the main theme from the first movement, the piece finishes with first the orchestra, and then my violin, fading away to nothing; the stopping of the world is forever this time.

I lower my violin and my bow as the audience begins to applaud. I bow, graciously accepting the praise, then exit the stage. The backstage area glows as the hall lights come up behind me and I hear the rumble of voices and feet as the intermission begins.

"Mr. Gaston," several voices call at once. A small crowd of reporters has gathered in the backstage area, waiting to descend upon me with their cameras and recorders in order to bombard me with questions. I am very strict about the absence of members of the press before a performance, but I am generally patient with giving limited comment afterward.

One young woman in the sea of reporters stands out. She is small in stature and in build, but forces her way through the tangle of larger people with great determination. "Yes," I say, responding directly to her as she reaches the front of the crush.

"That was a spectacular performance, Mr. Gaston," she says. She means it, but I'm well aware that she'd have said it even if she didn't.

"Thank you," I reply.

"So," she goes on, tipping a small digital recorder in my direction. "Now that you've finished your premiere performance of this piece, are you already working on the next one?"

I take her in more carefully. She is a few years younger than Catherine was, a redhead to Catherine's brunette. Her blue eyes sparkle, even in the muted backstage light, and her smile radiates. Watching her as she fought her way through the aggressive crowd, and seeing her now, in her triumph at having gained my exclusive attention, I see in her the very passion I longed for in Catherine near the end. "I think I've found a starting place, at least," I say, smiling back. "What's your name?"

She looks surprised, but responds readily enough. "Elyse," she tells me, something friendly and personal in the response. She then repeats herself, more professionally this time, adding a surname. "Elyse Milan."

"That's a beautiful name, Elyse," I say. "Musical, even. Would you be interested, Ms. Milan, in doing a more lengthy interview?"

She looks as though she's just won a sweepstakes. "Of course I would," she says.

As we leave the hall together, the first few notes begin to play at the back of my mind.

PAINTED IN RED

BY BRANDON FORD

No, this wasn't right. It wasn't *good*.

With contempt, with disgust, Jeff Alcott glared at the piece he'd spent the past week of his life working on. The piece he'd spent the past week *perfecting*. An involuntary sneer lifted and stiffened his upper lip and he groaned in defeat. He pulled the canvas from the easel. Holding it in both hands, he stared until the straight lines became blurred and uneven. He stared until the colors morphed into one huge, distorted mess. He stared until nothing made sense anymore.

What had once been a beautiful sunset over a deserted precipice was now a display so sickeningly amateur, so abysmally ordinary; he felt his stomach twist in knots. With gritted teeth, he snapped the canvas in half over his knee, leaving a multicolored smear of paint along the thigh of his faded jeans. He felt a sharp twinge when the wood cracked and splintered, but ignored the pain as he tossed the canvas aside.

Fresh paint clung to his fingertips as he reached for the whiskey bottle at his feet. He'd already had more than enough, the haze impairing his ability to balance, but he didn't care. He needed to feel a little numb. He needed the escape. For just a little while, he needed to forget the failure he'd become. The failure he'd always be.

Grasping the bottle by its long neck, he lifted it to his lips and chugged. The last of the soothing fluid burned down his throat. He closed his eyes and savored the sensation. When they opened again, he saw only picturesque perfection hanging from the wall before him. The bright, vibrant colors. The crisp detailing. The subtle, yet brilliant splash of cobalt blue that made the piece come to life, as though the image leapt straight from the frame. The painting showcased an extraordinary talent—a talent Jeff knew he'd never possess.

The whiskey bottle slipped from his grasp and bounced along the wooden floorboards without breaking. Staggering out of the room, he started down a corridor, reaching for the wall, stopping every so often to keep from tumbling forward. In the living room, he found a seat on the couch and collapsed. Turning toward the bare windows, he eyed the setting sun and swaying branches of the tall oak trees lining the block. He'd been drunk an awful lot lately, especially in the afternoons. Once upon a time, he thought the alcohol would inspire him and free his mind. He thought a bottle of vodka and maybe a few lines of coke would give him the ability to focus long enough, deep enough, to create a piece as masterful as the one he'd just staggered away from. But these days, he only used the booze and nose candy to forget Kyle.

As brothers, Jeff and Kyle may have shared the same parents, the same genes, the same blood, but they'd *never* possessed the same talent.

Jeff was studying the greats by age six. By age ten, he could name every piece decorating the walls of the local museums. Picasso, Michaelangelo, Da Vinci. He'd memorized them all, understood their drive, and longed to be among them. He painted and sketched throughout his teen years. Majored in the fine arts at State University. Earned his degree through hard work and determination. But his paintings never caught the attention of anyone in the industry. Galleries all over the city snubbed him, belittled him, tactlessly told him that he just didn't have what it took…and probably never would. At age 29, he'd accomplished nothing more than a strong sense of self-loathing and an insatiable urge to feed his addictive personality.

Kyle, who never really had to work for anything, made a few wise investments shortly after college, and it wasn't necessary for him to join the work force. At least not right away. Anxious to find a way to fill his time, he picked up a paintbrush for the first time less than two years ago and already had his own shows. Kyle, four years Jeff's junior, never really cared much for the skill and precision it took to paint an image worthy of a museum wall.

It was Lynn Devoreaux that first discovered Kyle. Lynn, owner of the city's most accomplished and respected art gallery, had been sent to examine Jeff's work. But his paintings had been overlooked, and Lynn fell in love with the pieces Kyle had devoted little to no effort creating. Horrified, Jeff could only stand by and watch all of his dreams and aspirations shatter. With pursed lips, he felt the stab of betrayal penetrate.

It was then Jeff began to feel hatred, raw and true, for his one and only brother. He'd always resented Kyle's breezy approach to life. He'd *always* been envious of Kyle, but when he saw Lynn write out that check—an advance for Kyle's next three pieces—it had morphed into loathing. Jeff had worked so hard for so long, and even still, he couldn't match Kyle's talent. Part of him knew he'd *never* be as talented as his little brother.

But things could've been worse. Kyle had always been more than happy to share the wealth, even giving him the spare bedroom rent free. Yeah, Little Brother sure was generous.

Watching as the room spun round, feeling his eyelids grow heavy, Jeff eventually passed out. He woke several hours later to the sound of the front door slamming, footsteps approaching the living room. His mouth so dry, his head pounding, Jeff wanted to escape to the kitchen for a few aspirin and a glass of water without being seen. The last thing he wanted was to look into the eyes of the brother he despised.

Pulling himself off the couch, he glimpsed the dark sky beyond the windows before rushing for the refrigerator. Woozy and unbalanced, he hadn't even made it two steps before he heard Kyle's voice.

"Jeff! What happened to you, man? I thought you were coming to the show tonight."

Show?

Kyle's latest exhibit. Jeff hadn't been to one in over a year. Watching people fawn over Kyle made him sick to his stomach.

"Sorry," Jeff said, turning briefly to meet Kyle's gaze long enough to see his girlfriend Gina.

"Are you all right?" Kyle asked. "You don't look so good."

What a surprise. Jeff hadn't showered in days and hadn't shaved in more than a month. Personal hygiene had become an awful nuisance he tried to avoid. Jeff gave a slight nod but didn't look up.

"I'm sure he's just tired," Gina offered. With an awkward laugh, she hiccupped and placed a hand to her mouth. She looked like Jeff felt—her eyes unfocused and half-open, her frame wobbling.

Jeff folded his arms, taking a moment to examine them both. "You two been celebrating?" he asked, pulling a bottle of Evian out of the fridge and popping two Advil.

"Yeah," Kyle said, leaning against the counter facing Jeff. "We sold the whole series. All twelve pieces."

Jeff closed his eyes, and in that flash of darkness, he fell out of himself. Another stab of envy and hatred left him broken.

Kyle leaned in and kissed Gina's cheek, telling her with his eyes to hold on just a moment longer.

"You sure you're okay? You seem a little… off."

"I'm fine." Jeff took another long pull from the bottle of water. "I've just been working."

"On a new piece?"

Jeff nodded. "Yeah."

"Great! Let's see it."

"After it's finished," Jeff said, knowing he'd probably *never* finish another painting.

Gina ran her hands along Kyle's back and began tugging his arm, her gaze flooded with impatience.

"I guess I'll see you tomorrow then," Kyle said, allowing her to guide him away from the kitchen and toward the bedroom.

Jeff was silent for several moments, listening to the sounds of muffled chatter and Gina's girlish giggles. The cold bottle dripping with condensation held steady in his hand, he could only stare off, seeing nothing, but hearing everything. What he needed was a different bottle—one that would relax him, one that would cure his thirst for an alternative existence, one in which he could actually feel alive.

Kyle didn't drink much, but he always kept the liquor cabinet fully stocked. "Never know when guests will arrive," he'd once said, hoisting inside a box of liquor bottles.

The cabinet stood only a few feet from the kitchen. Jeff swung both doors open and sighed with relief. He reached for a bottle of Jack Daniels—good old reliable Jack—twisting the cap off with one swift motion and placing the opening to his lips. He felt better already.

But the more he drank, the more he heard the noises from the bedroom—Gina's soft moans and Kyle's low, almost self-conscious grunts. Jeff found himself gritting his teeth and clenching the bottle tight. He couldn't remember the last time he'd gotten laid. He couldn't even remember the last time he'd kissed anyone, and he'd definitely never been with anyone like Gina. The same sadistic side of his mind—the side with visions of Kyle's death—told him he never would.

His body trembling, his upper lip quivering, he marched toward the line of drawers beneath the sink and tore each one open with a determined hand. He stopped when the glistening steel of the meat cleaver caught his eye, paralyzing him. Gripping it by the wooden handle, he held the blade at his side and stalked out of the kitchen. Breathing heavily, his blood pulsing, he trod down the hall towards Kyle's bedroom. He listened to the post-coital silence and muffled snores.

Inside, buried in the darkness, he found only stillness. Kyle let out a soft hum and shifted positions. Still lost in her own dream, Gina did the same, her head against his bare chest.

It would've been so easy….

Only a moment of panic and terror and it would be over. Kyle would be gone. Jeff's dream could live on. He could finally be who he wanted to be. But eliminating Kyle wouldn't make Jeff a better painter. He'd still be the same fuck-up he'd always been.

Inching his way back, Jeff reached for the knob and gently swung the door closed, maintaining a firm grip on the meat cleaver's smooth handle.

When he stepped through the doorway of his own room, the painting was the first thing he saw—the painting Kyle had crafted. It was a piece he hadn't devoted much time to, but still, he'd managed perfection. Kicking the easel aside, Jeff could only hear the words Kyle spoke when he'd given him the painting. He'd said it was meant to inspire and rouse his creativity. It was meant to trigger something inside, something hidden. It was a gift Kyle offered his brother with only kindness and love, but it brought forth only hatred in Jeff. With gritted teeth and eyes burning with contempt, he buried the thick blade in the center of the painting.

Cruel thoughts pulsed in him, but his drive to create overwhelmed them. He tore open the nightstand drawer and pulled out a sketchpad and pencil, stopping to glimpse the pointed lead, knowing he'd rather used it to puncture his own trachea. On the crisp white page, he drew his viciousness. He drew hate and unspeakable carnage. He drew Kyle's slit throat, gallons of blood spilling from the deep gash. He drew the eyes of his brother filled with shock. On *this* page, there would be no happy ending. There would be no future filled with success and praise—only a blood-soaked climax.

On the opposite side of the page, close to Kyle's mutilated corpse, Jeff drew Gina's eviscerated torso; organs and entrails spilling out in buckets. Like Kyle, her eyes were drawn wide and filled with dread. The two annihilated bodies lay sprawled on the page. They reached for each other, the tips of their fingers standing inches apart, like a twisted version of The Sistine Chapel.

When he'd finished drawing, Jeff could feel the cramping in his right hand and forearm, and though he wanted to continue perfecting this showcase of bloodshed, he had no choice but to place the pencil back in its drawer. He turned toward the gray sky beyond the open window, curtains swaying in the soft breeze. It wouldn't be long before the sun rose. He felt whole. It was the best work he'd done in a long time, maybe ever. Standing, he approached the toppled easel, straightened its legs, and placed it right side up. On its ledge, he placed the sketchpad and backed away, wanting to gaze on the horrendous beauty from a distance.

Yes. This was definitely his best work.

He crawled back into bed, and as his eyelids fell, a smile crossed on his lips as he drifted off to sleep. That morning, he dreamed only sweet dreams.

* * *

When Jeff opened his eyes, it was night again. Another day had passed him by. Rolling over, he glanced at the clock—just after seven. He stretched and waited to fall out of his sleep-induced haze. Pulling himself out of bed, he turned to the night sky again, knowing he couldn't have missed much that day.

From down the hall, he heard the squeal of twisting knobs—the shower—and then the creak of an open door. Footsteps padded closer, and Kyle emerged, dripping wet and clad in only a terrycloth bathrobe, a towel draped over his shoulders. Behind him, the hardwood floor of the short hall was covered in a trail of foot-shaped puddles.

"Hey," Kyle said, toweling dry the back of his hair.

Jeff merely grunted.

"We're heading out for some dinner in a bit. You want to come?"

"Who's we?"

"Gina and me. Who else?"

"Is she here?"

"No, she went home to change. So, how 'bout it? You're more than welcome to join us."

Jeff shook his head. "I'd rather not."

17

That was an understatement; he would've rather torn his eyes from their sockets than sit across from Kyle and Gina during their celebratory dinner.

Kyle only gave an awkward smile. "So…how's the piece coming along?"

"Piece?"

"The piece you've been working on."

Jeff shrugged, his stare distant, his mind blank. Lost and drowning in a daze, he couldn't remember doing any work. He couldn't even remember starting anything. All he could remember was failing.

As he stared off, Jeff imagined living in a world where he possessed all the talents of his brother. Never knowing what it felt like *not* to have something to say.

It wasn't until minutes later, when he heard Kyle gasp, that he was pulled from his catatonic state.

In the next room, Kyle stared transfixed, a hand to his mouth, his eyes filled with horror. "Why would you do something like this?" He turned to Jeff.

"Do what?" Jeff asked blankly.

"And this," Kyle said, motioning toward the meat cleaver embedded in his own work. "Why would you do *this*?"

Jeff couldn't remember doing that either. The night before remained a blur, and the only thing he clung to was his ever-growing hunger for what Kyle had—an incomparable ability to create.

It was then Jeff realized how he could possess that talent. The idea fell on him in a flash; it seemed so simple. Inside, he came to life, and his body pulsed with optimism. He knew how to claw his way out of life's sinking hole of failure.

Kyle lifted the sketchpad from the easel's ledge and held it in both hands. His eyes focused on the penciled images, and he became hypnotized by the disturbing likenesses. His lips parted and he stepped away from the easel. Without a word, he parked himself on the edge of the mattress and let out a deep breath.

Jeff focused on the glistening blade of the meat cleaver. He smiled, grateful it was still there waiting for him. With a steady hand, he reached up and pulled it free. Clenching it tight, he turned towards Kyle and slowly approached.

"I don't understand," Kyle murmured. "How could you do this? After all I've done for you…. Who *are* you?" His eyes lifted towards Jeff.

"I'm you, Kyle," Jeff said. "Or at least I soon will be."

Filled with a thriving will, he raised the cleaver into the air, and without hesitation, he brought it back down again. Everything happened so fast. It was over before either of them had even blinked.

When the shadows cleared and Jeff's eyes could focus once more, he found the thickness of the blade buried deep in Kyle's forehead, the handle jutting from between his bulging eyes. The sketchpad fell to the floor, a spatter of blood covering the page, distorting the image. Kyle's body slumped back, landing amid the bed sheets. The handle of the cleaver stood straight up, pointing towards heaven.

With a smirk, Jeff climbed onto the bed, his bare feet sinking into the mattress with each step. Seeing Kyle lying still and silent, knowing he'd never take another breath again, Jeff felt a strong sense of euphoria. All his fears had vanished. Everything seemed right. Everything seemed just. Still, there was much left to be done.

Placing his right foot in the center of Kyle's chest, Jeff pressed down, his hand reaching for the handle of the cleaver. He grunted and pulled with all of his strength, and just when he thought the blade would remain buried in Kyle's skull forever, it popped free. He lifted the cleaver to his eyes and admired the dripping steel.

"Oh, God…"

Startled, Jeff whirled to face the doorway. Gina was dressed to the nines. When she saw him, she gasped, and before Jeff could move or react, she turned to run.

Gripping the cleaver, he leapt from the mattress and rushed after her, his heart pounding faster with every breath.

Reaching the front door, she cried out in panic, her hands hard at work on the multiple locks. Jeff could only think of stopping her before she made it through that door. Raising the cleaver again, he brought the blade down. Fumbling with the deadbolt, her left hand met the edge of the falling steel. Three fingers fell, and Gina screamed, dropping to her knees as she held the mutilated hand close to her, both her cleavage and angelic white dress covered in fresh red. Before she could release another terrified wail, Jeff buried the cleaver in the side of her neck, severing her jugular and spinal cord. As a river of crimson erupted, a thick wave spilling over her shoulder, she fell sideways.

Pulling free his cherished weapon, Jeff turned on his heels and marched away from Gina's, his mind blank, every emotion washed away. He would take from Kyle the one thing he could never truly obtain—a worthy talent. Back in the bedroom, he dropped the cleaver onto the mattress and gripped Kyle by the ankles. With a hard tug, he pulled the body forward until it collapsed against the floorboards. Both eyes clear and focused, he pulled the terrycloth robe from Kyle's body and tossed it aside. Avoiding his brother's naked flesh, Jeff's eyes concentrated on one area—Kyle's right arm. Reaching for the cleaver, he pulled in a deep breath.

Though he fought to stay in the moment, it seemed he'd lost himself once more, his mind venturing elsewhere. When he returned, he watched himself hacking into Kyle's flesh, the blade tearing through tissue and bone inches from the right shoulder. It all came back to him in a flash and he realized his purpose again.

Jeff had seen more blood than he'd ever imagined, and as he continued swinging the blade, he knelt in a puddle of warm red that grew thicker and fuller with every passing second.

When the blade sunk into the wood of the floor, Jeff knew he was halfway through. With a light tug at the wrist, the appendage came free. Stopping to take in a breath, Jeff grinned, his eyes fixed on the dismembered limb. He knew Kyle's talents would soon be his. Before the night came to a close, he would be everything he'd spent years knowing he never could.

Leaping to his feet, he headed for the kitchen and tore open one drawer after another, digging both hands inside, sifting through the contents of each. With bated breath, he continued to search, knowing he couldn't complete his mission, couldn't find his talents without it.

Not here. *Dammit.*

He raced into the living room, and in the bottom drawer of the end table, he found it. In his hand, he held a spool of thread, a needle wedged between the thin strips of navy blue. With a smile, he headed back to the bedroom. The trail of blood had reached the doorway and slowly seeped out into the hall. Jeff's feet almost went out from under him as he made his way back over to the body.

Now came the hard part.

His heart pounded in apprehension, his left hand gripping the cleaver so tight it hurt. Gazing down at Kyle's dismembered arm, he breathed deeply and told himself this was the only way. It *had* to be done. There were no alternatives. He'd have to find the strength.

Dreaming of a future filled with success, he lay down next to Kyle. Visions of gallery owners like Lynn Devoreaux showcasing his work helped him lift the cleaver high in his left hand, and desperation did the rest, forcing the blade into his own flesh.

The pain was blinding, but he knew he couldn't stop. Tears pouring from his eyes, the chaos of his own screams echoing in his ears, he continued to hack, slicing into his own shoulder the same way he had sliced into Kyle's. Spatters of blood covered his forearm as the cleaver continued to chew through tissue and bone.

Sobbing, Jeff heard the light thud as his own tainted, talentless arm came free. He stopped, struggling to breathe. His body was weak and the blood loss steady, but his determination wouldn't allow him to stop. Sitting upright, he reached for Kyle's severed arm with his left hand, hoisted it, and placed it in his own lap. He reached for the spool of thread, and with his teeth, pulled the needle free, thanking God it had already been threaded. Once again, he collapsed onto his back.

Almost there, he told himself, placing Kyle's arm close to him, the exposed bone grazing his own obliterated shoulder. Forcing a smile, he tried to forget the pain, knowing the wound would heal.

Pulling two feet of thread from the spool, he began to sew. Every so often he let out a moan, but eventually grew numb to the pain. It all seemed to be happening to someone else. Jeff no longer felt as though his actions were his own. He no longer felt his *body* was his own. He felt he'd *become* someone else.

In the end, he'd triple-stitched and the arm seemed to hold well enough. He wasn't sure how long it had been, but when he turned toward the window, the orange glow of the sun warmed him. He smiled, promising himself this would be a day he wouldn't waste.

His body sticky with blood, he turned toward the easel and smiled. Now, it was *his* turn. *He'd* be the one showered with praise. *He'd* be the one with gallery openings throughout the city. Finally, his time had come.

Pulling himself up, ready to begin, he let out a long breath, but before he could reach for the paintbrush, his body gave out. He fell onto his back once more, and this time, he couldn't bring himself back up again. He couldn't even turn his head.

Jeff had only managed to paint one thing by the time he'd gasped for his final breath—the floor beneath him. It was painted red.

THE CITY OF THE DANCING LIGHTS

BY FRANK ROGER

It has been an exceptionally good year, but don't we say that every time we return from the varicolored, multi-layered cross-cultural extravaganza the Annual Festival of the Arts has become? Once again, we've seen exciting new trends, invigorating new approaches, even stunning new art forms. Minimalist offerings—such as Akira Yamamoto's "Smallest Desert in the Known Universe," comprised of four minute grains of sand only visible through a microscope—were counterbalanced with productions of mega-proportions too large to fit into the Festival Center—like the brilliantly conceived and dazzlingly choreographed ballet of blizzards and hail-storms and tropical rain-showers created by Roberta N'komo, images of which were shown in the Center's special theatre.

As was generally expected, the decline of Virtual Reality art continued. That form may well be on its way toward total obsolescence, and most artists working in that area until recent years seem to have channelled their artistic ambitions into other forms of expression. Melinda DaSilva is a case in point. She used to be Brazil's most original and prolific VR artist, flooding the market with high-intensity, gut-wrenching, skull-splitting VR pieces.

"It's dead," she told me at one of the Festival's countless parties. "Forget all that old stuff of mine. I've entered a new phase in my career, and I refuse to look back. I'm into sculpting emotions now."

Some of her recent work was demonstrated at the Festival, and I must say it's quite gripping stuff. Her emotion-sculptures are painstakingly concocted chemical substances, injected into the bloodstream, allowing the user (or "beholder," as Melinda puts it) to experience a head-spinning blend of emotions. The impact on one's mind and soul can be ecstatic, devastating or even permanently altering. Two fellow journalists literally succumbed to her art, and Melinda referred to their deaths as "a fitting tribute to my artistic rebirth, a richly symbolic act in praise of my new approach, rising phoenix-like from the ashes of my former way of self-expression."

As one art form is disappearing into oblivion, another seems to be enjoying an unexpected revival. One of the most remarkable new trends, indeed, is the surprising resurgence of an art form considered dead and buried: literature. Prose printed on old-fashioned paper and assembled into books, to be read by turning page after page by hand. The most prominent flag-carrier of this revivalist movement, George MacLannan, conceded to me during his Publisher's Party (another defunct tradition of bygone days brought back to life) that there is no true audience for this type of art anymore, as there are no traditional "readers" left.

"But this book of mine," he explained, "must be viewed as a symbolical statement rather than some artsy mannerist joke. Art has been lifted from its cultural niche and transferred to the world of commerce. All too often these days, art is being consumed, like any other type of product. I wanted my book to tie in with this deplorable situation, wanted it to be used by consumers rather than purchased by collectors or 'read.' So the book was given an expiration date. After that date, the printed text begins to fade away and the book slowly decomposes into dust. This way I present art as an ephemeral consumerist need. Think about it. But above all, enjoy the party!"

The creations of the twin brothers Jorge and Luis Casares y Ramirez have become a mainstay of the Festival, and once again, both of them were represented with recent works.

Jorge Casares y Ramirez, the oldest by three seconds (as he repeats in every press conference), had chosen his "Human Race Against Time" for this year's edition, a remarkable blend of sports and modern ballet that the artist himself labels "chrono-choreography."

It consists of twenty-four men (each representing an hour of the day) running an eight-shaped circuit (representing the infinity of time) continuously, with interruptions for sleep and meals only. At least sixteen of them (representing the average person's regular active hours) are running together at all times. These twenty-four actors (performers? participants?) have signed very unusual contracts, to say the least. They are contractually bound to run the circuit until they wear out, grow ill or become too old, in which case their sons or grandsons are to take their place. The contract extends to twenty-four generations, so that this piece of art is destined to last for a considerable length of time. The twenty-four families were picked from different races and colors, in an effort to represent mankind in all its diversity. The runners, and their future generations, are personal property of the artist, who literally *bought* them.

"We all could use the money," one of the runners told me in a short interview I managed to arrange during one of his breaks. "Most of us come from poor countries, and we had all run up insurmountable debts we never could have paid off. Jorge's contract relieves us from all that, meaning he'll cover our debts in return for this job and life-long support of us and our families. You could say it was the only way out for us. This was an offer we simply couldn't refuse. It's hard work and we're tied up forever, but at least we've left the slums behind and lives without hope. We've got financial security now. And our wives and kids are fed."

It appears these people, perhaps understandably, fail to see themselves as an integral part of an important work of art, which in itself is a brilliantly spot-on commentary on the human condition in these ultra-hectic times, marking the end of a turbulent period in mankind's history as well as the dawning of a new era, opening up haunting vistas and yielding chilling intimations about what the future has in store for us.

Jorge's younger brother Luis never failed to surprise critics and audiences with his architectural collages, and this year's entry—"The Rise and Fall of Mankind"—is no exception. If anything, his scope has become more encompassing, his vision more awe-inspiring, his conceptualization more boldly daring. Try to picture an intricately conceived and constructed mosaic of snapshots of world history. The gates of Santiago de Compostela's cathedral swing wide open to reveal a starving Third World child, its hand eagerly reaching out, its swollen belly and huge staring eyes caught in a blindingly white spotlight. The background darkens, as all at once a mushroom-shaped cloud billows up, and both the cathedral and the child are blown to smithereens. As the radioactive dust settles, a radiation-scarred family becomes dimly visible, scurrying among the rubble, desperately eking out a miserable existence, clinging to lives barely worth living. The gray sky turns blue and then black, craters appear in the barren ground, the blue disc of the earth winks into existence, pouring vivid light onto what has now become the lunar landscape, and two astronauts come jumping into view. One of them is about to plant the American flag he is clutching, claiming the moon for his country, an act of patriotism carried out many miles away from the nation that gave rise to and nurtured those feelings. A guerrilla fighter in a tattered green uniform darts from behind a rock and fires at one of the astronauts. The victim's spacesuit is punctured, the air escapes, and as decompression follows, the man dies in a shower of blood and bones. More soldiers in a variety of uniforms appear from all around and carnage ensues, transforming the moonscape into a corpse-strewn battlefield. The sky turns blue again; sunlight floods the scene, signalling that we're back on earth. From the mound of dead bodies a slender green stem arises, and in one gracious movement a bright-red rose springs into full bloom, majestically dominating the landscape. Then its color slowly fades as the rose metamorphoses into a poppy, which quickly crumbles into dust. The dust actually turns out to be opium, and drug-users come rushing towards it, eager to grab handfuls of their deadly wonder-stuff. One by one the junkies drop to the ground, lifeless, as the scene around them changes into the smoldering, lava-covered ruins of Pompeii. A few more transformations occur in rapid succession; the barracks of Auschwitz appear for a few seconds, to be replaced by the library of Alexandria, being set on fire by religious fanatics, the Taj Mahal, the Hollywood film studios, ransacked by raging hordes of moral purists, and the Vatican, bombed during the Great Religious Wars of the New Millennium. From the smoking debris the cathedral of Santiago rises triumphantly, and the whole cycle starts over again.

This mind-boggling, senses-shattering kaleidoscope is produced in a fascinating way, partly made with authentic, physical props, combined with a variety of holograms, and complemented by a well-balanced mixture of hallucinogenic chemicals pumped into the air of the presentation hall. As the artist considers the exact composition of his work, i.e. which elements are to be attributed to holograms, hallucinogenic chemicals or physical objects, to be a professional secret, we can only contemplate it and marvel at its deeply resounding, richly-textured meaning, and try to grasp its myriad allusions and connotations and hidden meanings. This work, for sure, will allow for as many interpretations as there are viewers.

As usual, the organizing committee selected a very special work of art for the crowning event of the Festival's closing ceremony. Once again, they stuck to tradition and kept the exact nature of this pièce de résistance secret until its presentation. To our surprise, we were asked to board a zeppelin and were told we would be presented with Michael d'Angelo's newest creation— "The City of the Dancing Lights"—while hovering over San Francisco. D'Angelo is well-known for his extravagant art, and the mere fact his latest effort could not be presented at the Festival Center itself left us expecting something truly spectacular.

The sun was setting as we arrived in San Francisco, tinting the clouds coming in from the ocean orange and copper, colors constantly changing hue as nightfall approached, as if nature's forces had decided to enrich the Festival with their own artistic endeavors in competition with the puny humans struggling with their comparatively primitive material. As the zeppelin hung motionless over Union Square, we were provided with a splendid view of the city sprawling beneath our feet, a tapestry of lights fighting back the darkness hovering above. On our left we could see the Golden Gate Bridge, on our right the Oakland Bay Bridge, both glimmering with pinpoints of light, the heavy traffic contributing a patchwork of red and white lights streaking the overall picture. The city's major hotels, towering light-encrusted columns, rose up toward us as if eager to grab us and pull us down. Then the Festival committee's chairman finally decided to address us.

"We hope you have enjoyed what you've witnessed so far," he said, "but we know that will pale into insignificance next to what you are about to experience. D'Angelo is not simply offering a major contribution to modern art here. He is modern art. 'The City of the Dancing Lights' will set new standards. Everything that follows will be judged against it for years to come. You who are about to behold this masterpiece cannot possibly realize how privileged you are in having been selected. In only a few moments, everything will be disclosed to you. Be prepared for the truly sensational."

He gestured, and the lights dimmed. "I hope to see you all again at next year's Festival."

We all looked down at the now night-enshrouded city beneath us. For a moment nothing happened. Silence hung heavily among us. Only our agitated breathing could be heard. Then d'Angelo's creation was finally unveiled, step by carefully measured step. Understanding dawned. We peered outside, afraid to miss the smallest of details. A new chapter in the history of art was being written in our presence.

It began with small tremors, sending faint ripples across the cityscape. It appeared as if this modest overture to the undoubtedly grand proceedings went unnoticed by the city's unsuspecting population. Not a single light winked out of existence. Not one car seemed to do so much as slow down. People didn't yet realize they were to participate in a major work of art. The second set of tremors was more powerful. Only this time there were some visually attractive reactions. On the two bridges, and in various parts of downtown San Francisco, a large number of drivers slowed down or stopped, resulting in a bonfire of bright red brake lights flaring up. As a number of lights, scattered all over the city went out, an equal number were switched on, perhaps by people already asleep who were now rising from their slumber, wondering what was going on, or perhaps more likely, as emergency back-up systems were activated.

At that point, d'Angelo's carefully orchestrated choreography of explosives embedded in key locations under the city slipped into full gear. Our appetite had been sufficiently whetted, and the main course was about to be served. After a minute-long interlude, which seemed to last hours to us sensation-starved spectators, the first serious quake shook the city on its foundations. Thrilled and breathless with anticipation, we watched as several segments of the Oakland Bay Bridge collapsed, crushing a number of cars in the process. Now the city truly came alive. Panic finally reared its ugly head. In some districts, the lights went out; in others, small explosions sounded and buildings erupted into flames, illuminating the areas of interest. All traffic came to a standstill. Screaming and yelling crowds slowly started to fill the streets and squares.

The dust had barely settled when three short but powerful quakes hit the city in rapid succession. The screams of the crowds thronging the streets, desperately looking for a shelter from the seismic onslaught, were drowned by the rumblings of explosions and collapsing homes. Virtually all artificial lighting had disappeared from view now, but the rapidly increasing number of fires provided sufficient illumination for us to follow how the situation was evolving. It crossed my mind that this replacement of the artificial by the natural might symbolize the return to a more primitive state in mankind's evolution, expressing perhaps d'Angelo's cyclical view of history. The crazed hordes clogging the streets in a frenzy of panic-ridden despair could then be viewed as man's return to barbarism, accompanying or possibly mirroring the return to the forefront of nature's forces. D'Angelo had pressed the rewind button of mankind's history, making the city and its inhabitants revert to their earlier stages.

A volley of "oohs" and "aahs" went up all around me, as directly beneath our feet, Macy's crumbled into ruins. Somewhat farther down, several buildings along Market Street had also succumbed to the quakes. Dust was billowing up, partly obscuring the orange and red flames increasing in size and numbers everywhere. Ironically, the tall columns of the major hotels and the financial district's skyscrapers behind us were still standing. Was this part of d'Angelo's scheme? Was he trying to indicate that ultimately technology would provide the key to survival, that man, if only he chose the right way, could emerge victorious from this battle? In a certain sense, that would echo interpretations given by knowledgeable critics to other recent works by the same artist, but then again d'Angelo has been known to veer off in unexpected directions on more than one occasion, intentionally misleading critics and audiences alike.

A short pause allowed us to check the current state of the agonizing city. The two bridges could only faintly be seen, but it was obvious they had suffered irreparable damage. We could only guess how many people had died as they had been crushed or had tumbled into the cold water of the Bay. Large parts of the city were on fire, and the smaller buildings had collapsed. The city now proudly displayed a nightmarish mêlée of shell-shocked people, frantically struggling through debris and rubble, acrid smoke filling their lungs, blazing-hot fires eagerly reaching out to engulf them with hungry flames. The innocent victims, or rather unwitting actors in d'Angelo's vision, were only given short respite.

The moment of the Grand Finale had finally arrived. It started with a deeply resonant rumbling that we, high up in the air though we were, felt rather than heard. We caught our collective breaths as understanding dawned. Only now did we grasp how thorough the preparations for this piece must have been, and we marvelled at the flawless perfection with which it was being presented. D'Angelo's team was made of dyed-in-the-wool professionals, setting standards comparable only to those their employer was setting for his peers. The tapestry of blazing fires that was now San Francisco started to tremble, casting an eerily wavering light over the scenes of destruction. A masterfully choreographed sequence of quakes was now hitting the city, and a round of deafening applause and cheers went up as it became clear the awesome powers being brought into play.

We no longer viewed what we saw beneath us as a city inhabited by human beings fighting for their lives in the face of an unexplainable catastrophe, but rather as a gigantic construction which was being dismantled systematically, with due attention paid to the aesthetic aspects of the process. The city was becoming less recognizable with every hit. One by one, the major hotels gave way to the pressure, sagged, crumbled, and finally collapsed in geysers of dust, concrete and stone. Massive applause went up as the towering financial district fell in one majestic awe-inspiring swoop. The quilt work of fires danced a pavane as the crust on which the city rested was shaken to the point of pulverization.

A standing ovation was reserved for the coup de grace, as wide crevices opened up and large parts of the city were swallowed, and finally the raging waters of the bay washed tsunami-like over the smoldering ruins, extinguishing the multitude of fires in towering fountains of vapor. Gradually, darkness descended, authoritatively reinstalling the night, and thus signalling the end of the presentation.

We felt our zeppelin gaining altitude, and the lights were switched back on. Discussions and analysis grew into an impenetrable brouhaha; notes were frantically scribbled down, entered into laptop computers or spoken into recorders. An appraisal of this amazing tour de force was already being attempted, comparing it with d'Angelo's existing body of work and viewing it against the larger background of contemporary art as a whole. Deeper meanings and hidden symbolism were being discovered, interpretation upon interpretation was being offered, layer after layer of insightful understanding was being removed as the gathered critics were probing for the essence of d'Angelo's latest addition to his oeuvre.

As we set course back to the Festival center, we barely noticed the invitation to come back to next year's Festival, completely engrossed as we were in our activities.

Needless to say, we'll all be back next year, wondering how this year's achievements can possibly be equalled, let alone surpassed. And no doubt we will be pleasantly surprised once again.

PRETTY FACE ON GENOCIDE

BY STEVEN L. SHREWSBURY

Had I been a single man with an ego to stoke, the revelation of me bedding Dr. Talia Li would have been a notch on the bedpost the size of an axe wound.

My indiscretion added spice to her acceptance of me in bed. Oh, I often told myself the searing passion came from my lanky body, rugged looks gleaned from a life of adventure, and brawls…or perhaps my expansive knowledge of history brought on from my profession as an archaeologist. In all honesty, Talia's lust was birthed when I uncovered numerous items that added to her true passion: Genghis Khan. Be it ol' Temujin's early leather deel, his various sashes or rusted helmet sans furry edges, Talia showed her appreciation better than most art directors. If I proved above average or superior in the bedroom, or in her case, the kitchen, living room, and balcony, it was a bonus adding to her infatuation.

As I looked up at the mirror over the bed, seeing her petite form curled next to my long frame in the flickering candlelight, I wondered how many men could successfully perform under these conditions. Not just with a mature woman of beauty, but in a chamber filled with ancient treasures and her wearing the tunic of the Mongolian warlord himself. Sure, she wanted me to mount her dressed in it myself, but I was far larger than the Khan. Talia donned it instead, assuring me she'd flied solo in the outfit before, and the rest proved easy enough. Her painted face bothered me a little. Talia's grease paint kabuki thing during sex fascinated me at first, but after several times, the oriental kinkiness faded and it felt more akin to screwing a member of KISS.

She had her secrets. What woman didn't? The head of the Art Institute of Chicago possessed more skeletons in her closet and the jars in her foray than most serial killers. I'm positive I am not the only one this rigid, ambitious lady brought to her apartment high above State Street. I reckon I'm the only psychometric archaeologist she's bedded, though. Only a handful of folks in the world know of my talent. I have my secrets to keep, too.

31

"You always give me want I want," Talia said, her breathing returning to normal and long, painted nails drumming on my chest. "Be it here or with your power to touch objects and see the past."

My gloved hand running down her spine, I said, "Well, I aim to please, ma'am."

Her thumbnail and middle fingernails pinched at my nipple as her voice betrayed irritation. "Please dispense with the corny redneck talk, Elijah. Even if you graduated from Miskatonic University, I know you're brighter than that."

I gave a yawning sigh. "I hate behaving, Talia, you know that. Being the renegade half American Indian archaeologist at the party, the proverbial turd in the punchbowl of these stuff shirted pricks gets old. I'm smarter than all of them. I've seen things none of them could live with."

Her hand flattened as my tone grew harsh. "Elijah…"

"Can those shitheads even guess at the beautiful horror and terrible beauty I've seen? You could fill a museum with the things I could put to canvas, if these hands could paint. Can any of them understand what it is like to live with the knowledge I have?"

"You've proved countless ideas and invalidated others," she reassured me, her tone gentle. "Consider the treasures you've discovered for me. Your incredible capacity to discover orgasms hiding in the strangest of places is almost akin in quality to the relics of the Great Khan you've endowed me with."

I touched her hair and she twitched.

"What?"

She rose, using my chest for leverage, and said, "Those damned gloves of yours are exasperating after a while."

I looked in the mirror over the bed again and flexed my covered fingers. "You know I have to wear them to avoid the visions. I don't have that much control over my psychometric skill."

She sighed and swung her legs over the edge of the bed. As she started to undo her right fishnet stocking, she mumbled, "Fine, fine…"

I could've been a smart ass and said if I can get past her clown makeup obsession and nailing her in a pointed helmet, she should overlook my gloves. Talia wasn't about fighting, though. We weren't married or in a relationship of any sort, so, no fencing was needed for control.

"I'd kill to have your gift," she confessed, sliding the garter belt from her narrow hips.

"A Neo-Druid in Canada wanted my ability, hell, tried to take my head for a totem pole."

She untied the left stocking from around her throat. Though not one for bondage, I complied with her desire for the stocking garrote this last time. "I heard of that adventure on the wind, Dr. Blackthorn. I'd heard you can pass on a revelation at times, let someone else see what you have experienced."

"Where did you hear that? That's silly."

"I cannot believe you'd hold back such a splendid visualization from me, would you?" Talia put the stockings together and folded them over, resting her hands on bony hips by the edges of a thin belly chain.

"That's nonsense," I lied. Though brilliant and a shrewd businesswoman, Talia proved way too obsessive for me to admit to that particular skill. Visions of her keeping me imprisoned to dole out ancient sights jogged across my brain, so, I deceived her. "I came here to read the new find. Thank you for the fun and tossed salad, though."

A smirk on her lips, she nodded and looked down. Her painted nails passed over her belly ring and then to her pubic ridge, shaven clean, and stopped above the tattoo of the dragon arising from her labia lips. At times I found that sexy. Now, after the act was over and the guilt of my sins lay heavy on my heart, I wished the candles would learn to lie, too.

After visiting Talia's shower to rinse her off myself, I donned my clothes and asked, "Where is the masked Buddha?"

Her face was scrubbed free of the grease paint, and she wore a scarlet robe and fuzzy slippers. The footwear killed me; it was out of character for a woman so embedded in Asian art and imagery. I guessed comfort could tell custom and fixation to kiss its ass on occasion.

Talia sat at a mirror, working on her base makeup. "Your wife psychometric as well? Can she read my DNA on your shorts?" She turned around, her bare legs splayed open to tease me with what I'd already devoured earlier. I tried to banish the idea of the dragon image as Satan in Biblical lore.

"No, but I've lived a long time being careful."

Talia nodded and stood up. She moved like a wisp of air, so light and waifish. I followed her out of the bedroom full of masks and Asian treasures into her dining room. The oak encrusted room, designed for entertaining dinner guests, proved less than typical of a sparse Oriental home. Her small hand rested on a ceramic cover to a pie plate. Talia winked and unveiled a small artifact hidden in the pie pan. Ignoring her peculiar attempt at a jest, I leaned over, squinted and reached out.

"May I?" I asked before my gloved hand touched the object.

"Please."

I loved how she talked, polite and erudite. (Precisely how she responded in bed when I asked if could go south on her, but I digress.)

Amazement struck me at the extreme weight of the small object—a fetish or idol, clearly a Buddha, but quite skinny.

"Curious. It appears to be the fasting Buddha, but the only one in the world is in the LaHore museum in Pakistan." My eyes scrutinized the object. "Is it a fake, like the starving Buddha's supposedly dredged up in northern Pakistan a few years back? I can't believe a huckster would get the best of you."

"Please. You're so quaint, Elijah." She walked over and gazed at the idol.

"What? You need my ability to see if it's real? C'mon, sweetie, there must be something more."

Talia held up her middle finger. Coy as ever, she then reached out and stabbed at the face of the slender Buddha. I nearly stepped back as the face fell from the idol, or rather, a thin outer layer flipped free, revealing a second face underneath. Though fabric coated my thumb, it passed over this new visage, one withered and aged, almost inhuman to the point of rot.

As my eyes widened, she said, "You know what this means, Dr. Blackthorn."

"The hidden faces of the Tangut folk," I said slowly, gripping the sides of the idol. A sharp popping sound echoed in the room as the idol split in half, revealing a metallic object within. "They were almost forgotten when your pal Genghis Khan destroyed them. He created a new form of the word 'pissed' with them, didn't he?"

"You see what's inside?" she asked, her emotions rising. "You know the tales of how Khan died."

I moved the idol up and down, thinking something else lurked inside the hollow shell. "There are quite a few tales about his death."

"I refuse to accept the story in the Galican-Volhynian Chronicle that he perished in battle against the crushed Tanguts, or that he fell from his horse."

I put the idol back in the pie tin and picked up the slender object that dwelt inside its core. After I ran my right index finger down the flat of the slim blade, I said, "You think that this is the knife that killed him?"

"The one that started him on the road to death, perhaps. If a Tangut princess really castrated him as he raped her, hiding a blade in her vagina like the folktales relate, this could be it."

"That story always sounded like bull feathers to me." I raised my eyebrows. "How the hell could she have done that? Talk about Kegel muscle control."

"Quite." Talia folded her arms under her small breasts. "Perhaps she smuggled the blade in her vagina and used it as she fondled him. I don't know. You could see it though."

Talia became so formal when seriousness took hold of her.

"Where did you get this?"

"Ironically enough, a former student performing arbitrary research in China found it in the dirt. Seriously, no major traps, no pitfalls or alligators in a moat. Just in the dirt for any dolt to find."

"Lucky," I said with a nod, and blew on the edge of the blade. "It must not have been important enough to keep in reverence or hide in such an atypical edition of Buddha. Tests from the thirteenth Century?"

"From all indications, a spot earlier. The piece is genuine, but the blade and the carvings on the Buddha testify about the instrument used to knock down the great Khan. It may be twaddle."

"Sure." I nodded, but never took my eyes from the knife.

"This is why I contacted you, Elijah."

Ah, back to first names when she wants something grave.

"I can take a look. Most of the time, red herrings abound in my visions."

Knife in hand, I walked to the leather couch and sat down. I placed the blade on the glass coffee table and started to remove my gloves.

Talia curled up in the loveseat nearby, watching me intently. "We've talked of this before, but you really discovered this ability in grade school?"

Hands free of the gloves, I nodded, looking at my bare digits. "Yeah, I turned up a hunk of an old soup bone buried by a dog in the sandbox. How was that for irony considering my later career?"

Her delicate fingers on her lips, she stifled a laugh. "I always wanted to ask if you felt the dog gnaw you."

"I don't experience the sensation of the objects. I saw it up close, though. Like touching a doorknob and seeing endless hands slap you in the face. However, with history, I usually see things around the object."

Talia watched me staring at my fingers and dropped her hands to her lap. "So you won't see the cut?"

"I doubt it. The ability shows me what it does. This may show me the student who found it joining the mile high club on the way home. I can't promise you anything. This may be a piece of junk, you understand that?"

Her words came fast and urgent. "But the inscription and all, if there is a slight chance that this Tangut princess used this on the Khan…"

"I gotcha, already," I responded, curious if the Tangut maidens were really so beautiful they had to wear masks to conceal their stunning appearances. The Buddha mask made me wonder if that was the implication here. Yet, the face under that mask was withered…

I took a breath, picked up the blade and the rest was history.

* * *

Sweat sprang to my brow as the glowing metal spearhead bisected my vision. Though never sure who I saw things through or if it was a function of omnipresent sight, I experienced the heat of the glowing lance near my face…just before it was applied to the bloody groin of an aging man.

Pain is an international language, but I understood the tongue of the men in the smoky tent around me anyway. I always did in my revelations. While the older man howled in pain from the application of the scorching sword, I wondered why these other Mongols, all armed with scimitars and recurved composite bows, only lightly held the struggling man down. Their words of worry and suck up praise to the old one soon spelled it out to me. This wasn't a prisoner under torture, but their leader, and the burning tool was meant to heal a wound.

The struggling man seized the forearm of one of the men near him and groaned the name "Ogedei."

Sweat ran from my face as that name sank in. Ogedei was the third son and successor of Genghis Khan. When they defeated the Russians, I recalled reading, Ogedei had Prince Mstislav and his two sons wrapped in felt rugs and stuffed under the floorboards of his tent. These three were crushed to death as Khan's son and his chiefs danced and sang to celebrate the victory.

Something in the mind I occupied told me the rest of those around Genghis were his sons, but my own identity seemed elusive. Nevertheless, I wondered if the crude field cauterization worked. Whoever I looked through beheld the reality that the old leader still suffered, but the blood around his wound wasn't fresh.

"I'll never survive," the one I assumed was Genghis said, eyes shut tight, grim gray brows fluttering.

One of the men took a knee. "Perish the idea, father. You shall recover in time."

With great violence, the man shook his head. "No, Chagatai, but I knew my time was not eternal." His voice broke often as he spoke. "You, my sons and blood, must carry on the mantle of the Khan. You have an empire that will span the whole of the earth at your fingertips."

The other men in the tent took a knee and I found myself doing the same. The disclosure I saw through the eyes of one of Khan's bloodline was the least of my worries as they soon faced me.

"Prove your worth, young one, not just to me, but the entire world," Khan said and motioned to Ogedei who resided nearest to his right hand. This man, a thick set individual with grim eyes and one eyebrow, held out an object to me. Without hesitation I took hold of it. My eyes peered down, seeing a perfect version of the blade glimpsed in Talia's living room.

Ogedei said to me, "She must die. She will be the first. The rest will fall in time. We will create something to be marvelled at for a thousand years."

"I understand," I found myself saying, but from my tone and hands, I wasn't a thuggish warrior like the others. In fact, I doubted I was sixteen years old in this new flesh.

"Her people will vanish from the earth; never will the beautiful ladies of the Tangut nor their sons tread upon the soil," Khan muttered. "She who has slain me will never be a glorious remembrance. Skin that bitch alive, boy, and if she begs to taste death, piss in her mouth. Make me a mask from her beautiful face. Do it in one peel if you can. You have good hands. Create something lovely for me."

After a brief bow, I stood and left the Great Khan. Hesitation wouldn't be tolerated. If I asked questions or waited a moment to contemplate the order, my own bloodline would be deriding me or beating me, instead of saying I deserved to rape the Tangut Princess held prisoner in base camp before she was staked out for the dogs to eat.

All the same, I waited outside the tent, hearing their father tell of what the boys would soon do. Various tales of Khan's death were manufactured—one suggested an accident on horseback, another of dying in battle—anything but the reality of being castrated by a vengeful Tangut maiden.

Something felt terribly wrong about my assumptions. For some reason, the idea that a gloriously beautiful Tangut maiden awaited me at the end of my journey seemed unreal to my new perceptions. A fear bubbled in the extremities of this youth. I couldn't quite understand it. Truly, I wanted to think I'd soon behold a glorious damsel, lovely and flawless like a rare woman of Asiatic splendor. The fiction of the gilded flower I searched for was never plainer than when I stopped at the place of holding. Another of Khan's sons guarded this locale, one the other guard called Tolui.

Genghis wasn't screwing around, it seemed, with the concept of his legacy. Already the reality that a princess had felled and flailed the Great Khan had set in. The posted guards looked severe and ready to die before they released any secrets. Over and over, my mind told me it was a gorgeous maiden waiting. So much so I wanted to deny the reality of what some part of me knew lurked within the tent.

Bound spread eagle on the ground inside the tent laid a woman, but no magnificence surrounded this lily of the Chinese mountainside. In the meager sunlight, smoldering fire of dung and straw, and single lantern light, I could see plainly enough. At first, I thought my siblings jested with me, sending me here to see my reaction. Was it a test of my resolve or a great jape on their end to send me to this old woman, knife in hand?

Stretched before me lay a small body, not hideous by any means, but decades away from being a virginal damsel. Her breasts sagged and one lay farther to the side than the other. Her ribs protruded above the stretch marks of several births. The knobbiness of her knees and the abundance of calluses on her feet all betrayed her as much older than an innocent maid. Her face? Well, I cannot testify to how this woman appeared in a natural state, for it was clear she'd suffered a heavy beating. Her nose was crushed and emitted a wet sound. Dried blood caked her nostrils and lips, but they parted to gasp at regular intervals. Bruises and creases filled with purple lesions littered her face. I recall thinking she looked pretty good for an old woman who cut the balls off Genghis Khan. Why she lived at all struck me as odd, though.

"You hesitate in your task," the old woman croaked, her left eye never opening, forever sealed by swollen tissue and dry blood. "Are you truly your father's son?"

I knelt by her, blade at the ready and asked, "Why do this thing to the Khan? Your people will be gone forever as an example of his brutality. You know the way of the Khan."

"I was born to favor a purpose," she rasped. "I was known unto the Khan decades ago. When he first knew of my folk and coveted a prized maiden or two, it was I who satisfied his torrid lust. Now, he will not get the satisfaction of slaying my people. I was offered the task of giving him what he wanted most." She coughed and seemed to laugh.

"I'm confused. You are beyond my father's years and not what he desires."

"Think you know so much? The great Khan has a failing ability where all warriors root their pride. My mouth always made him happy years ago. His desire to deflower a princess would end in her death when he couldn't perform. Oh, we women talk much, you blood kin of Khan, and I knew the fate of my people once he failed to pierce a virgin. Killing all witnesses is never enough. You are here to silence me forever, and that you shall."

"You are mad, woman."

"They searched me all over," she chuckled dryly. "A few groped me low down, but none dared penetrate the opening of one as old as I. All they understood was that the Khan knew me as a girl and met in private with me. Do you think he will let it be known an old woman robbed him of his manhood while his pathetic member was in her toothless mouth?"

My head spun as I found this elderly lady better at revelations than me.

"What can you do to me, boy? You are barely twelve years of age. What striking tale will be spun next, grandson of the Khan? Not even all of his weapons can rid my face of this smile."

"True," I said and inserted the blade under her scalp line and started to cut.

All of my strength and will could not stay the hand of young Kublai Khan or the reality of the past.

* * *

"So what did you find in the Tangut hills?" Talia asked, drinking deep from a glass of wine. "You resided with the Khan and his armies, didn't you? I can see on your face that a great truth now dwells within."

Gloves snugly back on my hands, I looked at the blade on the dining room table like a dead rat. I never witnessed what she wanted or learned anything useful, aside from a new form of graphic destruction. Only a few moments had lapsed since I picked the object up, but I wager my face betrayed my experience.

"They were all dead already, the tribes," I said, finishing up my story about the vision. "After I met the maiden that had the knife, the armies went to the hills where the Tangut tribes lived. The people we found there had taken a form of scorpion venom and killed themselves. The sons of Khan were flummoxed and bade us invent a tale of great death for the Tanguts before he passed."

"They were all dead, mass suicide?" Her voice sported real hurt.

"Yes, but we, er, the soldiers all chopped them to bits. Per his orders, we carved out a lesson on the faces of those there, to see the artwork of the Great Khan. "

Talia fell quiet for a long time, drinking more wine. "And you slew the woman that cut Khan? That was true?"

"No. She was alive when I left. I never killed anyone." I walked over to the table and picked up the Buddha idol. When I raised it over my head, she screamed. I dashed it down on the wooden table, sending pieces of it everywhere. Talia's howls ceased when she saw me point to the hidden object in the skinny Buddha amongst the shards.

"Careful," I said and started to peel the slender object apart. "I saw it cured on one side with a thin layer of copper. I cannot believe this is here."

Talia ripped the object from my hands and held it up. "Good God, the face of Khan's killer!" Her lips quivered as she started at the grisly object. "How can it survive?"

I couldn't answer her question but thought the piece of material wasn't that impressive, like wadded up paper backed with aluminum foil. But the face rang similar to my vision. I saw the left eye in the lurid mask of skin remained swollen shut.

"Did you hear of the Khan's burial plans? Do you know where he lies?"

I shook my head, hands flat on the table. "No. I saw an example of nobility unseen in centuries, though. I saw sacrifice, an act of giving for a dead folk beyond any example I could ever invent with my hands. Someone wanted to make sure of killing the Khan no matter what happened."

Talia put the mask to her face and held it in place. The one eye I could see flickered under the mask. "You saw more than that, I bet. She was really taken by the Khan, wasn't she? You felt it all and don't want to tell me." She threw off her robe and climbed on the table. "Take me, Elijah." Her small breasts heaved, nipples erect. "You experienced her feelings, didn't you? You felt the Khan infiltrate you."

"You're crazy. It wasn't like that at all."

"Don't deny it." Swiftly, Talia's right hand descended to her crotch as her ass wiggled in the pieces of the idol. "God, I am so wet. Give it to me, give me that feeling! I know you can pass it on, Elijah. Make me experience what that bitch felt."

I thought of the lady whose face she wore. How utterly beautiful the aging lady was who slew the ruler of the world before he could exterminate and disfigure her people by the sword. I also saw the writhing head of the Art Institute on the table and was never so turned off in all of my life.

But against my better judgment, I gave Talia what she wanted. I removed the gloves and placed my bare palms on her knees. Then, I imparted a vision from the past and conveyed the feelings I received from the Tangut lady bound in the tent.

Her screams started off as ecstasy but ended elsewhere.

* * *

41

On the whole, I'm glad the terms madhouse and asylum are out of date. Of course, booby hatch and loony bin aren't any prettier than Psychiatric Hospital. My visit to see an old friend, Dr. Shawn Marsh at a facility in Kankakee made me a trifle nervous at first. However, my feelings of trepidation concerning the patient in question, Dr. Talia Li, faded when Shawn nearly embraced me, shaking his head.

"Elijah, sorry I had to call you out here." Shawn was a small man, nearly fifty years old, bald. He had seen it all in his years at Kankakee. Or, at least the thought he had.

"No problem, but why all the fuss?" I asked innocently, hands behind my back.

Dr. Marsh let out a loud sigh as he ushered me into his office. "Your name keeps coming up."

I closed to door behind me. "Pardon me?"

He waved me over to the desk and pushed a disk into his computer. "It's the same thing for weeks. Look at her."

On the laptop screen jumped the raving countenance of Talia Li. Her face a mass of tears and sweaty hair, the words from her pale lips came out garbled, but I caught most of them.

"Hideous, can you see how hideous I am?" she wailed, over and over. "Skinned alive, skinned alive!" Her sobs echoed as hands wrestled her. "Let me die! God just let me die. Send for Blackthorn! He will know how to save me."

Marsh shook his head. "I've never seen such a deep rooted case of self loathing in dementia before. While there is no history of anti-depressant abuse in Dr. Li, I can't explain this condition. She doesn't have a mark on her face, as you can see; save for the bruises she's given herself when the meds lighten up. She seems convinced of something that isn't there."

"Bizarre," I said, looking at her weep on the screen.

"At first, I suspected gender dysphoria common in transsexuals. There seems to an unusually high level of serotonin in her system but tests results are still coming back."

Did her being such a shallow person ease my guilt? Was I happy to be rid of a thorn in my side and threat to my personal life? Probably.

"Dr. Li is beautiful but convinced she's revolting," Marsh lamented. "Must be a byproduct of her art obsession, no? I know that's a blanket statement and probably far off base, but I just can't comprehend her breakdown."

"Beauty is a strange thing, Dr. Marsh. One man's trash is another man's treasure. Is it skin deep? Depends how deep one is."

SCAVENGER HUNT

BY R.J. CAVENDER

The Weed-Master Plus was slapping up a beautiful mess of what used to be Amanda's face.

I mean, I say the name like I knew the girl. She was just as nameless as anyone else. Names were never of any importance. You make friendly with an ocean of skin. You hear and forget an army of names.

Imagine the things two swirly-eyed boys of just fourteen could buy with five-large a week. That's each. We were unstoppable. Every moment was a murder-junkie-rockstar dream. Children and demons and armed and drugged, we raped the city streets.

When referred to, if ever, the gutterpunks and bindlekids would call us The Scavenger Hunt. We had a list, we were paid well, and we asked no names. Oft times we traded psychedelics and powders for useful information. We were effective and precise. We were shadows on the cold city concrete.

So's, her magna-tag labeled her Amanda, not that we ever called her by name. We swiped her sweet and clean on her darkened walk to her shitmobile, and one nastily laid bonk upsides her crannie later...and we've got our newest star. Never underestimate the power of a brick in a pillowcase, friend.

See, we got her tied tight and right, and my good man Dodger and I were ready to earn our keep. Old Stu had set up the entire operation, and no matter what his claims may be, both Dodge and I knew quite well he was pocketing more bills than he gave us. Which was acceptable. At first.

After all, the scrot-wrinkled old fuckleknuck was about as daft as they come. But, he had indeed orchestrated the entire project, so some props should be given for that if nothing else.

Those who do the dirty work sometimes need a bit more green. We had habits to feed, and got admittedly greedy. It's like kings in our world. Kill your teacher. Destroy all idols. Climb up to the throne. To us, Stu had become dust.

We killed, he made the money. The dusty desert was pregnant with graves we'd dug by hand.

The old fuck had us connected with the right of the wrong people. Old Stu had the hook-ups on everything of worth; drugs, tech weaponry, contraband pornographics, and deathshows. We signed on with Stu for the latter of the list. It was his farm where the deeds were done, and his digividcams were the ones steeped in hour upon hour of our bloodied footage.

Which brings us back to Amanda, and the goulash mess she once called a face. She was number three on our list for the night. Just a messy interlude sandwiched between a hit-and-run and a better than worse dissection. Just goes to show you, you never know exactly what moment will be your last.

This one was a fighter. No one could ever diss this dolly, as she was most assuredly the strongest female I'd ever put to rest. She spat and cursed with the best of them, even with her face falling off in sloppy, wet chunks. A wildcat.

The vidi-film Stu was recording tonight was given the working title of "Deep Red." We'd already burnt two hours on Amanda, and still found ourselves far from done. The list we'd been given was rather specific on what was to be done to her. Stu's clients were very exact in what they wanted.

So's, you find yourself at the fork in the road. Less taken path seemingly oh so perverse and unbearable, yet still you know if ye dare not tread...it'll stay stuck in your head. You know I did something utterly repulsive to the sweet and holiest of Amanda. That name itself just screams victim. We've all known an Amanda once. Was your Amanda a hapless waif who'd lost her way? Mine was.

There still stands this truth. To continue on only perpetuates violence, yes? Are you an enabler? I think, yes. But, you read on nonetheless. Just another rubbernecker. Just another consumer of the human machine.

It reminds us that we're alive, when people die.

That's why people like you pay to read stories of "true crime." You want to hear what beasts other citizens can be. You want to know the fear and death that demons can bring. Death makes you cling to life. Love your life.

That's why people buy the vidi-films. These cruddy-fucks with their tech-connects and shareburns sending data and collecting pain at an astonishing rate. A million broken lives and dreams all saved and savored and sent. And I break these lives. And I break these bodies. I am the spiller of the blood.

It almost makes me proud. My best work has been seen worldwide.

A white sheet. White robes. A freaker strobe making our every move all nightmare fucking beautiful. A sparkling, razor-sharp knife in each hand, hot liquid sex and metal. Stu was watching from somewhere behind the mirrored glass. Digi-vid burnt film. Blood spattered, frozen, all stop-motioned under the strobe.

Dodger twisted the skin on Amanda's back with a jagged broken bottle. He used the pliers next.

It was more like some trippy creepjoint performance art piece than murder. Fuck yes a girl died that night. Fuck yes we destroyed her. She was recreated as a piece of art, as well.

The finale. With surgical precision, she was flayed. Skin parted from muscle, muscle parted from bone. That little dolly was quite aware as her stuffing was pulled out. Hating the whole time. Cursing us with her last breath. An amazing specimen. Almost a shame to snuff, really.

Not that there wouldn't be retribution. All within a week, Stu and Dodge both dead. Me thrown into a "center" all locked and caged and raped and rotting. So, don't you fog up your ghoul eyes with tears for sweet Amanda. She was lucky. Even the death we gave her betters my everyday excuse for a life.

Stu had provided the list. This client had specific tastes. He wanted us to abduct a waitress. Young. Blonde. Pretty. Catch it all on vid from beginning to end. And the end. The fucking end.

The white sheets had set Stu back a couple of stones. Expenses to be absorbed in the cost of the vid. White sheets everywhere. Cotton and silk.

Turn white to red. Specific directions for acquired tastes. Take her apart. We did as requested.

Here's the part that got to me. This skirt is just getting off work. She's had a long day. I could see when we got her shoes off just how sore her feet looked. Waitresses work hard, they deal with muppets and creeperfreaks all day, and they bring us food. They make next to nothing. For some reason, this client had a grudge against waitresses.

Howmotherfuckingever, this particular diner-bitch deserved nothing like this. What, you stuff a meager ten-spot or so in your greasy apron and call it another day, and you somehow fall into someone else's sick electric nightmare. You find yourself at the mercy of a couple of powerdusted murder-junkies with knives and boners and rope. No matter how well you've planned out your life, you still end up with your head planted on a wooden spike in the middle of a dirty barn.

We pulled her apart. More specifically, we disassembled her entirely and made a hollow cavity where her chest used to be. That's what we were paid for. That's what they paid to see.

We cut her long ways, down the middle and displayed her peeled open and pinned. Struggling and jiggling and fighting the whole time. I've yet to see someone hang onto life quite like Amanda did. She must have really loved her life.

Specific tastes. Take her insides out, display them as they're removed, and pin her open like a bug on a board. Dodge produced a hammer and nails. Her guts already scooped out and strung about the barn like Christmas garland. Her heart in a jar.

Even though we enjoyed our jobs, neither of us were shits and giggles while we worked. Pure professionalism. Complete concentration. Precision. With every knife stroke, with every gun blast. We were tops at what we did, even for mere boys.

I've lost track of how long it's been now. I've been moved from one correctional facility to another to another to another. Now that I'm sick, they have finally left me in one place, presumably to die.

But, I don't die. Or I can't die. I've tried on several occasions, believe you me. But still my heart beats, slow and murmurous in my chest. My blood still flows. My flesh still lives. But every waking second is a parody of life itself.

Hunger consumes me. So hungry I could eat a scabby baby. Once, in this hellhole, I even pulled out patches of my own hair just for something else in my stomach. Fortunately, I am no longer plagued with the company of the other offenders in this zoo. They tend to steer clear of me now. They can smell me rotting. They don't want to catch whateverthefuck I have.

I lost all my teeth last week. Just by brushing. They all fell right out like pretty pearls clinking in the sink.

My thumb turned black and just sort of fell off. I can feel myself crumbling from the inside. The smell of decay covers me.

And even though I don't know why this is happening, I find at the same time I don't care. I just want it done. I want it over. Whatever curse the diner-witch put on me, whatever flesh-eating disease I've contracted, whatever this is, it's a blessing.

47

My every dream is filled with bodies and arms and mouths, all scratching, and biting. I rarely sleep. When I do, I awake to find another part of me rotten. Another part of me gone. And all I really want to be is gone. If I cannot die, at least I can disintegrate and rot. Soon I will be gone completely.

Dust. Nothing at all.

You make friendly with an ocean of skin. Children and demons and armed and drugged we raped the city streets. We were angels of death in a time of everlasting chaos.

I only remembered one name ever.

STILL LIFE WITH SOUL JUICE

BY L. L. SOARES

Carlos scratched the bite on the inside of his arm. He'd been getting a lot of them lately.

"Another one?" Misty asked.

"Yeah." He scratched so hard his nails drew blood. "Fucking bugs."

"I don't have any bites on me," she said. "Maybe they just like you."

"I guess I'm just too fucking sweet to resist," he said. "That's why *you're* here, right?"

She didn't answer, just continued to look at the painting he was working on. A great swirl of reds and blacks so far. He kept stopping to scratch his bites.

"I never see the fucking things," he said. "Do you?"

"I see the roaches well enough, but I don't think it's them. Roaches don't bite, do they?"

"I don't think so. Maybe we just have really hungry ones."

"I guess they took a look in the fridge." She walked into the next room.

He scratched at his arm again, and some pus mixed with blood ran down his elbow. "Shit! Where the hell did you go?"

Misty returned with mercurochrome. "Maybe this will help."

"It couldn't fucking hurt. I'm bleeding here."

"Poor baby." She poured the liquid on a piece of gauze. "Where's the cut, loverboy?"

He showed her his arm, and she started cleaning the wound.

"You're fucking Florence Nightingale," he said.

"*I am not*!" she said. "I never touched the lady."

"Yeah, yeah, real funny." Carlos sounded annoyed.

"I just realized, I'm here because you have such a great sense of humor," she answered. The gauze was stained with blood. "Maybe you should put a band-aid on the damn thing."

"Where do I start? They're on my back, down my arms. I look like a fucking *junkie* with these marks all over me."

"I guess you wouldn't consider going to the doctor?"

"Why the fuck would I? I know what it is: some kind of fucking bug bites. Why should I pay some doctor to tell me the same exact thing? Or maybe he'll look at them and really think I am some kind of addict. I don't need that shit."

"But they look like they're getting worse," she said, trying to sound concerned. It was getting harder all the time.

"Don't you think I *know* that?" he asked. "It's pretty fucking obvious."

"You should get one of those bug bombs or something. Maybe call an exterminator."

"Fuck that. I have a painting to finish. The rest can wait for now."

"You're in one of your moods."

"Moods? I'm *creating* something here. How is that a fucking mood? I just need some fucking quiet. If you can't be quiet and stay out of the way, then go away for awhile."

"Yeah, yeah."

"Just go take a hike, okay? This isn't a spectator sport."

"Okay." She grabbed her coat and came back to give him a kiss, not because she really wanted to, but because he'd go ballistic if she didn't. Misty just wanted to get out of this place with as little hassle as possible.

"I'll come back later."

"Do what you want," he said, stepping back and looking at the canvas, trying to get back into the groove, trying to decide what he was going to do next.

"Sure."

Out in the hallway, she really wondered if she was ever going to come back to this dingy place.

* * *

Blood dripped from his arm as he painted, but Carlos was oblivious. On the canvas was a gigantic vagina, open with the crown of a baby's head beginning to emerge.

The source of life.

Streaked with red and black.

And then it began to change, becoming more primal.

He was entering a fever-like state and getting lost in the piece.

Carlos stepped back. It was the most beautiful thing he'd ever seen, but it was far from done.

It needed more color, and he went searching for more paint.

* * *

Mid-way through the painting, Carlos passed out. He woke to find himself on the carpeted floor, paint spatters on his clothes, and some kind of creature weighing heavily on his chest. It had large red insect eyes and a spear-like snout. His hands reached out and touched it, and it felt like a mouse's body—a thin, furry layer of skin stretched tightly over muscle and bone. Although in this case, he wasn't exactly sure what he felt beneath the skin (did insects have bones?).

His first instinct was the scream. Whatever was on top of him was wrapping its thin, spindly legs around him, and he could tell it was some kind of giant bug, the size of a large dog. Because of the snout, his first thought was it was some kind of mutant mosquito, except it didn't have wings.

"Don't struggle," the thing said softly, near his ear. He couldn't see a mouth. "Don't move a muscle."

"What are you?" Carlos forced himself to ask. "What do you want from me?"

"Soul juice," the thing said.

He knew then this was the thing leaving the puncture marks on his body, that it must have been feeding on his blood as he slept. He was amazed it had finally revealed itself.

"Blood," he said. "You drink my blood."

"No," the thing said. "Your soul juice. I've only taken a little at a time, enough to sussstain me, but I'm ssso very hungry. I need more."

"You're going to kill me."

"No. We can help each other, you and I. You will feed me and I will give back to you. I will give you what you need to create."

"Give back to me?"

"Yes," the thing said. "You provide me with food. I provide you with a fire in your belly. A desire to create your beautiful paintings."

"Food, what kind of food?"

51

"You will know when the time comes, but keep in mind, if you do not feed me with others, I'll have to take my nourishment from you."

It released a vapor then, which smelled awful and sent him drifting off back to sleep.

* * *

Carlos woke again and saw that Misty was back. He was stretched out on the floor, and she was in the bed, sleeping. She hadn't even tried to wake him up and get him into bed with her.

Then again, he was sure she was cheating on him anyway. Why else would she come back late all the time? Where was she going?

He sat up and looked under the bed. The beast was under there, poking its elongated snout at him. He could see it wriggling in the shadows, and he wondered how long it had been here, in this apartment. He wondered how many times it had been under the bed when he slept, when he and Misty fucked.

The thought filled him with revulsion.

The thing looked at him with its bulging, segmented eyes and moved forward, its thin legs clattering softly on the floor. Not enough noise to wake her, but enough to make him sit up and consider running away.

"Now," it said. "No time like the present."

And it climbed up the side of the bed, pulling itself up the length of the sheets hanging over the side and clambering toward her sleeping form. It crawled on top of her and hugged her with its legs.

"Wha—" Misty was jarred awake.

Help me; you have to help me he could hear the creature in his head repeating over and over. Just to shut it up, he grabbed a hammer off of a table behind the canvas and went back to the bed to hold her down. She struggled, calling out his name.

"Keep her still," the thing pleaded.

Carlos hit her on the side of the head with the hammer.

Once.

Twice.

By now, the creature had pulled the sheets away from her nude body, and it struggled as it pushed her over onto her back.

She was still conscious, but clearly dazed by the blows from the hammer. Blood trickled down her neck and onto the cotton sheets, creating dark red Rorschach blotches.

He'd hit her harder than he meant to; blood and flecks of brain matter stained his naked chest. Carlos dropped the hammer and held her shoulders down.

The thing scuttled down and brandished its sword-like proboscis. It reared back and plunged its nose between her legs, deep into her cunt. It ran forward as hard as it could, ramming its nose deeper and deeper. Misty groaned in pain and thrashed about weakly.

Then the thing lifted its head, its nose ripping her flesh, opening her up like a piñata. But instead of candy spilling onto the ground, her intestines and other organs bulged out of the long, deep wound. The creature thrust its razor-sharp nose into her again, tearing through more tissue. Misty struggled, and Carlos held her tight, although, by this point, she wasn't putting up much of a fight. Her eyes were wide and staring at the ceiling, as the thing eviscerated her at the foot of the bed. She was gurgling in the back of her throat, trying to scream.

"Why don't you just put her to sleep, like you did me?" Carlos asked.

"Because it tastes so much better when you humans are awake and trying to fight back," the thing replied. "I put you to sleep because I wasn't sure if I could overpower you. But now, with your help, I subdued *her* easily."

She started to spasm, and he lifted the hammer again and smashed in her cheekbone, closing one of her eyes permanently. The loss of blood took its toll and she drifted away—the separation of the soul and the body.

"No!" the thing cried out in his head. "We mustn't let the soul get away."

A long tongue jutted from the tip of the pointed nose, lapping up blood, licking the red off exposed organs.

"So you do feed on blood," Carlos said, stepping away from the bed.

"No," the thing told him. "Not blood. What's *in* the blood. What's still leaking from her...*Soul juice*."

He felt it nudge him telepathically and felt himself moving towards Misty, climbing onto the bed and imitating the creature's actions. He reached in and pulled out one of her kidneys and began to lick it clean, tasting the coppery blood first, but then something else. Something tangy he couldn't quite name. And he knew that the only reason he could taste it was because the creature had done something to make him more aware.

"Go to sleep now," the thing told him, as Carlos smelled the rank vapor again. "Let her essence sink into you. I will clean all this up."

Carlos stretched out on the bed beside her mutilated body, lying across a giant blood stain that was still growing. He could feel the wetness beneath him on the sheets, and hear the slurping sounds of the giant insect that was still licking up as much of her soul as it could.

"When you wake, you will be full of the desire to paint," the creature told him. "You will be caught up in a fury of creativity, and you will let it guide you. But until then, close your eyes."

It spoke in his mind with the voice of a hypnotist, and he had no desire to resist.

* * *

Carlos woke up on the floor once again, aching and covered in paint. He struggled to his feet and stumbled to the bathroom. He was naked and multi-colored, his head throbbing. He dry swallowed three Tylenols and washed his face. The paint on his body had already dried.

He went back out into the main room of the apartment, which he'd stripped of furniture long ago and filled with drop cloths and canvases. There, the painting waited for him. He didn't remember painting it, but it was clearly his style. And something extra.

Something amazing. It was the most beautiful thing he'd ever seen: a bright green vagina, the crowning head aglow, a thousand rays of color to greet its arrival into the world. He knew its name immediately.

The Birth of Birth.

* * *

When he finally managed to pull his eyes away, Carlos glanced across the room. No sign of Misty. The thing that killed her had told him the truth; it got rid of the body. There were big

54

splotches of dried blood on the sheets, but it had removed them as well.

Even the hammer he'd used to smash in her face was licked clean of blood.

* * *

"It's the most incredible thing you've ever done," Jaze said, standing in front of the painting, taking it all in. "I'm sure we can sell this one quickly."

"I almost hate to see it go," Carlos said.

Sun snuck in through the room's lone window, illuminating the colors. It looked like a rainbow had exploded and thrown its guts against the canvas.

"Let me make some calls," Jaze said. "You got any more like this one in you?"

"I hope so."

* * *

Carlos woke to the sound of feet running across the ceiling.

He opened his eyes slowly. The thing was watching him and crawled down the wall to get a closer look.

Carlos sat up. "What are you, anyway?"

It was in the corner of the room, then, staring up at him. At first, he wondered if it was the same one he'd spoken with before.

"I'm your muse," it said, eventually.

"Yes," he said, relieved there weren't more than one of these things.

"You liked the painting, then? The one you made with soul juice?"

Carlos scratched his arm. The puncture wounds on his body were healing now. "Yes. It was beautiful."

"You'd like to make more like that?"

Carlos nodded.

"I will inspire you."

* * *

"You Carlos?" A man was sitting on the front steps of his building, a little kid beside him.

55

Carlos had just come back from the grocery store and was carrying two bags.

"Yeah."

"I'm Frank," the man said, standing up. "Is Misty around?"

"She's out right now. Can I give her a message?"

"This is Frank Junior," the man said. "Her son."

Carlos looked down at the boy, who was wearing a black T-shirt and jeans, just like his father.

"Yeah?"

"I need to leave town for the weekend. I was hoping she could watch him for me."

Carlos had heard Misty mention her son a few times, but he never knew where the kid lived, how often she saw him, or why he wasn't with her. He never asked, figuring it must have been painful if she never talked about it. She talked about everything else.

But the kid here, she hardly said a word about him, and nothing about his father.

"Is she expecting you?" Carlos asked.

"Fuck, no. Something just came up. You know how it is."

"Yeah."

"So can the kid stay here or not? She hasn't seen him in a long time. I figured she might be happy to spend some time with him."

Carlos nodded. "Yeah, I'm sure you're right."

"I've got to go," Frank said. He had short hair and his eyebrows were shaved off. He looked like he worked out a lot.

"Look, I really don't have time to babysit."

Frank leaned in close. "I know she lives here, and you don't have a choice. I have to go, and she's the only one who can watch him right now. He's her kid, after all. Let her pretend to be a mother for once."

Frank was already halfway across to the street by the time he finished. Carlos stood on the steps, watching the man drive away. He looked down at the boy.

"Well, I guess you're staying here for a few days. You hungry?"

Frank Junior nodded his head.

"Let's go inside and see what we've got to eat."

* * *

56

Something scuffled in the closet.

"What's that?" Frank Junior asked, jumping at the sudden noise.

"The pipes." Carlos was making a ham sandwich. "You want cheese on that?"

"Sure."

Carlos didn't have the heart to tell the kid his mother wasn't coming back. The whole situation put him in a bind. There was no way he would be able to paint with a kid around. *And what about the thing that climbs the walls?*

"When's mommy coming back?"

Carlos bit his lip and dabbed mayonnaise on the sandwich.

"Eat up, kid. You're going to have a long wait."

* * *

Carlos was sleeping on the floor. The kid had been on the bed, but he wasn't there now. Maybe he went to the kitchen for a midnight snack.

Carlos got up and checked the place, but no sign of Frank Junior.

Maybe he ran away.

Carlos heard the scuffling again and turned on a light. He went to the closet and opened the door.

The thing was holding onto the clothes hanging in the closet, its long sharp proboscis jammed down Junior's throat. The kid was sitting on the floor, looking up, except his eyes were closed. He looked like he was still sleeping.

"No," Carlos said. "Leave the kid alone."

"But his soul juice is so pure," the thing said in his head. "So sweet. I've never tasted anything like this before."

"Don't kill him."

"I don't want this to ever end. Leave him with me. Tell his father he ran away. His mother took him away."

"I can't do that. Don't make me do that."

He heard the creature moaning with delight in his head. He had no idea how to pull the kid out of there. The thing's snout was down his throat, making the boy look like he was being impaled. He was afraid if he moved the kid, he might risk hurting him.

Instead, he stepped back, closed the closet, and shut off the light.

* * *

Someone was tugging his arm, and Carlos woke with a start.

"I'm thirsty," Frank Junior said. "And my stomach hurts."

Carlos got up and poured some orange juice in a dirty glass. It was only five a.m.

The kid drank it down fast. Carlos watched him, looking for scars, scratches, any sign of harm, but he didn't see any. Frank Junior was wearing striped pajamas and tiger slippers.

"You want more?"

"Yes, please. I'm still thirsty."

Carlos couldn't shake the image he'd seen in the closet.

Frank went back to bed, curling into a ball beneath the sheets.

There was a drawing on the floor near the bed. Carlos picked it up. It was rough, but very good for a kid.

* * *

"What's with the kid?" Jaze asked, looking around the room at the finished paintings.

"He's Misty's. This is the first time I've seen him."

"I didn't know Misty had a son…Can I take these three? I'll put them up in the gallery. I don't expect they'll take long to sell."

"Yeah, business has been good, hasn't it?"

"I'll say."

Frank Junior sat at the small kitchen table, watching them, not saying a word.

* * *

Carlos woke, and got up off the floor. On the bed, the insect thing was on top of Frank Junior. They were struggling. It was probably smothering him, with its needle nose buried in his flesh.

"Will you let me have him?" it asked inside his head.

"I don't know."

"I gave you an alibi," it said. "I can end this tonight."

"He's just a kid."

"His soul is so sweet, though. I can't ration it out anymore."

58

"Give me one more day," Carlos said. "I don't know if I can go through with this."

"You wouldn't reveal me, would you?" it asked. "You wouldn't betray my trust?"

"No," Carlos said. "But give me another day to come to terms with this."

"I can do that."

The furry body moved away from the boy and slid off the bed. It went back to the closet, and closed the door behind it.

Carlos stared at the door for a long time before he went back to sleep.

* * *

They were in the park, eating ice cream cones.

"What's the thing that lives in the closet?" Frank Junior asked, staring up at him.

"What are you talking about?" Carlos tried to be gentle. He followed it with a little laugh.

"The monster," the kid said, "in your apartment."

"There's no monster. You've got some imagination."

"Look," Frank said, pulling a folded up paper out of his pocket and handing it to Carlos. "I drew a picture of it."

Carlos unfolded the paper and looked at the drawing. It was fairly accurate.

"That's a scary one," Carlos said. "You say you saw this in my place? In the closet?"

The boy nodded, confusion spread across his face.

"I've never seen it there," Carlos said. "He must be a good hider."

He handed the drawing back. The boy folded it and put it back in his pocket.

"When's my mommy coming back?"

* * *

Carlos woke with a sharp pain in his head.

He opened his eyes just in time to see the hammer come down again. He jumped back, putting his hands out, pushing Frank Junior away. The boy stood in the darkened room, holding the hammer.

"What are you doing?"

"You have to be still," the boy said, "so it can drink from you."

"Put down the hammer, Frank."

"My mommy is never coming back."

He raised the hammer again, but Carlos grabbed his wrist and shook it loose, sending it skittering across the floor.

"You weren't strong enough," the thing on the ceiling said.

Carlos looked up; its nose pointed down at him.

"Why?" Carlos asked. "I was going along with your plan."

"You were having second thoughts. So I decided to be the boy's inspiration instead. Have you seen his drawings? He'll grow up to be better than you."

"He's just a boy," Carlos said. "What will he tell his father when he comes back? That he has a new pet to bring home, a giant bug that drinks souls?"

"I don't need you any longer," the thing said, and ran down the wall.

"You said the boy's soul was too sweet to ration," Carlos said. "You said you couldn't resist any longer."

"I can ration it out a long time." It moved toward the bed. "And he makes new soul juice. He's young and can replace it as fast as I drink it. I don't have to be hungry anymore."

"And what about me? Are you going to feed off me like you did Misty?"

"I don't need you any longer," the thing said again.

Frank Junior found the hammer again. He ran and struck Carlos in the side of the throat, trying to reach his face.

"Stop it," he said to the boy. "Stop it."

"Hit him," the creature said in his mind, in both of their minds. "Make him stop moving so I can feed. So we can feed."

Carlos wrenched the hammer away and hit Frank Junior with it. He did it without thinking, to get the kid away from him, but he must have hit him harder than he meant to because the boy dropped to the ground. Blood began to pool around his head.

He couldn't tell if Frank Junior was dead or just hurt.

He turned on the light and the thing ran under the bed.

"Come out of there," Carlos said, running toward the bed and turning it over. As the creature tried to get away, he struck it with the hammer, over and over, pulping its legs, pounding through its thin furry skin and crushing the bones beneath. He could hear it crying out in his head.

He caught a whiff of the strange-smelling vapor that had previously put him to sleep, and he held his breath.

It tried to spear him with its nose, but he struck it with the hammer again. He put his knee on the nose, even though it cut into his leg, and he hammered the proboscis over and over until it separated from the head. Then he pounded its head until it stopped moving, until the thin flesh of its body stopped rising and falling with breath.

Its blood covered his chest and face. He licked his lips, and it was the sweetest thing he'd ever tasted. Before he realized what he was doing, he buried his head in one of the creature's open wounds, sucking furiously at the nectar inside.

When he was done, Carlos stood and moved away, wiping his mouth with the back of his hand. He stared from it to the boy.

Neither moved.

Carlos reached over and turned off the lights.

* * *

Carlos was sitting on the steps in front of his building when Frank's father came back.

"I'm here to pick up Frank Junior."

"Sorry, you just missed him," Carlos said.

"What the fuck are you talking about?"

Carlos could see the veins in the man's neck.

"They left. Misty took the boy away. They were gone when I woke up this morning. They didn't leave a note."

"She wouldn't dare," the man said. "She knows I'd hunt her down."

"I don't know what to say," Carlos said. "I'm as surprised as you are. Misty and I had been talking about getting married. I thought she was the one."

"You're not in on this?"

"I think she was afraid I'd tell you where she went," Carlos said. "She didn't tell me a thing."

"That bitch," Frank said. "That's what I get for trusting a junkie. I figured I'd give her a chance to prove she could be a real mother again, but I should have known better."

Carlos was amazed how easily the man accepted the story. He hadn't even demanded to see the apartment.

"You hear from her, you call me," Frank said, handing him a business card. "I'll make sure it's worth your while."

"Sure," Carlos said.

Frank went back to his car and pounded on the hood a few times before getting inside.

Carlos watched him drive away and then went back inside.

Suddenly, he had the most wonderful idea for a painting.

A WILLING DONOR

BY KEVIN LUCIA

Craig Hartley stood at the tiny room's window at Clifton Heights Memorial, sweating his ass off in the summer heat.

It was easily eighty degrees outside. Despite a sign in the lobby boasting: "New! Air Conditioned Rooms!" it felt like this room was "Old! With No Fucking Air Conditioning at All!" It was so hot, Craig felt like he stood at Hell's gates—not a pleasant analogy in a hospital.

He despised hospitals. They represented life's futility. Didn't matter how much a person worked, what their goals or habits were, everyone wound up in the same place.

He grimaced as he watched townspeople scurry about the sidewalks outside. It's amazing, he thought, how they can run around in the shadow of this place, where they'll all come someday to die in their sleep.

He smirked. Idiots. That's why he'd left, wasn't it? So he wouldn't become one of them.

Craig's smirk faded. Here he was, back again. He'd gone out into the big, wide world and carved a life for himself—a good life, dammit—but he felt like he'd never left. Some part of him would always be nineteen—defiant, reckless, insecure, and scared of his father's bullshit religion.

Still haunted by the shadow of his brother's sacrifice.

Bullshit. That's Pop talking. You didn't believe it then, don't believe it now.

* * *

A dry spot on his scalp itched as he turned and inspected the room. He avoided looking at the horribly burnt patient, and ignored thee hissing, gurgling tubes and wheezing respirator that pumped life into his identical twin, Buddy Hartley.

The itchy patch on his scalp burned while tubes pumped air into Buddy's lungs and IVs flushed his scorched body with fluids, plasma, and nutrients. Craig couldn't ignore it, much as he tried. According to his father, it bore testament to his brother's sacrifice

63

for him. So his old man had always claimed, anyway, before falling into a combine three years ago and getting chopped to bits.

God rest his soul, Craig griped. Try as he might, he couldn't work up much grief over his father's passing.

With a deep breath, he forced himself to look at Buddy.

What remained was difficult to see. They'd been identical twins, but it was hardly evident now. Almost every inch of Buddy that wasn't wrapped in blood-stained gauze was scorched gut-red or deep black. Skin cracked and peeled, large swathes looked like melted plastic that had congealed and cooled in oblong globs. Buddy looked half his size, almost as if the fire had burned most of his muscle away. He was a skeleton coated with a thin layer of charred meat.

IV lines and a g-tube kept him nourished, PIC lines drained seepage away, while a catheter pumped what little piss there was out of him and into a bag hanging from the bedrail. An insistent cardiac monitor kept Buddy's heartbeat; sounding a rhythmic *ping, ping*. Despite the trauma, Buddy's heart still beat strong. Of course, Buddy's heart had always been stronger than his, in more ways than one.

Buddy's face was hidden by layers of gauze, and if Craig hadn't known it was his brother, he'd have thought it looked like a badly constructed prop for a mummy movie. There were no bumps on either side of the head where ears should be, and the mouth—which was intubated with a plastic air tube—was nothing more than a burnt hole. Thankfully, an oxygen mask covered the lower region of his face, but Craig could still see the ruined remains of Buddy's nose.

That was *not* his brother.

"He's dying, Craig."

Craig glanced over his shoulder at Dr. Stanley Newcomb, chief resident at Clifton Memorial. Tall, gaunt, thin-faced with bloodless lips and a black receding hairline, he looked like a ghoul that feasted on the flesh of the dead, or at the very least, a B-movie version of Vincent Price. In any case, Craig couldn't help but stiffen at the sight of the doctor. He'd freaked them out as kids, and Craig imagined no matter how many peppermints or lollipops he distributed, Dr. Newcomb would always freak kids out.

His scalp burned. He swallowed, composed himself, and in the process, thought he caught a breath of *Old Spice*, Pop's favorite cologne.

Dammit. Man's dead and gone, and that's it.

Mentally, he shoved the scent aside. Aloud, he asked, "How long?"

The doctor pursed his lips. "A few days. We've done all we can, but the trauma is too severe. His body is breaking down, I'm afraid."

"How'd it happen?"

"Since your father died and the farm sold, Buddy had been boarding at Miss Walpole's and working at the landfill. It was burning night, and a load of garbage shifted and fell. Buddy was too close; it pinned him to the ground. By the time anyone reached him, this was what remained…It's good you came. He needs your help, Craig."

Something twitched in his belly, but he ignored it. "I can't do anything about *this*," he muttered. "There's nothing *anyone* can do."

"Not necessarily."

Craig frowned as he studied the doctor's pinched face.

"There are measures that can be taken. Your father left explicit instructions in his will regarding the events of either of your deaths, as well as a healthy trust fund to pay for such care. He left *specific* instructions regarding efforts to save Buddy's life, particularly."

Craig barked with laughter. "I'll never understand why you guys even let Pop past the front doors with his hoodoo-healing magic. I'm surprised no one ever sued you."

Dr. Newcomb shrugged, his expression placid. "This is an experiential hospital, Craig. We're open to all kinds of alternative medicine."

He gave Craig an appraising look that made him squirm. "Your father healed many folks over the years." Craig glanced away, cheeks glowing. "Placebo effect. Healing power of the human mind. Trick people into thinking they're better, they get better."

"Yes, the healing power of the mind," Dr. Newcomb muttered. "You'd do well to remember that."

"I don't understand how Pop could've saved that much money. He did all right on the farm and conned lots of hill folk up in the 'Heights with his hoodoo." Craig looked everywhere but at the doctor's gaze and his charred brother. "But not enough to set up a trust fund."

Dr. Newcomb tilted his head. "As I said, he did much good around here. After awhile, you could say we had him on a retainer of sorts."

Craig snorted, not sure if he should feel disgusted or…well, he didn't know what. So that's how the old man had been able to send him to all those summer enrichment camps and pay for his freshman year at Binghamton. And to think, the asshole had made Craig think it was because of Buddy slaving away on the farm.

"It's not going to work," Craig managed. "He's dying, burnt to hell. I'm too old to believe in Pop's superstitious nonsense."

He wasn't sure, but he thought the corner of Newcomb's mouth twitched upward at his last remark.

The doctor clasped his hands behind his back and rocked on his heels. "Regardless, Buddy's too weak for the necessary procedures. He needs a blood transfusion, and as his identical twin, you're a perfect match."

Craig looked at his feet.

What the hell am I doing?

As if reading his thoughts, Dr. Newcomb whispered, "Saving his life." A pause. "Also…repaying a debt, if I understand your father's will correctly."

Craig shook his head. *Bastard. Even when you're dead, you can't let up, can you?*

His scalp itched, but he managed to stuff his hands into his pockets.

"All we need is some blood." Dr. Newcomb assured him.

Craig swallowed. He faced the doctor with a stiff smile and rolled up his sleeve. "What the hell?" He stopped rolling at the elbow and folded his arms. "I pay my 'debt,' you get some blood, and I go back to my life. Why not?"

Maybe Dr. Newcomb meant his grin to be comforting, but the thin smile that spread his skin taut over his face made Craig shiver. "Indeed."

Craig's scalp itched and burned the whole time.

* * *

It didn't take long to organize the transfusion. In moments—quicker than Craig was comfortable with, actually—he was seated in a small, featureless room, with several racks of empty blood bags suspended next to him. Craig knew nothing about transfusions, but there seemed too many bags for just a pint or two.

Seated, shirt still rolled to his elbow, Craig felt a quick pinprick on the inside of his forearm, as painless as the wide-hipped, dour-faced nurse had promised. As Dr. Newcomb entered and the nurse exited, closing the door behind her, Craig felt many things. Surprisingly enough, one of them was pride. Finally, he *was* doing something for Buddy. He may not believe his father's hokey religion, but it felt good to give something back to his brother.

Dr. Newcomb smiled as he checked the IV lines. "This is a good thing you're doing, Craig. Not many people these days would sacrifice so much."

Still a bit high on his own altruism, Craig offered Dr. Newcomb a wan look. "Well, a few pints aren't all that much. It's not like I've given to the Red Cross lately, so I've got some karma to redeem."

Dr. Newcomb smiled even wider as he withdrew a syringe from his jacket pocket. "Yes," he replied, "a few pints. So modest. 'Karma to redeem,' an apt choice of words. Tell me, Craig—did you truly disbelieve your father's faith?"

Craig grunted, doing his best not to scowl. "Faith? You mean his crazy mish-mash of hoodoo and regional folklore?" Craig shook his head. He tried to find some middle ground between familial duty and truth. "Don't get me wrong. Pop raised us best he could all alone. He was hard but fair, never laid a hand on us, and provided."

Dr. Newcomb tapped the syringe. Apparently satisfied, he secured it to the IV. "But you didn't approve of his practices." It was a statement, not a question.

Craig waved his IV-free hand. He felt light-headed, warm. "C'mon, doc. Casting spells, conjuring and binding spirits, mixing herbs and potions, researching old, arcane incantations—that's no way to raise kids, especially one as…" he swallowed and said, "challenged as Buddy."

"And yet, you turned out fine. College degree, well-paying job…fancy car?"

"That's because I got the hell out. If it'd been up to Pop, I would've stayed here the rest of my life, working on the farm with Buddy."

A wave of vertigo hit him, making his eyes heavy. Looking up at the syringe with a tired squint, he mumbled, "Lissen, doc…what's in that syringe? I'm startin' to lose it, here."

The doctor smiled again. Maybe it was the strange drug, but Craig realized how *hungry* he looked.

"You've got quite a procedure ahead, Craig. We want you to feel as little pain as possible."

Whatever was in the syringe acted fast. Craig wanted to be sarcastic, but all he could manage was sloppy. "Boy, you guys take blood transfusions seriously, huh?"

Dr. Newcomb knelt next to him, his hungry look deepening. "I'm afraid I misled you, Craig. This is much more than a blood transfusion. Over the next few days, we're going to save your brother's life, and pay back your *Weirguild* to him."

Something cold pierced Craig's drug-induced delirium at the mention of a word he'd last heard from his father. "Waitaminute. Whatthefuckdidja say?"

Dr, Newcomb's smile faded, his expression grave. "*Weirguild*—your life debt to Buddy."

The sedative hit Craig hard. His head lolled to his shoulder. His tongue flopped and his throat tightened. He tried to speak but only managed a weak gurgle. He searched Newcomb's face, and then his eyes saw the glittering, metallic pendant hanging around the doctor's neck, under his open-collared shirt.

It was simple, yet ornate. In pewter, braided by gold, hung an inverted 'Y' in a circle—the 'Eye of the Dragon,' the same as the one his father wore.

With what sluggish control he had left, Craig jerked back, only to find his arms and torso restrained. When had that happened? Craig rolled his head, alarmed at the line of cold drool leaking from his mouth and down his cheek. Dr. Newcomb still squatted, fingering the pendant.

"Your father was a great man. His knowledge of the Netherworld and the Abyss was unparalleled. Fortunately, he passed along what he knew to me before he died. You can't imagine how many lives I've saved these past three years with his knowledge."

Craig tried to jerk away again, but barely managed a shoulder twitch.

Dr. Newcomb softened. "Believe it or not, he was proud of you. But he was prouder of Buddy and his sacrifice. I was the attending physician when you and Buddy were born, the night of your mother's death. You were conjoined twins, and not only was it my first such case, you were conjoined at the head in such a way I couldn't separate you cleanly…"

The spot on Craig's scalp flamed, but he couldn't do anything about it, and he burned in agony and shame.

"….because of the conjoinment angle, I needed to cut nearer to one scalp than the other and inevitably punctured the skull. The blood loss caused irreparable brain damage to the twin I cut nearest to. I was literally faced with choosing your intellectual futures."

Though every nerve screamed as Dr. Newcomb prattled on, Craig slumped further into his chair. He felt a small tug on his arm, flicked a glance to the IV, and saw a tiny red river flow away from him, filling the bags above.

His scalp continued to burn and burn.

"I watched in amazement as your father communed with the elements and touched your souls, even in your mother's womb. He looked for which would be more willing to sacrifice their future for the other." He paused and his eyes flickered. "In Buddy, he found such a willing, kind spirit. In you—not so much."

Craig's head fell back and all he saw was the blurred white of the ceiling. His extremities cooled as blood fled his body, like rats fleeing a sinking ship.

Dr. Newcomb must have leaned close, because as Craig faded, he felt warm breath tickle his ear.

"Everything you've achieved is because of Buddy's sacrifice. It's time to repay the *Weirguild*. It was your father's last wish." A pause. "Rest assured, though. I consider myself an artist. We'll make this—make *you* and Buddy—works of art, I promise you."

There were no more words, only darkness.

* * *

Light. Harsh, bright light. *Pain.*

Immobility.

With a gasp, Craig awoke in a bright, shining *hell.*

He lay on his back. Above him, a mirror reflected his naked torso. A white blanket covered the rest. He tried to move his head but found it strapped tight. His eyes darted, the light dazzled them,

69

its glare excruciating. Bodies walked past, wraiths of pure white, the color of bleached bones.

He tried to scream. His throat gurgled, nothing more.

A wraith leaned close, a strip of flesh on its face revealing eyes and the bridge of a sharp, aquiline nose. Dr. Newcomb.

Craig tried to thrash and buck against the restraints, but the neurons in his brain fired blanks. Electronic signals faded into nothingness as soon as they were sent.

Tenderly, as a father would a son, Dr. Newcomb rested a rubber-gloved hand on his brow. "You'll be happy to know the transfusion was a success. We got plenty of blood from you—without leaving you dry, of course—to give Buddy several more days. We have some room to work now."

Fuck you! Craig's mind screamed. Lunatic, psychopath! Get me the fuck out of here!

As if sensing his anger, Dr. Newcomb chuckled. "You may wonder why we've brought you out of sedation. No worries, we've adjusted the anesthesia so that you *will* feel pain, but it won't be unbearable. You may think us cruel, but we're simply obeying your father's last wishes. He felt the *Weirguild* would have more meaning if you were awake for most of the procedure. That way, there'd be a measure of balance between your pain and Buddy's."

Craig's eyes rolled, a wave of sickness and nausea buffeting him. He felt the overwhelming urge to piss, and though it seemed horribly out of proportion to the circumstances, he felt more afraid of that than anything else: pissing himself in front of strangers. Dr. Newcomb's eyes softened as Craig found his gaze.

"All these years Buddy suffered, watched you live a normal, successful life while he stayed behind as the 'slow' one. He never blamed you," Newcomb shook his head. "Tender hearted as he was, he felt the pain of being left behind, nonetheless. It was in his eyes."

Another wraith—Craig recognized the dull, gray eyes of the big-hipped nurse—floated near. Dr. Newcomb turned and accepted from her a shining, silver scalpel without a word. Light reflected off the scalpel, and Craig thought deliriously of a perverted *Excalibur*, freed from its stone at last.

In a flash of dreadful insight, Craig realized that stone had been his heart all these years.

No! Craig railed. His voice echoed in his mind. *God, no! Stop! Please, you're right. Please.*

He felt it. A pin prick first, then a sharp, painful stab, a line of fire, and worse...*pressure*. As the cut deepened, he felt pressure push out, as if something *inside* strained to be free and pushed against his flesh as the scalpel cut.

"For thirty-three years," Dr. Newcomb whispered, "your brother suffered alone. Never once did he complain, nor treat you harshly."

OH GOD! I'M SORRY!

"Your father admitted you were never cruel to Bud, but you treated him with a dismissive kindness, as an afterthought. His greatest hope was for you to someday *understand* what Buddy gave up for you. As a physician, it's my charge to see that hope fulfilled."

Hu-help m-me...someone help me...PLEEEEEASE!

"There," Dr. Newcomb paused and probed the incision, which sent rockets of pain into Craig's abdominal walls. "I don't mean to be conceited," he whispered, "but *that* is the true work of an artist...the first plain, yet perfect brushstroke of a masterpiece to be."

He reached up, adjusted the mirror's angle. "You may watch, of course. In fact, your father insisted upon it."

Craig tried to shut his eyes, to bask in forgiving darkness, but found that he couldn't. His eyes lids were firmly taped open. No matter how he strained, they remained so. He sobbed inside, the only external evidence the way his mouth sagged open in a lopsided O.

"He wanted you to see everything taken away. Just as Buddy watched you grow without, you must watch yourself be whittled away."

Craig was unable to help himself. He looked into the mirror. Amazingly enough, he saw that Newcomb was right. The incision in his abdomen was perfect, straight. The flesh inside pushed out evenly and pulsed—a thing alive, bubbling, almost...God help him...beautiful.

Blood pooled to the edge of the incision's cresting flesh, but didn't run over. It formed a calm, red lake. Dr. Newcomb's hand descended again, and Craig watched, transfixed. This time, though he still felt the pain, it seemed dull, far way, so focused was he on what the doctor carved into his flesh.

"Unfortunately, though the blood transfusion gave us more time, Buddy's kidneys and liver are failing." Dr. Newcomb turned and gazed into his eyes. "This will be your first repayment to him, the first work of our masterpiece together."

He resumed cutting, and Craig found himself watching those skilled hands as they parted his flesh. The incision spread. As Newcomb made three more perfectly spaced, identical incisions across his stomach, Craig marvelled at the cut's symmetry and balance.

The blood spread, running in all directions. A stray part of him thought nurses were supposed to suction and sponge all that away, but as he lost himself in the meticulous motion of Dr. Newcomb's hands and the brilliance of his own blood; he was glad they didn't. The blood flowed, pooled, swirled, and created little whorls and spirals. As Newcomb sliced, his crimson fingers crept like ivy. Craig was reminded—on some bizarre level—of those Spirographs he'd drawn little designs with as a kid.

Bloody Spirographs, all over his body…all his. All for Buddy.

At that point, something inside, the small orgasmic moment, vanished, to be replaced by a scream Craig hadn't uttered in years.

DADDY!

Like a flap, his skin peeled back. He caught just a glimpse of the pulsing, squirting organs—purple, pink, smooth and rubbery and sliding around his gut—before it became too much. His mind shut down, and he saw no more, taped open eyes be damned.

And yet, as the image of the turgid, slippery things nestled together in his abdomen faded, he couldn't deny their order and perfection…their *beauty*.

Blackness came.

* * *

Light.
Bright light.
Pain.

Craig awoke. Because his eyes were still taped open, there was no opening-door effect from oblivion to awareness. Black spotted to gray. Gradually, white dissolved the gray. White wavered, cleared, and coalesced…to his open chest cavity and two perfect, quivering lungs. They pulsed with each breath, and despite the trauma, they filled in rhythm.

All was symmetry. All was beautiful.

This isn't beautiful, he thought, stumbling against the drugs. *It's an abomination.*

Even so.

"Good news, Craig," a voice spoke near him. His head sagged more than rolled, and Dr. Newcomb's face eased into view. "Buddy's immune system accepted the transplants. No sign of infection or rejection. Of course, you'll need dialysis now..." his hand rand down Craig's open body cavity to his abdomen, which had been stitched up. The entire stomach was skinned, showing throbbing muscles. "...but equipment for that is very advanced these days. You'll be fine."

Craig's eyes must have lingered on the wet patch of his skinless abdomen in the mirror, because Dr. Newcomb added, "Ah, yes. Buddy's body received eighty percent tissue damage. He's eventually going to need skin grafts, so we took some from your stomach to close over his abdominal incisions."

He passed a hand over Craig's brow, and it was oddly comforting. "We'll talk more about that later. It'll be our final step. For now..."

He turned, accepted the scalpel from the dour-eyed nurse, and it again flared with Arthurian light. His hands and scalpel descended into Craig's chest cavity and on his upper bronchi. "As you can imagine, Buddy's lungs were nearly scorched to a crisp through excessive smoke inhalation. One was recoverable, the other, however....."

Dr. Newcomb cut into the bronchi. A great slash of pain exploded from Craig's chest, powerful enough to cause him to spasm, in spite of the anesthesia. A slight moan escaped his lips, and in the mirror, he watched himself spit up blood. He panicked as the blood filled his nose, his air choked off.

"Don't be alarmed," Dr. Newcomb soothed. "A backwash of blood and mucus up the trachea, into the mouth and nasal cavities is completely normal. We've inserted suction tubes down your nose, and your throat will clear soon. We'll intubate just to make sure, of course." He paused, shifted his hands so the nurse could help hold Craig's lung as it fell slack from its bronchi. "You'll be happy to know that many, many people have lived normal, productive lives with only one lung. Of course," Dr. Newcomb remarked, "I'm sure your definition of normal and productive has changed."

73

Even if Craig could answer, he wouldn't have. The pain had dulled, and true to Newcomb's word, two red lines suctioned away the blood and mucus flooding his nose. The blood on his lips, however, shone brightly, like fantastic lipstick on a mime or clown, and if he allowed his drugged dementia to take hold, he could image he was just that. He stared at his reflection as the doctor and lifted one lung from his body, quivering, dotted with bits of blood and bodily fluids. He *was* a clown, with shining red lips, red rivers running from his nose and a pulsing belly.

He was still imagining himself as Booboo the gibbering, eviscerated clown in Dr. Newcomb's traveling *Weirguild* Road Show, when the room spun everything went away.

* * *

They took his intestines next.

They didn't rip and tear, though, like in all those zombie movies he and Buddy used to watch as kids. It wasn't like that all, actually. Dr. Newcomb and his nurse's hands moved with a deft, secure touch. They coiled ropey, slick yards of intestines into a great bin. Somehow, they kept it together, piled in an even, sloping hill. Craig thought of wet clay and imagined they were molding his inner tubes into something new and beautiful.

Dr. Newcomb hadn't lied. Perhaps Craig was that much closer to dying, perhaps his mind had broken completely….but he thought now, that of all the arts he'd ever seen, *this*—what the doctor was doing and what lie hidden inside the body—was real art, after all.

"You may be wondering how all this is possible," Dr. Newcomb mused as he extracted length after length of slippery flesh from his gut. "You may also be wondering why I, a man of the Hippocratic Oath, would consent to such an undertaking."

The last bit of his intestine pulled free with a slurping sound. Dr. Newcomb threaded the rest of it to the nurse and came back to Craig's side.

"Of course, medicine by itself could not manage transplants this extensive." Craig's eyes still taped open; he had no choice but to meet the doctor's gaze. "This, of course, is also why I'm doing it. It's *my* Weirguild to your father, for giving me the gift of his knowledge. Without it, such a thing wouldn't be possible. Both you and Buddy would bleed out instantly, dying of shock or the transplants not knitting together as quickly."

He looked about to say something else, but reconsidered. Instead, he laid a hand on Craig's shoulder. "Rest, my boy, the last—the *hardest*—follows."

Mercifully, the fuzzy cloud of an anesthesia mask descended and darkness returned.

* * *

"We will, of course, leave you enough tissue to survive," Dr. Newcomb had promised, "and we'll also increase the medication for this. It's the most painful step."

It was.

They started at his feet, cutting through the skin and muscle. They slashed tendons, ligaments, connective tissue. They made concentric, connecting, looping cuts. Then, they *peeled* him like a banana. Dr. Newcomb didn't strip him to the bone, but what he left was barely gristle.

And the pain.

Oh, God…the pain. Craig hadn't screamed when they took his liver and kidneys, but *this*. He did nothing but wail silently as every nerve in his body blazed until it was snuffed out and ripped away from him.

Even then, some part of him was fascinated by what emerged. As the doctor and nurse pulled away the thick, corded flesh around his thighs, Craig saw something appear, like a statue emerging under the hand of its sculptor. This kicking stick-figure was somehow beautiful. As gentle hands cut, lifted, folded, and peeled away flesh from around his chest and rib cage, the awful thing jittered and rolled. Spiny, red limbs dripped with ropey tendrils of matter that could only laughingly be called flesh.

When they peeled away his face, his nose….when the last bit was pulled free and his skull popped out of its skin with a *plop*, he stared with horrific fascination at what this master sculptor's hands had revealed. Suddenly, his nerves torn free, all sensation died, and he was left to marvel quietly at the red-slicked skeletal form that stared down from the reflection above.

He was new, reborn. He was art—true, visceral, *cutting* art. He was no artist, but Dr. Newcomb…*he* was master of them all.

Something was different when Craig woke.

He sat upright. The light wasn't as bright. Though he felt nothing, he didn't feel drugged, either. There were no restraints, but he couldn't move

He still couldn't close his eyes. With a cool rush of shock, he realized it was because he didn't have the skin to do so.

A mirror hung on the opposite wall. In it, his reflection—not the horrific final image he'd seen flopping in the mirror in all its terrible glory, though. *This* was pathetic. A pitifully thin figure reclined and wrapped from head to toe in gauze, except for eye, nose, and mouth holes. Gore and fluid seeped through in spots. He saw all the usual medical and monitoring equipment at his bedside. Saw he was intubated, and felt with a start the plastic tube down his throat. He realized he wasn't breathing on his own.

This wasn't art. *This* was the abomination, something weak and useless.

This, this was…

…his brother.

The door opened and Dr. Newcomb walked in, followed by a smiling young man dressed in khakis and a white polo shirt. Though his face looked slightly inflamed—like he was recovering from an allergy or something—he bore a strong resemblance to…..

Craig couldn't scream.

The escalating *ping, ping, ping* of his heart monitor did it for him.

Looking concerned, Dr. Newcomb moved to adjust one of his IV drips, presumably his sedation. A warm, heavy blanket instantly fell over Craig. Though he still felt aware, the edge of his panic dulled. The *pinging* of his heart monitor slowed as well.

"That's better," Dr. Newcomb said as he pulled up a chair, the man—the *impossible* man—following suit. "We just got you back, Craig. Thought we lost you on the table for a moment. Would hate to almost lose you again."

He paused, waved a hand at the young man sitting next to him. "Here he is," Dr. Newcomb said with a wave, "my greatest work of art. Buddy Hartley; alive, well, and in the flesh."

Son of a bitch, Craig stuttered, his first coherent thought in what seemed like forever. Blind rage filled him…but it went nowhere, trapped inside. *Son of a bitch!*

"The swelling has receded nicely," Dr. Newcomb said as he traced a line down Buddy's face with his finger. Buddy laughed and knocked Newcomb's finger away. They acted like old friends. "Fortunately, most of that was done with rather pedestrian analgesics and anti-inflammatories. In a week's time, he should be completely healed."

That's my face….My fucking face!

Dr. Newcomb clasped his hands in front of him and leaned over, looking serious. "Unfortunately, there are limits even to your father's knowledge. We weren't able to repair the damage to Buddy's vocal chords and removing yours seemed too risky— though we *did* sever them. Your father *explicitly* stated in his will you were to survive the procedure. We wanted to adhere to that directive."

Buddy smiled and nodded his head. He looked at Craig, and there was such shining, bright gratitude there that Craig could do nothing but silently sob.

"Also, our work on his ears is completely cosmetic. To that end, he's both deaf and mute, but he's picked up sign language very well," Dr. Newcomb paused and signed something that must've been joke. Buddy guffawed, his laughter strange and mewling…but *sound* all the same.

"Finally, of course, there was nothing we could do about Buddy's mental limitations. He is as challenged as he always has been. However, your father *did* set aside two sizable trust funds. One to fund your care and another larger one to see that Buddy never has to work another day. I imagine with his communication limitations his mental challenges won't be quite as apparent."

Dr. Newcomb glanced at Buddy with a knowing leer, signing as he spoke. "In a week, Buddy will be quite an attractive fellow. I don't think he'll lack for female companionship."

Unbelievably, Dr. Newcomb mimed a generous hip thrust, at which Buddy broke out into scratchy peals of laughter.

I'd kill you if I could…

Dr. Newcomb sobered and waved a hand, calming Buddy down. "Most importantly, Buddy is extremely grateful. You have repaid him his *Weirguild*, and more than that, you have acted liked a true brother." He stopped signing, raised his eyebrows, and added softly. "As far as he knows…you volunteered for this."

To punctuate his point, Buddy rose from his chair and knelt next to the bed. Gently, he reached out, grasped Craig on either side of his head—which Craig couldn't feel—and stared at him with baby blue eyes Craig wasn't sure he'd ever really seen before. Buddy bent his head, touched foreheads with him, and grunted something that needed no translation.

Thank you.

Craig broke into little pieces. *Aw, fuck….fuck it, Buddy…I'm sorry I left you; sorry I didn't do more….*

Buddy nodded once, grunted again, and stood. Dr. Newcomb stood as well, and the pair headed for the door.

Wait, Buddy, don't leave me! Not after this, not after what I did!

Buddy gave a big, friendly wave and flashed a thankful smile that would burn itself into Craig's memory forever. Dr. Newcomb clapped him on the shoulder, and Buddy Hartley—identical twin to Craig Hartley—walked out the door.

Dr. Newcomb turned to follow, but stopped in the doorway, almost as if he'd heard Craig's plea. Hands in his pockets, he regarded Craig with a mercurial smile. "Now don't you worry, Mr. Hartley," he said formally. "Our staff is kind and professional. We have the best equipment around, and your father *has* saved quite a bit to pay for your care. We should be able to keep you alive for a very long time. Thirty years, at the very least."

He turned and walked out the door. Before he closed it, he said over his shoulder, "You should know, this is the first time I've used your father's knowledge in such a fashion. I'm rather glad you never paid back Buddy, because look at what a true work of art you are now: the everlasting art of your father."

He closed the door.

Craig screamed silently, and though he'd never feel or taste or smell again, the scent of *Old Spice* lingered in his nostrils.

At the very least, the patch on his scalp no longer burned.

ONYX NOIR

BY JESSICA LYNNE GARDNER

Death never looked as alluring as it did in the glossed pages of *Onyx Noir Magazine*. The ads alone were masterpieces.

As the woman beside her turned the page, Elise gasped at the timeless beauty of the photograph. It was of a girl with a long mane of shining red hair that flowed down over the white satin sheet beneath her like spilled blood. Her skin was so smooth and clear—nearly pearlescent. A ruffled black dress clung to the curves of her body, one strap loosely fallen over her shoulder, exposing the side of her perfect white breast. But best of all were her eyes, closed and painted with the most exquisite shade of shimmering shadow she'd ever seen. The color danced in the beam of light with facets of violet and brilliant emerald green.

Elise marveled at how each model looked so peaceful, so lost in the art of their poses. The next page was a man, his well-muscled body propped against the side of a striped, shadowed wall, one leg pulled to his chest and the other straight out. His chin lolled to his chest as if heartbroken, his long dark hair covering his eyes.

"Do you mind?" the owner of the magazine, a long-legged blonde, snapped.

"Oh, sorry I was just…"

"Go get one of your own."

Elise frowned and shifted in her seat as she looked up. She hadn't noticed the crowd of beautiful girls that had arrived within the last few minutes. The door opened and she felt her stomach flip. It seemed like everyone in New York was after this job.

"Denise Stiles?" an older woman reading from the sign-in chart called the next name, and a wisp of a girl with an elegantly boned face walked in.

It was no use; she'd never even make it to a call-back. What was she thinking? She stood, her cheeks burning. She didn't belong here…

"Elise Mayer?" She turned to see the other girl who had walked in only a moment before covering her face in her hands, small sobs escaping as she ran past her.

Elise swallowed and followed her inside. The hall seemed to go on forever, the uneven click of her faltering heels echoing against the floor. When the old woman finally stopped, it was in front of a cracked red door. Trying to stop her hands from shaking, she shoved them behind her back as she entered. The room was much larger than she'd anticipated. It was here the exceptional pictures breathed their first life. Here, in this empty, white place. There were a few props—sheets, mattresses, light— but the rest of it was startlingly bare. The gothic backgrounds so commonly seen in past issues must have been offsite or post production because she saw no hint of the windows or forests or stone walls here. There was a whiff of sweet and sour, an organic smell that was covered by the alcohol-laced bite of a cheap air freshener.

Sitting on a humble stool was the genius behind *Onyx Noir*. He was a lot taller than he looked in his pictures. His long hands rested in his lap, fingers moving compulsively. His eyes belied his impatient posture and a gentle darkness.

"Elise?"

"Oh…yes." She looked for somewhere to sit down but there was nothing.

"Daniel." His bony hand shot out to shake hers.

"I just want to tell you that I really admire your work…"

"Let's get something straight Ms. Mayer, I called you in for a secretary interview, *not* to hear how wonderful my work is." His words were tepid, but the smile afterward was dripping with charm.

"Of course…Here's my resume. I've had similar jobs before, and as you can see, I'm very proactive..."

He was hardly listening as he scanned quickly through the papers. "Mmhmm, I can see that. Well, Elise, congratulations."

She wasn't sure she'd heard him correctly, "I'm sorry?"

"You can start tomorrow morning, eight o' clock sharp."

Her heart felt as if it were going to burst. It didn't matter she had no idea how much the pay was or the specifics of the job. Just working there, in the acclaimed studio, was enough. She knew she'd never be able compete with his models, but as a secretary, working so close to him…who knew?

* * *

Daniel massaged his temples. That girl's voice grated his already bare nerves to shreds, but he needed someone to handle the paperwork after the disappearance of his last secretary— someone who didn't ask as many questions. It was difficult being the mastermind behind *Onyx Noir*. He rubbed his hands together and pulled down a black backdrop screen. He'd have to move quickly or his materials would dry up on him. As he slid one of the mirrors to the side, he entered the hidden space behind it and sized them up, looking for the best fit for a funeral bride. A small knock at his door alerted him, and he quickly closed the closet. Ms. Flannigan appeared looking apologetic, an irate middle aged woman behind her, clawing her way toward him. This wasn't good.

"Mr. Ives...please, I need to speak with you. It's urgent!"

"Come in."

Ms. Flannigan let her pass, but continued staring daggers at her as she straightened her now crooked glasses.

"My name is Pattie Byron. I'm looking for my daughter. I know she's been here. I'm ashamed to admit it, but I had my husband follow her once. She was on drugs. I was trying to find out who was selling it to her..."

"Mrs. Byron, slow down, I hope you're not implying—"

"Oh, no, I realize a man of your position wouldn't be involved with that. I came to find out if you've heard from her since Monday. It's been four days and not a word. I don't know if she was kidnapped or if she overdosed...God help me." She started sobbing, and Daniel tried not to curl his lip.

"I'm sorry, Mrs. Byron, but I haven't heard from her. She posed for a shoot, and I've been trying her cell phone myself but keep getting her voicemail. Have you tried the police?"

She wiped her tears and nodded. "Nothing yet...You'll call me if you hear anything won't you?"

"Of course, just leave your number with Ms. Flannigan at the front desk."

He sighed as she walked out. Despite her annoyingly soft, nasal voice, he was looking forward to having Elise come in tomorrow. Old Ms. Flannigan could only handle so much, and his nerves were just about shot. He couldn't work with distractions like these.

* * *

Elise was up and almost ready by the time the alarm sounded. She'd made sure to wear her best pencil skirt and pink blouse. She looked in the mirror, and while the face staring back at her wasn't the type that appeared in magazines, she was attractive. Her large, hazel eyes were defined with purple eye shadow over a small, cleanly cut nose and glossed lips. She squirted her wrists with a cheap musk.

Who would have thought that the British fashion icon would travel to Manhattan to complete his next two issues? This could be her chance. She hurried out of her one-room apartment and into the busy street, sparing a glance at her watch. The bus would be there in five minutes if it was on schedule. She waited at the crowded stop, holding her bag tight against the inside of her arm.

"You know that girl that disappeared on Monday?"

"Oh you mean that teenager, Brianna, or whatever her name was?"

"That's the one. I heard she was a model for that smut rag *Onyx Noir*. That Ives fella is supposedly a suspect now."

"That just goes to show you what young people are into nowadays. Terrible, just terrible. I saw in the paper her mother said she was on drugs. If she knew that why didn't she do anything about it?"

Elise stopped listening to the gossiping old ladies as the bus pulled up. She reminded herself to get an mp3 player after she paid off her credit card. When she got to the office, the emptiness startled her. The building that she had always expected to be full of busy writers, graphic artists and models was completely empty except for the old woman, whom she guessed was more a manager than a secretary. She nervously cleared her throat, and Ms. Flannigan looked up over her glasses. "You're early. We prefer you not arrive any sooner than scheduled. It runs up the numbers on the payroll."

Elise's mouth opened to speak then closed abruptly. This was going to be a lot different than her other jobs...

"But no matter, we'll begin now. The first thing you have to remember is never to walk in on Mr. Ives unless paged. You are not to knock and not to let anyone past you without his permission. He needs his privacy in order to capture perfection.

"Writers and agencies will call from time to time to offer their services or ask for a photo for their ad. You are to take the messages and ask for a sample of their work and a resume. Then give them to Mr. Ives in separate, labeled manila folders from this drawer. If he's interested, Mr. Ives will let you know and you can contact them. You will have paperwork and paychecks to send the models from time to time. I'll show you how that's done later." She paused for a moment to see if her words had sunk in. "And if anyone should call for him directly, send them to his voicemail no matter how urgent."

Elise nodded. It appeared to be a very strict and orderly system, but a shockingly simple one. And living alone, silence was something she was already accustomed to. She smiled. She couldn't believe she'd made it here. This was going to change her life. She could feel it.

* * *

Daniel growled as he looked through the digital display of his camera. None of the photos were turning out how he'd expected. He carried his materials back into the closet, grunting from the weight, and sat on the mattress, his head in his hands. There was nothing else he could do. The materials were supposed to last a week but this last one was already going stale. It was too stiff and starting to smell. Maybe the humidifier wasn't working properly. He'd dispose of them next week, closer to his move back to Britain. Until then, he'd have to make do with the plug-in air fresheners. There were so many different scents that the studio smelled like a French brothel. He sighed and got up, slipping on his gleaming leather loafers and Armani suit jacket. It was time to find a fresh one.

He passed the front desk on his way out and turned. Elise sat with Ms. Flannigan, her brow creased over the paperwork as if her life depended on it. His lips folded into a little smile. In a way, it did. He continued out the door onto the humid street and into his black Jaguar.

Which clubs were left? He'd been to the *Electric Spider* and *Red Code*; the only other one in the area was the *Twisted Sands*. He smoothed down his hair with his hand and pushed open the palm tree decorated door. The electric beat of the music vibrated in his throat and the strobe lights flashed over a mass of undulating bodies. At the bar he ordered a Jack and Coke. He'd have to keep his head clear tonight, though; there was work to be done. He swiveled on the bar stool and watched the nearly naked girls gyrate over the men they were with, rubbing, pumping, nearly fucking.

Most of them weren't the right type. They were too short, too fat, too plain, too pink. He was in a sea of butterflies—creatures of beauty and transformation, creatures whose lives had to be sacrificed so that the others understood their importance to the world. He captured images that transcended life, a chrysalis of perfectly preserved slumber, but for this piece he wanted something different, something that screamed of subdued power. His gaze fell on a girl in a halter and black leather pants. The first thing he noticed was her stomach. An inky scorpion wrapped itself around her, starting from the right of her puckered navel and ending in the middle of her back. As she danced, the image moved as if alive, the pinchers snapping up and down. His eyes switched to her face. It was thin with high cheekbones and pouting black painted lips. She was the one.

He caught her attention and placed a hand on the stool beside him. She flashed a sly "come hither" grin and continued dancing with the rich Mediterranean guy she'd been working, her eyes flicking back to his in an occasional seduction. He ordered another drink from the bartender and waited. She saw the drink and, after the song ended, took the bait. He watched the scorpion pulse as she walked, her small, shapely hips moving from side to side. She sat next to him without a word and emptied the glass. The bar lights rained down on the small imperfections of her skin, but they could be easily concealed. The structure was perfect.

"Want to dance?"

He shook his head and reached out, stroking the black scorpion body all the way around to its deadly stinger. He felt her taking him in, looking for a wedding band, sizing up his bank account from the way he held himself. A girl as hypnotic as her could get away with murder.

He gestured the bartender for another drink. She laughed. "I don't need to be drunk to fuck you." She took the glass and downed it anyway. "Let's go."

Daniel led her to his streamlined car. She didn't seem surprised, but ran two fingers along the surface of the door. He unlocked it with a flick of his keychain and got in. She took a moment longer, and he could see her in the rear view mirror, pretending to check out the back of the car. She was memorizing the license plate number. He was going to have to be careful with this one. When he heard the car door slam he put it into drive without looking at her.

"You're in a hurry," she said through lips muffled by a dangling cigarette. The sterling silver charms around her neck clinked together as he went over a speed bump a little too fast. He wondered if they each represented a different man she'd conned. She wasn't affected by the drinks, either. Her large, quick eyes took in everything, including the sweat on his forehead and around his neck. She was a huntress, this one, but that's what had drawn him to her.

"So what is it you do?"

"I'm a photographer. My name is Drew."

"You don't look like a Drew." She flicked cigarette ash out the window.

He drove faster and felt relief when he pulled into the parking garage. He made sure Elise's car was gone before going inside. "Welcome to my studio." Back in his element now, charm returned.

Her eyes narrowed and she gave him a sly smile. "You should never mix business with pleasure."

"Oh, but I do, quite a bit as a matter of fact. I live here."

"I hate men who put work above everything else." She looked at the mattress with the satin sheets and caught the scent of skin. "What kind of pictures are you taking exactly?"

"Would you like to see them?"

A pause. "Sure."

He reached over his desk and pulled out the drawer containing his portfolio. She flipped through the pages, obviously impressed. Girls like her had never heard of *Onyx Noir*; they'd be lucky if they'd seen *Cosmopolitan*.

"These are really beautiful, but there's something…creepy about them. I just can't put my finger on it." She flipped through, trying to ferret out the jagged piece of the photographic puzzle. "Why are all of their eyes closed?"

"The magazine is devoted to a gothic subculture, the closed eyes are a symbol of the sleeping potential within us all, the transformations we all go through in life and beyond…"

"Death."

"You could say that, yes." He stood close enough to her to smell the cheap Pantene shampoo in her shining tresses. "How would you like to model for me?"

Her eyes stopped on a particular photo of an angelic young girl lying in an open casket, arms folded neatly over her chest. It was one of his earliest works and hadn't been published. Her facial muscles were too tense under her golden brow, the white skin tight on her forehead. But it was the lips that gave it away. They were pale, nearly blue. The book began shaking in the girl's hands. "Oh fuck—"

He advanced, his hand grasping at her face. The other hand pulled her hair. She fought as he held the rag over her nose and mouth. A pointed heel struck his calf, sending an icy prick up his leg. Grunting, he pulled her hair farther. Her fist was jutting out blindly, striking the air in front of him. Another kick landed just above his groin. She had some training. Nearly doubling over, his grip loosened and she broke free. Hands to her throat and red eyes streaming, he could tell she had nearly succumbed to the Carbon tetrachloride. She took a small knife out of her black boot, her whole arm shaking as she raised it. She fought to keep herself upright. He'd hoped it wouldn't come to this; he didn't want to damage such fine material.

She was ready for him as he moved toward her, and he cried out as the knife sliced open his palm, the pulsing blood gushing out of the wound and down his forearm. Daniel breathed heavily and snatched at the knife with his other hand, but she held tight. It was almost a shame to see such fierce fiery passion snuffed out. *Almost.* He pried it from her grip and struck the back of her head with the handle, catching her as she collapsed. A bold monarch butterfly tangled in his net.

He laid her in the tub on the third floor. Ms. Flannigan wrapped up his bleeding hand and helped him wash her body. The water was a deep red by the time they finished.

"It's alright Daniel; at least her face isn't damaged. It'll be covered by her hair."

"No, no, no. You don't understand. I needed her to be perfect, undamaged. She died knowing she was going to die, and it shows, Bonnie."

"Really, she looks fine to me…"

"Look!" his finger pointed to a small worry crease in her forehead. "It'll all be ruined."

"You can always smooth that line out during editing" she said in a soft voice.

He shook his head. "I've never used effects on the materials. Never. Maybe I'm losing it. Maybe the magazine needs a new leader." He grasped at the sides of his head, rubbing in small, circular motions around his temples.

"Finish cleaning her," he snapped. "I don't want her skin getting pruned. The September issue is due next week. I've run out of time."

* * *

Elise was early again and waited outside the building until eight before hurrying in. She was surprised to see Mr. Ives standing beside her desk. He grinned, but there were deep circles under his eyes. In his hand was a photograph.

"Good morning Elise. I'd like your opinion on this. I was up late working on it last night and I need a new set of eyes."

Her face lit up.

The model in the photos, suspended by her thin arms from a large rope, was partially naked, her silken black hair just covering her nipples. Elise's eyes dropped to her side, where a scorpion tattoo wrapped itself around her waist. Her pelvis was hidden by a black gauze cloth that reminded her of the white rags wrapped around the loins of Jesus.

"They're great." She wasn't lying, the pictures were beautiful, but something about them disturbed her.

Daniel looked relieved. "What about her face?"

Elise took another look at the model's face. She was an exotic beauty with ruby lips and darkly shadowed eyes. Her skin was flawless and radiant. "She's…" She paused as she caught something on her forehead.

Daniel frowned. "What is it?"

"There." She pointed at the girl's hairline as he ripped the picture from her hand. "I see something wet in her hair. Probably just gel, but—"

"Yes, thank you. I'll be in my office the rest of the day."

* * *

He'd been careless and fed the photo through the shredder before bringing the image back up on the screen. If it would have slipped through to publication he would've been shut down. He couldn't afford to do that, not when he'd worked so hard to establish himself.

Daniel digitally removed the blood from the picture and matched the slightly reddish sheen to black. Lately he'd been letting his emotions get the better of him. With each picture, doubt clouded his judgment. He saw the way the new girl had looked at it. She was disturbed, disgusted even. He didn't want to become a forgotten photographer for a fading magazine; he wanted *Onyx Noir* to stay on top.

He was the father of a new artistic renaissance. Death was something aesthetic and collectable, and now everyone could see his vision even if they didn't understand it yet.

* * *

It was the third model she'd called that hadn't picked up, but Elsie left another message and recorded the name, date and time on a sticky note inside her file. She was getting bitter. Those girls were so busy with parties and photo shoots they didn't have time for anything else.

Ms. Flannigan had left Elise to fend for herself, complaining of an aching back. She had the hang of the paperwork, but dealing with the phone calls was still giving her trouble. She'd gotten into it with someone demanding to speak with Mr. Ives immediately. They'd claimed it was important—just like every other call that came in—and after a barrage of insults she'd transferred him to the voicemail, the same as everyone else.

The day's paperwork now complete, she had nothing left to do but wait for the phone to ring. Eventually it did.

"Thank you for calling *Onyx Noir*, how may I help you?"

"I need to speak with Daniel Ives."

"May I ask who's calling?"

"Detective Sherridan. I need to speak to him immediately."

"I'm sorry, he's in a meeting, but I can transfer you to his voicemail if you'd like."

"Listen, miss, this is the third time I've called this week. None of my messages have been returned. I need to speak with him immediately or I'll come down and see him in person."

"Uh," she hesitated, "please hold."

She tried Ms. Flannigan's cell. No answer.

Shit.

She buzzed Mr. Ives' desk, but he didn't answer, either. Gathering up her courage, she walked down the hall, nearly turning back several times. She knocked on the door and was surprised to see it wasn't closed all the way. It swung open and Mr. Ives was there with the scorpion model. She was very still on the mattress while the shutter of his camera snapped over and over. He spun when she entered and ran to meet her. The emotions behind his normally calm mask seemed to be reaching the point of a barely contained explosion. Elise took several steps back.

"What is it?"

"I, uh, answered the phone and—"

"Ms. Flannigan instructed you not to interrupt me during a session."

"I'm sorry, but the man on the phone said he's a detective and that if I didn't put you on the line he'd send officers down here…"

He slammed the door in her face, and she walked back down the hall, fighting back tears.

So much for getting on his good side.

When she got back to her desk she had an apology ready for the detective, but the phone line light had already turned green. He'd picked it up. She sighed and straightened the papers on her desk, but her mind kept going back to the model. How had she gotten in? She hadn't seen any other cars in the parking lot and no one had come through the office… Maybe there was some kind of back door. Since she'd never seen any of them before, that would make sense.

Elise blushed.

Or maybe he brought them in at night and they stayed with him until the shoot in the morning. The idea of being a model looked better than ever.

Mr. Ives walked out. His face was red and he was rubbing his temples. He pressed his palms onto the desk beside her and stared through her with his dark eyes. "I'm sorry I got a little angry with you. It's just these detectives won't leave me alone. Ever since that girl Brianna disappeared they've been questioning me."

Elise nodded. "I understand. It must be difficult for you realizing that one of your models is…" she groped for the right word, "gone…but they shouldn't blame you. Models lives are sketchy anyway."

His eyes grew warmer with her words. "Elise, you've made a great secretary, but ever since I saw you at the interview, I thought you'd make an even better model."

Her eyes grew wide. "Really?"

"You have that girl next door look and I could really use it for the upcoming issue. I'd have to take a few rolls of you first to make sure you're photogenic enough, but why don't you come in tomorrow morning? Don't worry about your hair and makeup, I'll do that myself. Just wear a black dress if you have one."

* * *

She couldn't sleep that night, her mind racing as she pictured herself on the glossy pages of *Onyx Noir*. Images of France and Belgium and London, with pink champagne in one hand and caviar in the other, danced in her head. Her life would finally have meaning.

The next morning Daniel was at her desk. "Ready for your first shoot?"

"More than ready." She followed him into the studio, chattering the whole time. "I really can't thank you enough. This means so much to me…"

The door swung open and a different girl was lying on the mattress.

"I'm going to try something a little different this time." The door closed behind them. She stared at the blonde model and felt a chill work down her spine. She looked so pale and thin, her skin almost translucent, nothing like the gleaming girls in the finished pages. The smell in the room reeked of spoiling meat. Elise held her breath and wondered when he was going to wake the other girl up. She supposed it didn't matter; they all had their eyes closed anyway.

A horrifying thought struck her, and she scanned the room for any sign of the nightmarish truth. She saw nothing; everything was in perfect order, the same as it was the first time she'd been there. But that god-awful smell… it seemed to be coming from the back of the room.

Her stomach clenched. There, through the gap at the bottom of the mirrored closet door, she saw fingers poking out of the darkness. A scream escaped her but it was too late, something was around her nose and mouth, already making her head swim.

Elise fought the iron grip but was fading fast. Her last thought, after the realization came and the fear passed, was that she'd made it; she was now a model.

The tagline of the magazine played with her last bit of consciousness: *Death never looked so beautiful.*

ONE HEADLIGHT

BY ERIC ENCK

Saturday

6:39 a.m.

Six people were found dead by the growing light of early dawn. They were all decapitated.

* * *

8:12 a.m.

The police, as usual, didn't have much to say. Detective Frank Jasper gathered six of his best officers together for a search. It happens in this revolving marble of blood and bone. What doesn't happen are murder victims found with toys in their mouths, in their open cavities, in their bloodless chests. Eyes no longer blinking. Chalk lines waiting to be drawn.

"Why the hell would someone murder Tina Jones, Doug?"

Jasper stood over Tina Jones' body waiting for his partner's answer. She was decapitated at approximately one in the morning. Her head was missing, and whoever had killed her had spent a few hours disemboweling her and looping her guts around the furniture in the room. On several pieces of furniture, her killer left toys—Match Box cars.

"Better yet, what do toy cars have to do with anything?"

"Symbolism?"

"Symbolism for what?" Jasper asked.

"He wants us to know something."

"I already do," Jasper said. "He's one sick son of a bitch."

"Besides that," Doug Maddix said. "Killers always leave clues behind. It's part of their repertoire. In some sick way they want to be found."

"Oh I'm *gonna* find him," Jasper said. "This girl did nothing wrong. She's Pastor Bernard's daughter for chrissakes."

Bernard led the local Baptist congregation. He believed in God. Everyone does until something vile happens to them.

Both cops stared at the wreck before them. What remained was once a cheerleader. On the floor were spent dreams of teenage boys and a future demolished forever. On the floor was a work of art.

Right before Maddix vomited his eggs onto the strips of carpet untouched by the gore, his partner's phone rang. Doug didn't pay attention to the one-sided conversation. Instead, he focused on the tiny toy cars. Most of them were replicas of muscle cars, all of them colorful and shiny and dotted with a droplets of blood.

"We gotta go."

"What's going on?"

"There're five more…just like this one."

* * *

10:06 a.m.

The next were the same.

A butcher in Ridgewood was found spoiled on the walls of his chop shop. On the counter next to the "Ring for Service" bell was a Hot Wheel—a black Camaro.

Frank Leppold was found in the freezer, his head missing. His arms were folded across his chest, saving the funeral director the trouble. His pants were gone. His cock and balls were removed with eerie precision.

Down the street, old Susan Knowle was found torn to pieces. She'd been skinned, alive and screaming, tied to the toilet with duct tape and twine. Her killer used a fruit peeler to do the job. Her skin was nowhere to be found.

Across town, three more victims were found, all with heads and other body parts missing. All with toy cars found near the bodies. Upon further examination, the coroner noted whoever had murdered the six locals from Freedom had recently polished his car. Traces of Turtle Wax were found in all of the victims' hair.

* * *

Sunday

Before the taxi driver could pull back into the afternoon storm, a man wearing mirrored sunglasses got in and closed the door behind him. He took a breath, as if smelling all the past romances of the cab. He was young and looked familiar to the driver.

"Where to?"

"Baker Street."

"And what's on Baker Street this afternoon?"

"Murder."

The cabby said nothing. He lit a cigarette and breathed deep. He started to drive. "That's a sick joke, my friend. You know about the murders here in town?"

"Who doesn't?"

"Little tipsy?"

"Yes," the passenger answered. "I don't drink and drive."

"Wise move. You wouldn't want to kill anyone."

"Actually, I want to kill *everyone*, but not tonight. Tonight, I only have one headlight."

"I think you'd better be getting out now."

The passenger pulled a gun and pointed it at the driver. "I think you should just take me to Baker Street."

"Mister…I…I got a family," the cabby pleaded.

"And I'll come for them too," the passenger said.

They looked into each other's eyes like long lost friends, and the passenger pulled the trigger. Blood, bone, and brains covered the inside of the shattered windshield. Droplets of crimson sprayed the passenger's mirrored sunglasses. Stepping out of the cab in the middle of an empty street, the passenger moved along onto the sidewalk, sheathing his pistol.

How many must I sacrifice for it?

How many must die to see it come to life?

* * *

Monday

9:04 a.m.

From WDOX 18 News:

In the wake of the Freedom and Ridgeport murders, local folks are staying home and locking their doors.

Local gunsmith, Roy Calverton has sold half his in-stock merchandise in the past few days.

The State Police have not ruled out the possibility the killer is a local himself, however. The only clues left behind are toy cars at each crime scene. The police have nicknamed the killer "Match Box.

Tina Zigler reporting.

* * *

2:08 p.m.

Tina Zigler was brutally murdered.

* * *

3:34 p.m.

Doug Maddix came into the station as a handful of local officers gathered around the conference table. On the desk were files of the recent murders. Frank Jasper spoke first.

"I've come to the obvious conclusion that we're dealing with more than your regular psycho."

"I didn't know there was such a thing as a *regular* psycho, chief," Sergeant Taff chimed in.

"Look. This guy isn't like Dahmer or Bundy. He shot a cab driver in broad daylight and left one of his fucking Match Box toys in the back of the car. He killed Tina Zigler for chrissakes. Who knows who's next? This town's not ready for a goddamn serial killer. We need to find this fucker now."

"So where do we start? I mean, how many people in Freedom match the profile?"

"I know this much," Jasper said. "This son of a bitch is gonna be at the car show this weekend. I'd bet my soul on it. Hell, I wouldn't be surprised if this he has a nice fine ride himself."

* * *

Tuesday

12:10 p.m.

A glimmering, black '69 Camaro was seen driving down Sunset Boulevard. Frank Jasper sat on his porch, with files by his side and a cigarette between his tired lips. The car was high-toned and mean. A red pinstripe ran its course from the front of the car all the way to the raised trunk. As it reared, the car became a jagged line. It reminded Jasper of hospital monitors, like when his father died from a heart attack and the jumping line finally went flat. His father died with one eye and...

(One Headlight)

...a case of mono.

"Is that you?" Jasper asked. He blew out smoke and stood from his chair. The Camaro gunned forward, the sound of its engine terrible and mean—a thundering holocaust. That car was definitely going to the show on Saturday, and so would the Freedom Police Department. It was too far away to read the license plate, and the windows were too tinted to see the driver.

The light turned green.

* * *

Wednesday

12:18 a.m.

The Daytons were in their family room, watching for news about the local madman, when Alice Dayton's husband came out of the bathroom in obvious pain.

"What's the matter, hon?"

"I think I'm sick."

"Something you ate?"

"Maybe."

"That's a shame. I was hoping for a little *oomph* tonight," Alice said. She walked over to her husband with a seductive smile, but he didn't want any part of it. His bowels felt full and his mouth was dry. He'd definitely caught some sort of bug.

"Maybe tomorrow," Simon said. "I'm sorry babe."

"No problem, hon. I'm gonna go make sure all the doors are locked before we go to bed."

"I'll get them," Simon said. His face was covered with cold sweat. Summer colds were the worst. Outside, he heard a distant sound of thunder but saw no lightning to support the idea of a storm brewing.

"No, you just rest," Alice said. She went to lock the back door of their mobile home, but Simon was already up and moving. "I need to move around. When I sit down, I feel like I have to shit."

Simon made his way slowly but surely to the door. He hated living in the woods; there was nothing around them for miles. The closest semblance of civilization was the post office four miles away. His hand fell on the deadbolt. One twist was all it would've taken to save his life, but the door jerked open and the knob pulled free of his clammy hand.

A man stood before him. Hair slicked tight to the skull, he was smiling below mirrored sunglasses that reflected the moonlight.

"Good evening."

Before Simon could respond, the stranger stepped forward with an enormous KA-BAR. The knife was serrated on one side, beveled on the other.

"What do you want?" Simon asked. The stranger took one more step before the night ended for Simon Dayton.

"Just to tell you, sir, that you should lock your doors at night."

Simon's eyes widened as the stranger forced the knife into his gut. His pants filled with hot shit peppered from the flu coursing through him. In one terrible second, Simon no longer worried about his bowels. They were all over the floor. He fell back against the washer and dryer with one audible yelp that sent Alice hurrying into the kitchen.

"Simon?" Turning her head around the corner, she saw her husband with his white T-shirt split down the center. She saw the worried look on his face and his eyes shifting in terror. He sat upright against the washer, holding bloody ropes of his intestines, trying desperately to keep them inside his body.

Through his agony, he apologized to his wife, who saw a black foundry boot tracking mud onto the linoleum from around the corner. A face with mirrored sunglasses followed it.

97

Alice screamed, her tender vocal chords producing a sound an octave above normal.

"Hello," Match Box said. "I was just in the neighborhood telling people to lock their doors at night. I don't know if you're aware or not, miss…but there's a killer out there somewhere."

Alice backed away.

"And they say he's been doing some terrible things. He's been murdering everyone. Stealing their skin. Some of the victims have body parts missing. Have you seen the news?"

Alice mumbled something inaudible. She saw her husband finally succumb to the wound on his stomach. The maniac before her stepped into the kitchen and carefully placed a Match Box car onto the bar.

"He leaves toys behind," he said and smiled.

Alice screamed.

"No need for that, you pretty thing. See, I'm doing something for this town. My father was a joke. People like you stepped all over him. People like you took him for everything he had. So now I'm giving something back. He was an artist. He made beautiful paintings. Fortunately, he passed his creativity down to me. After I killed my mother, I thought it was just about time."

"Time for *what*?!' Alice screamed.

"Time to create a masterpiece, of course," Match Box spoke. "I'm not killing all these people just to satisfy some bloodlust. I'm doing something with my work. I'm making art. But it's a bit different then my father's kind."

"Please…I'll do whatever you want, just don't kill me," Alice begged. Her face had become a wreck of heat and tears and terror.

"Kill you? I'm not going to kill you. You're going to become part of it. I still need an engine of course. A *heart* so to speak, but you're much too beautiful for that."

Match Box was close enough to lift Alice's dark hair with his bloodied knife. She could smell the blade.

"I'm going to need your flesh Alice."

"No…"

"Oh yes. I'm going to need your flesh so I can continue my masterpiece. I think you'll do quite fine for the seats."

"You don't have to rape me."

"Ha!" Match Box stepped back and grinned. "Rape you! I think you've missed the point, and besides, you're definitely not my type."

Match Box grabbed Alice by her throat and whispered into her face.

"I like my women dead."

* * *

2:24 a.m.

The garage door opened, and the black Camaro eased into the space beside another vehicle covered with a blue plastic tarp. Match Box grimaced at the rain. His father had died during a terrible storm, and it brought back unwanted memories. When the door came down, meeting the concrete, Match Box went to the trunk of the car and opened it. Inside was Alice Dayton. Her mouth duct taped. Her wrists bound with electrical wire.

"Still upset are we?"

Alice screamed.

"Don't take it personally, but this may take a while. I hate the rain. The night my father died it was raining. He was helping me rebuild the car you just had the pleasure of riding in. We were almost finished before we took him to the hospital. All we needed was one more headlight and we would've been finished, but dad died before he got to see it completed."

Pulling Alice from the car, he carried her like a groom crossing the threshold with his bride.

"So...Alice...I created a new car in his honor, one that my father would be sure to love."

Match Box placed Alice on a pool table, the felt torn and grimy with the stains of past victims. "I really hate to do this, but it's for a good cause you know. I'm going to have the best car at the show. You should be proud in knowing you'll be a part of it."

Bound and gagged, Alice watched as her captor bent under the table and brought out a black hunting case. She knew what it was; her husband had used it when he went hunting in Orviston. It was filled with the tools he used to process deer. To *skin*.

Match Box placed a die cast car beside Alice's head and smiled. He raised the meat clever.

Thursday

9:51 a.m.

Jasper walked outside with his morning paper. His thoughts raced for an answer to who was murdering people in his town. He looked up at the bright sky and prayed to God for an answer. A few minutes later, he lit a cigarette and went to his mailbox, reminding himself he needed to cut the grass. The mailbox handle was rusted. His wife had been on him to oil it, but of course he hadn't, and as the months came and went, it was becoming harder and harder to open. He was glad Clara was with her mother in the Cayman Islands; she didn't need to know what was going on in Freedom. But walking back towards the front door he realized how much he missed his wife.

He took their heads.

He took their skin…and the Birard boy…he took his goddamn legs. What kind of an animal does that? This is a small town for chrissake.

We can't deal with this shit.

Jasper glanced at the headline below the flag of the paper; the "Match Box Killer" was still as much of a mystery as he had been the day before. Across the bottom of the front page was the event section featuring the weekend's car show.

They need to cancel that show. I'd have it done if I didn't think that Camaro had something to do with all of this. And who was driving it?

Frank paused to put his coffee cup down on the kitchen table when he froze.

Clara liked her house clean. Not a speck of dirt to be found. She even dusted the walls.

On the coffee table, sitting by itself was a small toy car—a police cruiser Match Box.

* * *

2:44 p.m.

The phone rang, and a hand reached for it. The hand belonged to bloodstains. Under the cuticles were particles of enough evidence to send him to jail a hundred times over. But he'd been to jail before.

"Hello?"

"Mr. Carr?"

"Speaking."

"This is Mike Walls with the Convention Committee in Ridgeport."

"Yes sir," Match Box said. "What can I do you for?"

"This is a courtesy call. We just wanted to make sure you still mean to enter your 1972 Dodge Challenger this weekend."

"I do."

"We were also curious, Mr. Carr, why you wanted to enter it into the concept class. Usually, concepts are owner created."

"I know, but the car is a modified Challenger. It's got the body of a '72 Challenger, but you'd hardly know it by looking. I've done some amazing things to get this out of the garage. It should be ready to go by tonight."

"Sounds good. The judges make their decisions on several different factors. If it's as unique as you claim, well…quite frankly, I can't wait to see it."

"I can't wait to *show* it. It's still missing one headlight, but I'm fixing that up as we speak."

"Good," the voice on the other end said. "Well…registration is at seven on Saturday. See you then."

"You sure will."

Click.

Match Box walked to the front of his masterpiece. The tarp was folded back onto the hood of the monstrous machine. It bore one headlight, a human skull with Xenon bulbs in the eye sockets and a gaping mouth that was relieved of its flesh in mid scream.

"Just one more."

* * *

4:34 p.m.

Maddix sat in his recliner drinking the last bottle of a six pack. It was his only day off. The State Police had taken over the investigation of the killer in Freedom, and the town itself was at a standstill. Doug brushed his dark hair back with one hand and breathed deep. Suddenly, he wanted a cigarette. He hadn't smoked in years, but things had changed lately. Before he could finish the thought of going to the drug store to buy a pack, his phone rang. It was Jasper.

"What's the news?"

"I didn't get a chance to tell you this."

"Frank?"

"Yes…it's Frank."

"Tell me what?"

"Yesterday, I went out to check the mail. I came back in and someone had left a toy police car on my coffee table."

"What?"

"It's getting serious, Doug. I think we have something major here. I think it goes beyond us, beyond the Staties, maybe the F.B.I even."

"Jesus Christ."

"I know. I haven't been able to sleep. I've been keeping my rifle close by, and my nine. I suggest you do the same."

"Who else did you tell?"

"Nobody."

"Why?" Doug finished off the bottle of beer.

"Because it's gonna cause a shitload of paperwork and headaches, and I don't need Clara finding out some sick son of a bitch strolled into our house right in front of me. I dusted my place for fingerprints…nothing of course."

"What about the toy?"

"Nope," Frank said. "He's *toying* with us. Although, I gotta be honest, I'm a little freaked out by all of this. I don't want to let anybody see it, but it's got me shook up. When I saw it sitting on the table I couldn't move, it was like my shoes were full of glue."

"I bet."

"Anyway, I just wanted to let you know. Don't say anything, though?"

Maddix considered the penalties for withholding evidence, but decided it was worth the risk."Of course."

"And get your gun."

"I will." He already had it on him, tucked into the back of his jeans with his T-shirt pulled down around it.

"And Doug?"

"Yeah."

"Watch your back."

"I will."

102

Maddix heard the click and placed the phone on the receiver just as a cold shadow fell over his shoulder.

"Turn around and I'll stab you in the face."

Maddix froze.

"Put your hands up."

He obliged.

"You don't know me detective, but I know you. When my father was a kid, you ran him under didn't you? Chased him down like a dog. He didn't do anything to anyone. He had problems just like me, just like all of us, and just like *you*."

The blade grazed the back of Maddix's neck, barely piercing the skin.

"You're gonna wish you never became a cop you son of a bitch."

"I didn't do anyth—"

"Shut up!" Match Box screamed. "Shut up you filthy fucking pig! You have the right to remain silent, so remain silent you piece of shit!"

The knife went in all the way that time. The blade slipped through the vertebrae of Maddix's neck, the metal sliding off the bone, making him scream. His scream ended when the tip of the knife protruded through his Adam's apple. Match Box pulled the blade free and threw the cop across the room. Maddix went off his feet and slammed into the china cabinet. It rained porcelain for a few seconds, but Maddix saw the man in front of him.

He was a nightmare.

The man wore mirrored sunglasses, but strips of his flesh were gone, in some places down to the bone. His cheekbones showed through his peeled face.

Maddix couldn't talk. So screaming wasn't necessary.

"Look at me," Match Box said. "Look at what I've sacrificed. Look at what I've become for this town. This goddamned *town!*"

"I need more flesh, officer, and I only have so much time. But if I can sacrifice a little of me, so can you."

Maddix held out one hand as the other went for the gun in his jeans, but Match Box moved with surprising speed and grabbed the gun.

"So!" Match Box said. He turned in a circle on one boot heel and ripped the glasses from his face. When Maddix saw his eyes, he knew who the man was, and more importantly, he knew who his father was. His father had been mentally retarded, but he knew his way around an engine.

Match Box's face was worse around the eyes. He had the black bags of sleepless nights there, and one eye had obviously gone blind.

Just need one more…
One headlight…

"Even now, you try to apologize for what you did to my family with a *gun*? You want to shoot me, pig?" Match Box pulled the trigger and the bullet ripped a smile into Doug Maddix's T-shirt. His back bled through the shirt, forming a morbid Rorschach.

"Come outside with me." Match Box dragged Maddix's wasted body into the backyard, where the Camaro glimmered in the afternoon sun. Match Box walked to it and got in, the engine rumbling as it screamed to life. Maddix saw it come for him as angry as the man driving it. He tasted the grass in the tires, the pebbles that filled his throat, the smell of oil and fuel and blood and bile.

Behind the wheel, Match Box screamed, his stretched face peeled away farther from the bone. Match Box got out of the car, and with his KA-BAR, began to saw.

* * *

Friday

9:02 a.m.

Frank Jasper slept soundly, even though his partner hadn't answered the phone the night before. His wife had called him that morning. She was the type of woman who knew when something was wrong, and she was on her way home.

Frank strolled across the lawn to the mailbox, his morning cup of coffee in hand. The rusty hinge opened with a creek. He'd oil the clasp tomorrow. Until then he had work to do. The morning light revealed the envelopes and flyers from stores, but sitting on top of everything was someone's version of a cruel joke. He reached in with shaking hands, and forgot about being a cop, forgot about evidence. All he remembered was the last thing Doug had said.

104

I will…

Doug Maddix's blood-soaked badge glimmered in the post dawn light.

* * *

3:25 p.m.

The bikini car wash was wrapping up. There had been lines of cars for most of the afternoon, but the customers had trickled off. The four sorority girls raising money for the local SPCA were lingering, pruned and wondering just how much they cared about puppies after all, when the black Camaro rounded the corner and slowly circled the soap and hoses and young flesh.

"What the fuck?" Craig Walton said. The girls looked on in a mixture of amazement and disgust.

"Dude…I'm not cleaning that," one of the girls spoke.

"Maybe he hit a deer or something."

The Camaro was soaked in blood. The driver had the wipers on and the windshield was smeared with dried mud and what looked like shreds of uncooked bacon. The whole front of the car was wet and shiny and glistened in a deep red. Craig walked to the driver's window, which was as black as the rest of the car.

"You hit something?"

No answer, just a rumble of the engine. It whispered murder. The girls walked around the car cautiously.

"Sir?"

The window came down a crack, just enough to slip a fifty-dollar bill through.

"It's ten bucks man."

"Keep the change."

Craig grimaced, but shrugged his shoulders. He started spraying the car down with a pressure washer. Underneath the body of the Camaro, pink water formed on the black top. The girls didn't go near it like the others they had serviced. Instead, they used long poles with brushes on them to soap up the windows. When they were done, Craig made with his hand that everything was okay. The Camaro rumbled to life.

Mr. Carr had everything he needed. All night he'd prepped and prepared for the show. Everyone in town went to the car show, and he would display his masterpiece. As he peeled the flesh

105

from the cop's head with a garden claw, he realized he would have his second headlight after all.

The police would come.

"Let them come," Match Box said. "Let them suffer."

* * *

Saturday

7:09 a.m.

The Ridgeport fairgrounds were packed for the show. Mustangs, hotrods, Camaros, Corvettes, and all kinds of custom-painted rides rolled in, including one car of particular interest. It was long and covered with a pool tarp. The windows were the only part exposed. A few people complained of a strong odor, but other than that, it didn't seem to be of any magnificence. The driver wore a ball cap and mirrored glasses, bandages all but covering his face.

* * *

12:00 p.m.

The cars lined up based on categories. And then came the concept arena. This year there were only five concepts. One car had only three wheels. Another changed colors in the sunlight. The headlights were on the side view mirrors.

Two of the judges approached one vehicle in particular. It was covered in a stained pool tarp. A group of people surrounded it with anticipation. The owner of the car exited the vehicle and stood with a smile on his face.

"Mr.....let me see here. Mr. Carr?"

"Yes sir," the man said to the judge.

"What's that god awful smell?"

"Ran over a skunk on the way here. I apologize. Please don't let that sway your judgment."

"It won't," the judge said, pushing his glasses back up on his nose. "What's the exhibition called?"

"Freedom," Carr said.

"May we see?"

"Sure."

Match Box walked to the side of his prize and gripped the pool tarp with one hand. The tarp slid off the vehicle with a slick, almost unnatural ease. Both judges dropped their clipboards. The screams followed.

What sat in front of them was not a car. It had an engine. It had wheels. It was once the chasse of a Dodge Challenger turned into a human nightmare. The entire vehicle was covered with human flesh, dried out in some places and fresh in others: a rush job. The flesh was stitched together onto rusted metal, the tires slick with dripping blood. The rims, once shiny chrome, were wet with gore. The center caps of the rims were replaced with human eyes encased in glass. The entire grill of the car was made of teeth, gums still attached in places. Two human skulls with bulbs in the eye sockets served as the headlights. The tail end of the car had fins made of bone. Inside the car was a hell unfound.

The steering wheel was femur bone bent and wrapped in human skin. The seats the same but covered in human hair. The floor was matted with congealed blood and brains. The shifter arm belonged to a child—Alice Dayton's son, who came home to find an unfortunate surprise waiting for him in the kitchen. The shifter knob (the ultimate memento) belonged to one Detective Doug Maddix—his penis, glazed and in rigor. The remaining judge saw it and screamed like a little girl.

"Oh, come now," Match Box said. "It feels good in your hands."

The back seat was made out of women. Where buttons should have supported leather, there were nipples. The seat belts were made of arteries and veins wound together.

"Aren't you gonna look under the hood?"

"You're...my god in heaven!" The judge stumbled on the words.

Match Box lifted the hood. Inside was a chrome engine. The air filter was made of petrified lungs; tendrils of flesh and hollow bones served as pipes. A baby's skull with a glass top served as the water pump. The engine was inscribed with a simple message:

For dad...

"So I won then?" Match Box asked. The judges ran into the crowd of screaming people. Behind them, "Freedom" came to life. The pedals made of human feet were pushed to the floor, and the macabre hotrod tore through the grass and into the crowd as the police arrived on the scene. Match Box's car ran people down left and right, while the driver laughed like a coyote. Blood sprayed into the sky like bursting water balloons.

"Pave the way for a new foundation." Match Box said. Behind him came Detective Jasper and his men. The car continued to roar across the field, flames blowing out from the exhaust. As Jasper's crew got closer, they saw the bodies rolling out from under the abomination. Months of planning, weeks of killing, all for the sake of art.

"Stop that freak!" Jasper screamed as the police opened fire. Match Box slammed the brakes and went backside to side with Frank Jasper's car. Jasper pulled his gun. Match Box smiled.

"Check your mail, cop?" Match Box asked.

"Fuck you!"

The detective opened fire and missed twice. Match Box returned the favor by slamming his car into the side of the cruiser. Jasper saw the human skin stretched across the door. He saw something that may or may not have been a bellybutton.

Matchbox pulled a sawed off shotgun from between the seats, aimed both barrels at Frank Jasper and fired. Jasper's hat stayed on his head as his face, brains, and skull became a spray of gore. The cruiser rolled to a stop, and Match Box went on.

He didn't see the ditch before he hit it at an angle. Freedom flipped several times across the field, bodies strewn in the aftermath. One headlight continued to blaze. The other was dead.

Cop cars circled the mess before them, and officers exited their vehicles, guns drawn. From the wreckage crawled Match Box. The bandages hung from his face, revealing the infected wounds and shining bones beneath. He stood on one leg; the other was twisted and broken.

"You're under arrest!"

"No shit?" Match Box said. "That's okay; I'm done making art anyway."

Two officers rushed forward, guns aimed at Match Box's chest. Their commanding officer slowly walked towards the wrecked car.

"You call this art?" he asked. "You murdered…no, you butchered all these innocent people."

"Yeah I know," Match Box said. "I was there when it happened."

"And you call this art?"

"No," Match Box said. He pulled something from his jeans that looked like a remote control for a television. "I call *this* art."

Match Box pressed the button, and the car exploded, shredding the entire Freedom police force and the few remaining onlookers from the convention.

For the next thirty seconds, the only rain the skies let go was body parts.

THE EXHIBITION

BY JAMES ROY DALEY

Scott and Penny Beach stood in line for a long time before they were admitted into the exhibition.

While they waited, they couldn't help wondering if the show would be worth the bother. Penny didn't think so. She didn't think anything was worth a wait of longer than fifteen minutes. She suggested to Scott—not once, but several times—to forfeit their spot in line, toss the two hundred dollar tickets into the trash and head to the nearest bar for cocktails, her treat. Each time she suggested it, though, Scott only smiled.

Normally he would have gone for it; Scott hated waiting in line as much as she did, but he didn't want to miss the exhibition or throw away money needlessly. It wasn't in his nature.

The exhibition was called *The Horror Show*, and Scott was a horror enthusiast. He had the books, DVDs, posters, video games, and autographs, but he had never seen a horror *exhibition* before.

The front door opened, the line inched ahead two spots and Penny dragged a finger through her hair. "I forgot to ask…what are the reviews like? They any good? Is it gross…is it creepy?"

"There are no reviews," Scott said, a smug expression materializing on his face.

"Is this opening night?"

"Not really."

"Okay, I'll bite. Why are there no reviews?"

Scott nodded and grinned. "This is a one night only event."

"You never told me that."

"I thought I had."

"No. You said it was scary, but you didn't tell me *that*."

Noise from a streetcar disrupted their conversation. Scott watched it move along the avenue, and his eyes fell upon a three-story building that was shamefully vandalized. Two men stood near the building's front door. One man—a tall fellow with thick eyebrows—kicked a dead pigeon with an oversized boot as the other coughed and mumbled. Both were dressed in tattered, unstylish clothing. Shaggy beards and scruffy hair seemed to be the look of the day.

"By the way," Scott said. "Thanks for coming."

Penny shrugged. "No problem."

"Yeah, but this isn't the greatest neighborhood in the world. I'm sure you're not used to it, and I know you don't like this type of thing."

"That's not true. I like art shows quite a bit. I just don't like those stupid movies you're always watching. Most of them are terrible."

"It's hard to argue, but I still love them."

"Yeah, I know, but…they're so fake. They're poorly written and the direction is awful." Penny stopped herself from saying more. Scott's fascination with that trash made her doubt his intelligence. Were all men enthralled by such foolish rubbish?

She looked to her shoes, her sixteen hundred dollar peach *gala* shoes, the ones she'd worn to her sister's wedding thirteen months earlier and hadn't put on since. Without meaning to, she let out a sigh and held her Prada handbag in her arms like a baby.

Scott knew what she was thinking; she was bored and ready to go home.

"You know, Penny," he said. "You're really beautiful tonight. You look extra gorgeous."

Penny's eyes lit up like little suns. "Really?"

"Oh yeah, as lovely today as the day I married you."

The suns eclipsed. "That was only two years ago, jerk."

Scott laughed. "I know, and you still look good!"

Penny punched Scott playfully and kissed him on the mouth. Scott ran his hand down the back of Penny's dress and gave her ass a little squeeze. As Penny pushed him away, the front door opened. Two people stepped inside the exhibition and the door began to close.

Before it did, Penny stepped free of the line and said, "Excuse me, doorman?"

The man at the door hesitated. "Yes?"

"Can't you let *more* than two people in at a time? We've been waiting for an hour!" Penny flashed her dimples and tilted her head. A curl of hair swooped across her thin eyebrows, bouncing up and down.

The man at the door smiled. Long teeth sat deep within his mouth. He had cheekbones like elbows, and when he spoke there was a rumble in the back of his throat that sounded like someone digging gravel with a shovel. "I'm sorry Miss…two at a time, that's the way we do it. It makes for a better show."

Penny's eyebrows lowered. "Oh."

"And for your information," the man said, "I'm *not* a doorman. This is my family's exhibition. My name is Denoté."

Before Penny considered a response, Denoté closed the door with a thud. The people in line, who had quieted down and listened to the exchange, began talking again.

"Well…now we know," Scott said. "Two at a time."

Penny opened a pack of cigarettes and lit a smoke. The guy waiting in front of them bummed one and shared it with his date. He was an older man with long hair and a tattoo of an eagle on his neck. The tattoo was well designed and inked by a skilled hand. Penny thought it made the man look dignified, not trashy. It was something she would never have admitted.

The tattooed stranger introduced himself as Gary Somers. In time, he told them he worked in real estate.

Scott laughed. "You don't look like a real estate agent."

"I know." Gary responded proudly. "But I'm a nice guy and pleasant to work with. I get a lot of referrals and repeat business. You'd be surprised. This city is loaded with people that prefer working with an agent they relate to. Most sales guys have no soul; it's like they're manufactured in a real estate factory where sex, drugs, and rock 'n' roll never existed. *Here's your haircut, suitcase and nametag. Don't forget to smile politely.* How can you have faith in someone when you don't trust them?"

Scott nodded. Gary was a little over the top maybe, but he seemed honest and straightforward.

The door opened and the next two ticketholders stepped inside. As the door closed, Gary's date—a woman who had introduced herself as Angel—asked, "Have you noticed that people go in but nobody comes out?"

Penny dropped her smoke on the sidewalk and crushed it with the toe of her shoe. "No, but now that you say mention it..."

"Why is that?"

"I don't know. Backdoor?"

"I guess."

Time crawled. Penny touched up her makeup in a dark window. More people entered the exhibition in pairs and nobody left through the front door.

Finally it was Gary and Angel's turn to go in.

"See you on the other side," Angel said.

Scott smiled. "Have fun."

Thirteen minutes later, the door opened and Denoté led them to a ticket wicket. The lady behind the glass said, "Tickets please." Her name was Paige.

The tickets were big and gaudy and said THE HORROR SHOW – ONE NIGHT ONLY in giant bold letters. Below the text, a mediocre drawing of an evil looking skull looked semi-daunting. In the bottom corner of each ticket was the price: $200.00, tax included.

Scott handed both tickets over.

"Names?"

"Scott and Penny Beach."

Paige typed the names into a computer, and Scott and Penny were led to a door. Above it was a security camera.

"Mind your step," Denoté said before he opened the door. "The art isn't merely on the walls. It's on the floor and ceiling too. It's in the air, the atmosphere. It's everywhere; it's alive. There's only one exit, located at the far end of the building. This show is a one-way street. You can't leave through the front door unless you do it now. You won't have a chance to revisit the exhibitions once you pass them, so enjoy the art while you can. I hope you're not faint of heart. This exhibition is designed to scare you to death."

"Sounds good," Scott said. He noticed a smudge of blood on Denoté's shirt; it looked like a handprint. Scott figured it was part of the show. "Looking forward to it."

"Thank you," Penny replied. Her voice was hardly a whisper. *Scare you to death.* She didn't like the sound of *that*.

As Denoté opened a second door, Penny wondered why she had allowed Scott to bring her to such a place. This wasn't a gala, this wasn't the theater, this was…well…she didn't know what this was, but it wasn't for her. She knew that much.

Scott and Penny stepped inside the next room. It was small: twelve feet by twelve feet. There was a single light hanging from a black ceiling. The walls were black; the floor had black tiles. On the far side of the room was a white door. There was no art inside the room, no furniture either. It was just an empty room that seemed very dark. The corners were only shadow.

One corner was hiding something: a small camera.

The door behind them closed; they heard the CLICK of the lock.

113

Penny turned around, startled. She grabbed the doorknob and twisted, but it wouldn't open. She knocked on the door with her knuckles hard enough to make them red; she slapped the door with her palm.

Scott placed a hand on her shoulder. "Babe, what are you doing?"

"I don't like this," she said flatly. "I don't like being locked in."

"Why not?"

"It—" Penny stopped short and looked Scott in the eye. She was going to say *it frightened her*. But wasn't that the point, to be frightened?

"Are you scared?"

Penny laughed in spite of herself. "Yeah, I guess I am."

"Should I remind you that—"

"I know," Penny interrupted. "That's the whole idea, to be scared. But I expected paintings and sculptures, not to be taken prisoner."

"Prisoner! We're not prisoners!"

"They didn't answer the door."

"*He* didn't," Scott corrected. "It's just one guy."

"What about the ticket lady?"

"What about her?"

Penny wrapped her arms around Scott's body. "Just don't try any funny stuff," she said. "I mean it. This *stupid* event is going to freak me out enough without you shouting 'BOO' in my ear."

"I won't."

"Promise?"

"Penny, I love you. And at two hundred bucks a pop, I shouldn't *have* to shout 'BOO' in your ear."

"That's true."

"Actually, you know what I heard? I heard that tickets for this thing were going for ten thousand."

"Really?"

"Yeah, and we paid two hundred."

"Not just us," Penny said. "I heard other people in line saying the same thing. Two hundred bucks."

"Huh."

"Ten grand is bullshit, babe. Either someone lied or they were talking about a different show.

Scott nodded. "I guess. Ready to move on?"

114

Penny looked at the room. "Is this it?"

"Looks that way."

"Well…this is dumb."

Scott made a face that suggested she was right. "There goes two hundred dollars."

"Each," Penny said with a smile, but she didn't care.

Her folks were rich.

* * *

Lawrence Whitely and his wife Elizabeth sat in the back of the car, listening to Mozart. When the car stopped, the driver turned off the music, stepped out, opened the back door and held out his gloved hand gracefully. The driver's name was Nathaniel Lewis; he was dressed in a pristine black suit and had been driving for Mr. and Mrs. Whitley for eleven years.

Elizabeth took Nat's hand and was assisted onto the carpeted sidewalk. "Thank you," she said, shuffling from the car.

"I'm fine, Nathaniel," Lawrence interjected. "No need to help. This old coupé is still running smooth, thank you very much."

"No problem, sir," Nathaniel said, tipping his hat with his fingers. He wasn't surprised; Lawrence never wanted help, even when he needed it.

Lawrence grinned. "I'll call you around ten-thirty, maybe eleven. You can pick us up then."

"Very good, sir."

Lawrence and Elizabeth walked up the carpet. A young man in a burgundy suit opened a door. A man in a black tuxedo asked if he could be of assistance. His nametag said Donnie Polanski.

"We're here for the Horror Show," Lawrence said.

"Ah, very good, sir. The party is being held in the President's Conference Suite. Right this way."

Don Polanski led Mr. and Mrs. Whitely through luxurious hallways. When they arrived at their destination Lawrence handed the man a fifty-dollar tip.

"Thank you, sir," Don said, and he tucked the fifty into his breast pocket just as neat as he pleased. "Have a good evening."

Inside the room, a man in a grey suit approached. "Good evening, sir. Good evening, my lady. Here for the show?"

"Yes."

"Excellent. May I see you tickets please?"

Lawrence reached into his coat pocket and pulled out two tickets. They were small and elegant, with stylish gold letters written in script. There was no photograph on the tickets, but in the bottom left hand corner it said: $10,000.00 – one night only, limited to twenty tickets.

"Very good," the man said with a brown-toothed grin. "A car is waiting."

* * *

Scott and Penny Beach stepped inside the next room and the door closed behind them. They heard the CLICK of the lock, and with that, the music began—though 'music' may have been the wrong word. It was a note, a low and hauntingly steady note; the type often heard in horror movies when things turned tense.

Scott smiled; he liked it.

Penny didn't.

The room was twice the size of the first. Like the other room, it was painted black with a single light hanging from the ceiling.

On the left side of the room, three photographs were pinned to the wall. Each photograph was taken with a Polaroid, and placed five feet away from the next. Above the photographs, a small reading light illuminated the image.

They approached the first picture.

It was the image of a dog, a large brown Rottweiler. It looked strong.

Penny took Scott's hand, squeezed it, and together they approached the second photograph—an image of a table saw, the kind commonly used in a wood shop.

"I don't get it," Penny said.

"Me either."

They approached the third photograph, slowly, almost cautiously. There was a feeling growing between them that the couple didn't want to address. They were becoming nervous. They expected art, not this. Not cheap photographs and canned music. This was dark and disturbing, true, but there was nothing artistic about it—at least, not from what they had seen so far.

As they reached the third Polaroid, Penny turned away.

It was the image of a body—a corpse, mutilated beyond comprehension. The stomach was gutted, the chest was mangled; entrails washed the floor around it. A hand had been chewed off. The throat was opened to the bone. Glossy eyes were forever frozen in a gaze of terror.

It took Scott a few seconds to recognize the corpse as a woman, and a few more to see the Rottweiler in the background.

"That's fucked up," Scott said.

Penny glanced at the image a second time. "Do you think it's real?"

In the far corner of the room, near the door they had entered, a wall began sliding up. It made a sound like an escalator. They heard a deep, sharp bark, followed by two more. There was nothing *canned* about it.

There was a dog in the room with them, a Rottweiler. It bolted for them, its snout arched into a brutal snarl, with teeth long and white. Its ears were pulled so far back they looked aerodynamic.

Penny stepped away, lost her balance and fell. Her dress yanked against her shoulders; her purse slipped from her fingers and slid across the floor.

Scott watched his wife drop.

His mouth was agape; his eyes were wide with terror.

Looking away from her, he saw the animal leap and he screamed. With his hands held in a distressing pose of defense, he thought he was about to be torn to pieces.

Miraculously—as if God himself intervened—the dog came to an abrupt halt in mid-air.

It was chained to the wall.

"Jesus Christ!" Scott cursed as the animal was hurled to the ground.

The dog lifted itself to its feet, yelping. The hair on its back pointed north. White foamy drool hung from its mouth like a beard.

"What the fuck is that!"

Penny was shaking; she was close to tears. "Help me up," she said. "Scott, give me a hand."

Scott helped his wife to her feet, still cursing and angry. "This isn't art! This is bullshit! Are you okay honey? Are you all right?"

Penny wrapped her arms around her husband. Her dress—her beautiful, peach colored dress—was torn on one side. "Look at me," she said.

The dog growled and barked several times, drowning her words.

"I'm not happy about this," Scott said. "This is bullshit."

"I know it is. Let's get out of here."

As the dog barked again, Scott screamed, "SHUT UP!" He was furious now. That fucking dog was *not* cool.

Hand in hand, Scott and Penny walked towards the white door, eager to move on. The floor was sticky. The white door had spots of blood on it.

They entered the next room; the door closed behind them with the familiar CLICK. This time, the sound pissed Scott off. He tried opening it. Sure as shit, it was locked. Not that it mattered—they *couldn't* go the other way. Not with that fucking dog in the room.

The new room was bigger than the one before it, but its design was similar: black ceiling, black walls, black floor, white door, and spooky music. But this time, four pieces of art hung from the wall on their left, placed inside three-foot glass cube cases. Actual art, not Polaroids.

"Wait here." Scott took a step away from Penny and away from the cases, wanting to investigate the dark corners of the room.

Grabbing his arm, Penny said, "Are you crazy? Don't leave me here! You're going to trip some invisible wire and a gorilla will jump out and tear my fucking head off!"

Scott felt the urge to pull away from Penny and tell her to shut up.

He didn't.

"You're right," he said, feeling terrible. This wasn't her fault; it was his. He was the one that brought them here, not her. "I'm sorry. I'm just a little upset about that last room."

"It's okay, just don't leave me."

"I won't."

They walked away from the art, checking out the dark corners. There was nothing to see: no secret doors or hidden panels, no levers or tripwires. Having found nothing waiting in the darkness, they approached the first piece of art.

In the top right-hand corner of the glass cube was another print, labeled FIFTY-ONE – MARTIN McCAMMON. It was the photograph of a twenty-year-old man. He had dark skin and dark eyes; he was not looking at the camera. In fact, he didn't seem to realize that he was being photographed.

Beneath the photo, a corpse was humped together in a pond of blood; it looked like the same person. The legs were cut off, the arms were off; each limb looked like it had been sliced a thousand times. In the center of the kid's face, a deep cut traveled from chin to forehead.

The glass was smudged red, like someone had opened the lid and dropped the corpse inside.

The case must be airtight, Scott thought. Otherwise the blood would be dripping out of it.

They walked across the sticky floor. Inside the next case they found another photograph. This one was labeled THIRTEEN – CHRISTINE S. HUSTON. It was the image of a woman. On camera, she looked pretty. Inside the case, she looked like ground beef.

If Scott had to guess, he'd say someone had taken a chainsaw to her.

Inside the third case they found a comparable piece. The photograph was labeled EIGHTY-NINE – OWEN GLENN. The teenager had been ripped apart.

"God," Scott said, amazed. "These look real, don't they?"

"What if they are real?"

"Yeah right."

"No, think about it," Penny said, completely serious. "What if this is real? That doesn't look like a special effect to me. That looks like a dead body."

"You've seen a lot of dead bodies, have you?"

"That's not the point. Look at it! It's real!"

"Why would anyone do that to a person, and then display it? You're being stupid."

"No, I'm not. They'd do it for the money."

"Money? What money?"

"The two hundred dollars."

"They only sold a hundred tickets, babe. That's all that they put on sale. What's two hundred times a hundred?"

"It's twenty grand."

"Twenty? Really?"

"Yeah."

"Still…twenty grand isn't enough money to kill for."

"No? This is a 'one night only' event. Think about it. They set up shop, rent this shithole for next to nothing, kill a couple bums, take our money and hit the road."

"I think you're being crazy. I also think the people putting on this event were hoping to draw this type of reaction, and with you, it's clearly working."

"Don't talk to me that way."

"What way? I don't want to fight, babe, but…think about what you're saying. So this is what, a snuff show? I bought tickets in advance! It's promoted in the newspaper!"

"So what? They could take the money and run, couldn't they?"

Frustrated, Scott put a hand to his head. This sucked. First the dog scares the shit out of them—and not in a good way—and now this. He wished he had stayed home. "I suppose."

"I'm ready to leave, Scott. I'm tired. I want it to be over."

"Me too."

They walked to the fourth display. It was different than the first three. It still had a photograph (without a number), and it still had a body, but this time the art was a dog. It looked like the same dog that tried to eat them, only mutilated.

* * *

Lawrence and Elizabeth were led from the conference room, down a hall and through a set of doors where several black limousines waited. They sat inside the nearest one and the car began moving. Fifteen minutes later, they arrived in a part of the city that neither Lawrence nor Elizabeth had been to before. The buildings were condemned. Derelicts loitered on the street.

"They sure are making an effort to capture the mood, aren't they?" Lawrence said.

Elizabeth huffed. "This is dreadful. I can't imagine what encouraged you to buy tickets for such an event."

"Variety is the spice that makes life worth living, my dear."

"Well, I could do without this."

The driver opened their door but didn't offer a hand.

Mr. and Mrs. Whitely pulled themselves from the car and were led into an alley. Elizabeth wondered if they would be mugged. They reached a door. The driver knocked three times, paused, and knocked again. The door opened, and Denoté led the couple up a flight of dilapidated stairs.

Lawrence opened his mouth but decided not to say anything. His blooming questions would be answered soon enough, he figured. There was no point in inquiring about the location.

They entered a room that *had* been renovated, walking past two very large, very ugly, men that looked like escaped convicts forced into suits. One man was missing a handful of teeth. The other had a scar that ran from his eye to his chin and a tattoo of a swastika on each temple.

The walls of the room were freshly decorated; pot-lights had been installed in the ceiling, and antiquated paintings adorned the walls. Fresh cut flowers sat in stylish vases, and there was a fully stocked bar and a man in a tuxedo handing out cocktails. There was a piano with a highly talented musician. His fingers rolled across the keys effortlessly; light jazz comforted the room. The piano sat upon a circle of fresh, coffee colored carpet. Where the carpet ended, the room had been remodeled with dark hardwood floors. Stainless steel baseboards circled the space. And on the far side, several large windows had been installed next to each other. Television monitors were above them. Tables and chairs created a living room atmosphere.

Mr. and Mrs. Whitely were offered a drink and led to their seats. Lawrence requested bourbon. Elizabeth asked for a glass of cabernet.

The man seated beside Lawrence introduced himself as Buck Million. He wore an oversized brown suit and cowboy boots made of alligator skin. He said, "You've missed quite a show so far folks. Don't know how they do it, but it's fascinating, worth every penny."

Lawrence and Elizabeth smiled at the man and looked through the glass. They saw nothing.

"Not there!" Buck said. "Don't look down there, not yet anyhow. The action is on the monitor right now. See? Look at 'em. They're getting ready to move! You'll know when the action is down there. The lights shine."

"Down there?" Elizabeth asked.

"Yep…down there, and they're putting on quite a show."

Lawrence looked at the monitor. A man and a woman were standing in a dark room; it looked like they were arguing. The man lowered his head and reached for the doorknob.

Buck said, "Oh boy, here they come. You're gonna love it!"

Lawrence thought for a moment he recognized the couple, but he wasn't sure. The image was too grainy to distinguish faces.

* * *

Scott stepped through the door with his shoulders raised. The floor creaked. The room was dark. He couldn't see anything. Standing inside, Penny held the door open, the light from the other room the only thing illuminating the way.

"What should we do?" Scott asked, his voice echoing off the walls.

"Why is it so dark?"

"I don't know."

The light in the room behind them flickered and turned off. There was only darkness.

"Close the door," Scott said.

"Honey, I'm scared." Penny squeezed Scott's hand hard enough to let him know she meant it. "I don't like this."

"Close the door."

"Why? What do you know that I don't?"

"The only thing I know for sure is that I want to get out of here. I was in a funhouse one time, inside a very dark room, like this. The objective was to find the door on the far side, but they were tricky, see? I put my hands on the wall and I circled the room. But the door I was looking for was closed. Touching it did nothing; it felt like the wall. I had to circle the place twice before they opened it. Point is…I think we're in a funhouse babe. We need to find the door on the far side."

"I hate this place."

"Me too. Is the door closed?"

Penny stepped ahead and allowed the door to close. New music came on, which was a lot like the old music, but with a slow and steady pulse: *boomp, boomp, boomp*. Hand in hand, they followed the wall to the nearest corner. The floor seemed shifty and unstable.

"What's wrong with the floor?" Penny asked. She stubbed her foot on something sharp. "Fuck!"

"What happened?"

"I don't know. I cut my foot on something!"

They turned the corner and walked about ten feet before Scott touched a glass case. He wondered if there was a body inside, but he didn't wonder for long. A light began shining from within the glass, growing steadily brighter.

A corpse was revealed. A photograph was revealed too: SIX – RICHARD GOLDSMITH.

Floor creaking, they moved on.

When they reached the next case the same thing happened; Scott put his hand on the glass and a light began to shine. This time, the art was different. The case had a photograph, but no body.

SEVEN-THREE – CURTIS RYAN BERRY.

"Why is it empty?" Penny asked.

"I have no idea."

Scott was starting to make out the shape of the room, now. It seemed like a gymnasium. After he put his hand to a few more cases, he'd know for sure. He stubbed his toe on something solid, dismissed it, and moved on.

"There is something sharp sticking out of the floor," Penny whined. "I think my foot is bleeding."

"Just keep walking."

Scott touched the next case with a trace of excitement. Each case revealed more of his surroundings, like he was unwrapping a gigantic gift. Unfortunately, the sensation was short lived and replaced with a feeling of imminent horror.

The light inside the case crept on.

Both Scott and Penny recognized the corpse.

SIXTY-EIGHT – GARY SOMERS.

The real estate agent.

His body was in pieces.

* * *

Lawrence took a sip from his tumbler, looked at his wife and shrugged.

"I don't get it," he said. "What's happening?"

Before Elizabeth had a chance to respond, Buck Million barged into the conversation. "Of course you don't get it! You're catching this act halfway through the performance. Maybe you guys would be better off waiting for the next round. Go talk to the piano man or something, tell him he's doing a good job."

"Next round?"

"Yeah…next round. Every ten minutes or so they sweep up the mess and start again."

"Do you think we should wait?" Elizabeth asked politely.

Buck looked Elizabeth in the eye. "Naw. This here is the best part, the *main* part. You should shut-up with the questions and enjoy. Hell, it's a magic show, that's what it is—a goddamn magic show."

* * *

"That's the man I gave a cigarette to."

"No it isn't," Scott said. His voice was barely a whisper. "It…it only looks like him. It's part of the experience."

"Part of the experience? Look! Look at him! Blood is pouring out of his head! See the tattoo? See his eyes? It's him!"

Scott didn't say anything, couldn't say anything.

He pulled Penny away from Gary's box, grinding his teeth together. His heart was beating faster now; his thoughts were reeling. What if it *was* the man from outside? Could it be him? Was it at all possible?

Had they stepped into a snuff film?

Were they about to die?

Scott dragged Penny across the creaky floor and heard a strange sound. He knew that sound. *Oh God, he knew—but he didn't want to admit it; he didn't even want to think it.* He slapped his free hand on the next box, wanting to see, needing to see. The light inside the box turned on. The box was empty, with the exception of the photograph. He read the name, not that he needed to.

FORTY-FIVE – PENNY BEACH.

"What the fuck is this?"

In the photograph, Penny's eyes were bright above her smile. She was wearing the same dress. Her hair and make-up was a perfect match. The photo was taken today. There was no denying it.

Scott didn't recall seeing anyone with a camera, but then again, he hadn't been looking. Someone could have snapped one easily enough.

Penny began weeping. "That's me—"

124

"No," Scott whispered, but his eyes spoke the truth.

The box was for her.

Suddenly there was a deep, low, growl. The strange sound, he realized, had not been his overactive imagination. And this time, he couldn't dismiss it.

They were not alone. There was a dog in the room.

"Oh shit," Penny said.

The lights came on—all of them.

They were standing in a warehouse. In the center of the room was a large cage. Inside the cage was a dog. It had teeth like daggers.

But could not attack. *Yet.*

The cage was sitting on a riser, three feet from the ground, attached to what seemed like a pulley system. There was a metal cable linked to the top part of the cage that extended high above the animal.

Florescent lights hung from the rafters, and glass cases were attached to the walls. There must have been a hundred of them. Half the cases were empty, save the photo inside. The others were stuffed with the mutilated dead. On the far wall, maybe twenty-five feet from the floor, several windows overlooked the room.

People watched through the windows with excited, smiling faces.

Looking at the floor, Scott gasped.

Unlike other floors, this one was made of unfinished plywood, and protruding from the wood were hundreds and hundreds of spherical blades. Some of them were fourteen inches in diameter. Some were twelve. A few looked to be sixteen. They reminded Scott of semi-circular shark fins, or teeth, or both.

"Table saws," he whispered, remembering the photograph. Hundreds of saws had been attached beneath the floor. This took time; someone wasn't fucking around.

He stepped back and looked at his wife with a new sense of fear.

"You were right."

* * *

Buck Million stood up from his chair and lifted a glass in the air. "That's what I'm talking about," he hollered, slurring his words slightly. "Let the show begin!"

125

"Here, here!" someone else shouted.

Standing at the window, Lawrence and Elizabeth gazed into the room with the saws. Lawrence crumpled his face into a ball.

What the hell is this, he wondered, some kind of game?

Elizabeth saw a man and a woman acting afraid, fake carcasses lying inside glass cases, and saws—probably made of plastic—sticking through slots in the floor. She didn't bother to look at the actors closely, or to analyze the props. She didn't care for this type of entertainment.

She walked away from the show and sat in a chair near the pianist. The music he played was beautiful. It reminded her of a simpler time, when family was king and people were simple and content.

After a fair-sized drink of wine, she opened her purse, deciding it was a good time to phone her daughter.

She hadn't talked with Penny in days.

* * *

Scott saw the people watching through the large windows. He waved his hands in the air. One man waved back, smiled, and nudged the woman on his left. Scott waved twice more before his eyes returned to the blades in the floor.

There was a moment of silence, followed by the sound of a phone. It was Penny's phone, ringing from inside her purse.

Scott's eyes widened. The concept of getting outside assistance hadn't yet crossed his mind. "Answer it! We need help!"

Penny unbuckled her purse and went for the phone.

A door—snuggled between two glass containers—opened, and Denoté stepped through the doorway, grinning like a wolf. He held a shotgun in his hands.

Penny pulled her phone free. "Hello?"

"Hi Penny," Elizabeth said, watching the pianist. She sat her glass of wine on a table. "How are things?"

"Mom?"

Before Penny had a chance to say anything else, Denoté pointed to the far wall and shouted, "That's your exit!"

Scott looked at the exit and at the saws blocking the path. He screamed, "What the hell are you doing to us?"

Denoté only laughed. "Start the saws!"

As if obeying his command, the saws came to life. The sound was gigantic; it was all Scott could hear. With the saws, the dog began barking hysterically and the music was turned louder to make things more powerful, more surreal. But how much stronger could things get? Wasn't this intense enough?

Penny shouted into the phone: "Mom? Mom? Can you hear me? Is that you? Oh God, I need help!"

She looked at the floor.

The blades were placed in odd angles, giving her room to walk but not much room for error. One missed step and you'd lose a toe, maybe a heal.

In between the blades, blood, meat, and bones were scattered in small piles.

Denoté smiled. This was his favorite part of the show. He loved watching people scream. And although many victims ran into the saws like they wanted to get it over with, most just stood there, too scared to move, afraid of the foreseeable future.

Seeing the woman's phone, Denoté decided to accelerate the event. The people upstairs might not like it as much but so what? They had enough entertainment to satisfy the sickest elite minds.

He reached into his pocket and clicked a button on a small devise. The dog's cage began lifting towards the ceiling, setting the dog free.

Once it was able, the animal leapt from its cage, oblivious to the danger on the floor.

Scott saw it coming and screamed in fear.

Penny didn't see the dog until its blood splashed her face.

As the animal bounced across several saws, she carelessly stepped away from the carnage. A 14-inch blade ripped her left foot—and her peach gala shoe—in half.

The pain was immeasurable. Falling backwards, she dropped her phone and screamed. Before she hit the floor, her fingers stabbed her face and her hands squeezed tight. A second blade caught her in the elbow, severing the arm. A third blade hit the small of her back. Blood misted the air, and she was pulled across the blade, losing bits and pieces as she moved.

Her eyes rolled back and her mouth fell open.

The people upstairs applauded.

* * *

127

As Elizabeth listened to her daughter screaming, the people in the room began putting their hands together. She heard Lawrence shriek.

"Oh my god!" he said with a huff, once he was finally able to string the words together. He clutched his chest, thinking a heart attack would be unavoidable. He wondered if he was dreaming. "That's Penny down there! And Scott! What the hell is this?"

Elizabeth came running towards him, pushing away whoever was in her path. She squeezed herself between Lawrence and Buck and looked into the room.

"Where? Where are they?"

The two men standing near the door saw what was happening. The man with the smashed teeth grinned. His name was Russell. "Looks like we've got a situation, Chez."

The disfigured man agreed. "Looks that way."

Chez flicked a switch on the wall and reached into his jacket pocket. A moment later both men were releasing the safeties on their guns.

* * *

A red light began flashing, but Scott didn't notice. He was too busy watching Penny being dragged from saw blade to saw blade.

Denoté *did* look at the flashing red light, however, and he knew what it meant. There was a situation, and it was time to bring this show to an end.

He lifted the shotgun up, and aimed it at Scott.

Scott noticed; it was time to move.

He began running like an athlete, successfully dodging blades for the first twelve feet. Then the shotgun went off, his toes clipped the jagged edge of a spinning saw blade, and he went down—arms wide, head back, screaming.

* * *

Chez and Russell eliminated people systematically. Russell shot the bartender first, putting a bullet in his head. The man fell back holding a bottle of sherry. Russ shot the waiter and the pianist next. The waiter flipped over a chair, and the pianist smashed his face against the keys on his way to the floor.

128

Those mangled notes would be the last he'd ever play.

Chez shot the couple standing closest to him, hitting each of them in the face. They fell like dominoes, one slamming into the other. Then Chez killed whoever seemed easiest, and at this point, they were *all* easy. Nobody was moving yet.

The time for fun was now.

One man fell to his knees, begging. He was shot in the heart. Another man wet his pants. He was shot in the balls. A woman well past middle age put her hands in the air, and proclaimed: "I surrender!"

Chez laughed and shot her once in each tit.

Lawrence put his arms around Elizabeth as if trying to protect her. He felt a pair of bullets enter his back. Elizabeth took one in the eye. They fell to the ground together, lumped in a contorted ball.

When Denoté entered the room he didn't look upset. He was a professional. This was the business he was in. Sometimes the exhibition went smoothly; sometimes it didn't. Either way, they got paid and traveled to another country.

He walked from body to body, shooting indiscriminately.

And while Denoté and his two brothers finished their work, Paige stepped outside and told those waiting in line the bad news. "There was an accident," she said. "Someone's been hurt. The show is cancelled."

When the question of refunds came about she lied, saying a full refund would be issued the following day. Some complained. Some didn't. None realized how close they'd come to death.

CRY LITTLE SISTER

BY JOHN EDWARD LAWSON

Gerard is what you'd call an escargot prep specialist. He works in a dry room shut off from sunlight, surrounded by white pine containers full of Helix aspersa—AKA brown garden snails. All day long he feeds them bran to cleanse their digestive tracts; snail waste is toxic to humans. He doesn't mind being the only EPS on site. Contact with the other workers tends to leave a bad taste in his mouth.

"Yes, mother," he grunts into the cell phone. He does this whenever he senses a break in the monologue.

"I wouldn't ask if it wasn't crucial."

"Dinner with the freak you married is crucial?"

"Yes."

"Okay." The snails scrape their teeth over the bran, the body-long foot of each working overtime to push and pull them along. "So you, me, Wasserman, and a Christless Cuban pork loin. Does it have to be tonight?"

"You forgot Christina."

"Ma! Talk about letting the freak outta the box!"

"Son," his mother patiently begins. Her accent has almost been smothered by decades of exposure to North American smog. Just a hint of her Japanese-Brazilian heritage lingers at the back of her throat like emphysema damage. "Nobody is talking about releasing deformed persons from their enclosures. It is just a simple family dinner."

"I'll be there." Gerard observes the snails glistening in their crates. Before he can add anything to the conversation the line goes dead.

His father had been a Muslim cleric in Yemen. Everyone finds it better not to think about him, as doing so summons to mind the decapitation images from the Internet, the endless news cycles, the eventual late-night-show-joke status his father's death was reduced to.

Fast forward three years: Yoriko Ali marries Wasserman McMann. Gerard, put off by having to welcome somebody into the family with two "mans" in their name, lurked in the shadows of the wedding while struggling to be a standup guy and keep it cordial. During the reception, Wasserman broached the subject of fatherly advice. Hoping to provide his stepfather with a chance to "bond," Gerard asked, "Does it ever get easier?"

"'Does it ever get harder?' might be the more pertinent question," Wasserman replied. He then brushed some lint from Gerard's shoulder and moved on to the other guests.

Thinking about the looming dinner he can only mutter, "Cock blocker." He runs a pale hand over his shaved scalp; despite his ethnicity, he is unusually pale, having taken more after his Japanese grandparents in that regard. His job prevents him from ever being exposed to sunlight.

Today is Wasserman's birthday, the first—and perhaps only—time he'll have to visit his stepfather's home. Being a standup guy dictates he put his personal feelings aside and do this for the good of the family.

* * *

Gerard has arrived at the appointed time, and the reward for his punctuality is a twenty minute wait outside the front door. Nobody is inside the black painted home, and just when he is ready to give up and leave, he sees Christina on the sidewalk just beyond the hedges. He feels vaguely guilty about reacting so violently when his mother mentioned his stepsister. They have never met, but he has…heard things.

McMann and daughter hail from mixed roots: Jewish, Lithuanian, Roma—AKA Gypsy. Christina's skin is pale, perhaps an even lighter shade of sickly than Gerard's.

She is sizable for a female and would easily be Gerard's equal in height, if not for the loss of her legs. She rolls to a stop in her wheelchair, which is an antique model customized with studded leather. She's dressed for a night of clubbing, not a family dinner.

There is an awkward moment of recognition and indecision regarding how they should address each other.

"Hey."

"Hey."

He moves to push her, but before he can do so a middle-aged Caucasian man, in a cheap suit and toupee to match, shoves him aside. "Wait your turn!" He takes hold of the wheelchair's handles, and when he speaks to her, it almost sounds as though the man refers to Christina as "Amputina."

"Hey! Hey, what the—?!" Suddenly the man is heavy and warm in Gerard's grasp, pinned against brick and whimpering.

"Please," the man gasps, "I'll pay on time next time!"

Christina smirks. "Norbert, meet my stepbrother…Gerard."

"Oh." Despite the blood vessels throbbing under Gerard's skin, Norbert has grown apathetic. "Same time, next week?"

"I just go where they tell me too. Call *them* to make an appointment, jerkface." She wheels herself up the ramp, forces the two men apart, starts to unlock her door and stops. Her glare sends Norbert scampering out of sight.

Gerard's eyes linger well after the man is gone. "Do I even want to ask?"

"Probably not."

They go inside.

* * *

The walls inside Wasserman McMann's home are as black as the exterior. The man himself has just arrived, a full thirty minutes after Christina and Gerard entered. That has given her time to change into clothes—and a wheelchair—more appropriate for the occasion.

The three of them are sitting at the dining room table, the wait for Gerard's mother bearing down on them all in equal measure. Any attempts at conversation by Gerard are met by sarcasm from his stepsister and a complete lack of acknowledgment from his stepfather.

Wasserman is in his early 50s, equipped with permanent sneer lines, a pot belly, and salt and pepper beard, sideburns, and mustache. He is dressed in a dark suit and loafers, a silver-tipped cane at his side—for show only—as he sips his drink and stares at the wall opposite him. Mounted on it is a photograph of turbine parts, rusted and broken.

He finally speaks, gesturing with his brandy snifter. "Didn't I ever tell you I'm a machinery aficionado?"

"Uh…no."

The chance to launch into a pseudo-intellectual rant smears Wasserman with ten shades of self-satisfaction. "Machines are symbols of autoeroticism," he says, finally hitting on something that catches Gerard's attention after minutes of dreary nonsense.

"Autoeroticism."

"Indeed."

"You know, comments like that are why I never came here before."

Wasserman laughs it off. "So, I suppose you'll want to skip my talk about how technology is a vehicle for societal change, particularly that of the United States affecting developing countries."

Inwardly, Gerard sighs. Making a conscious effort to relax the muscles of his face, to release his fists, he replies, "Don't think of it. It's your day, after all." He catches a glimpse of his stepsister's disgusted expression and realizes he's said the wrong thing. Another half hour of pseudo-intellectualism drags along until Gerard decides to cut his losses.

"I should be heading out," he informs Wasserman, "but first I wanted to at least give you this."

Gerard slides an envelope across the table. Inside is a store-bought birthday card signed, "With Love."

"You may well be a developing young man, and the fruit of my Yoriko's flesh, but hear me now when I say this. *You will never be able to earn my love!*" So saying, Wasserman tears the card apart, sets the pieces on fire, and exits.

Gerard, shocked by the outburst, hesitates, leaving it to Christina to dump her drink on the flames. "Happy fourth freakin' birthday, Dad," she calls after him. "You get to wear big-boy underpants now!" She and Gerard share a look, then a laugh. Staring at the burned spot on the tabletop she asks him, "What was that all about before, when I was trying to come up to the house and you were all grabby with my wheelchair? Makes you feel like a big man to push around some crippled girl?"

"Well...you're a woman, not a girl, and no. Of course it doesn't." He finds the question highly disturbing for some reason. Her silent gaze prompts further response, in the form of: "Was that the deal with the other guy, that Norbert?"

A smile spreads and takes root in Christina's features, like the unease slowly undermining the stability of Gerard's stomach.

* * *

The Shangri-La nightclub is illuminated only with blue light. The shadows are deep and many, pulsating in time with the drum beat. Christina managed to con Gerard into going after his mother failed to show for her husband's "crucial" dinner. Christina covers the door fee and drinks; renting herself out for amputee fetishists to push around all day, it generates what she calls "mad money." Gerard still can't get his head around that, and downs another screwdriver in an attempt to clear the image from his mind.

The features of the dancers come and go in flashes as they slip in and out of shadow. Some sport dreadlocked body hair, the hands of others are visible because of the laser henna glove patterns outlining them, others still have opted for cosmetic mildew. It grows on tooth enamel in bright yellow, green, or black, depending on your "taste."

So far, this experience only serves to reinforce negative notions about his sister's lifestyle.

She tugs on his sleeve. "Wanna dance? I've still got moves. I was in dance school, before...you know."

"You mean like on *Fame*?" She just gives him a look. After he shakes his head in the negative she wheels herself out onto the dance floor, proving her familiarity with the mechanics of her wheelchair with a series of gravity-defying moves, putting her four-limbed counterparts to shame.

Watching her sway back and forth in her chair, Gerard can easily see his stepsister snagging guys—hopefully none of the freaks in this place.

From his perch, he quietly observes the freak show in progress. Not his stepsister, but all the others overcompensating for the normality of their physical configuration. In the dark recesses of the club somebody shouts "Ain't no Alphaville up in dis bee-otch?!" Shadows surge en masse into the DJ booth in a fit of "street justice" as prescribed by Dee Snider. The playlist situation is soon rectified as DJ Gobsmasha is replaced by DJ Lickable.

When she comes off the dance floor, Gerard gets another round of drinks for them. Taking a gander at the spikes adorning her wheelchair, he wonders if he should bother opening his mouth.

"Did I hear that guy call you Amputina?"

She nods casually, as if it's the most natural thing in the world.

"And these fetish people, they just push you around, polish your chair, et cetera? It doesn't go any further than that?"

She laughs. "People don't need me for that. I'm strictly for eyes only, outcall. You want to tap a legless honey, you go to my employer and they arrange for you to come in for a visit."

"Should I be afraid to ask who your employer is?"

"You ever heard of the Meat Puppet Cabaret?"

The ill feeling formerly undermining the stability of Gerard's stomach returns.

* * *

With the departure of the children, and Yoriko's failure to show up for his celebration, Wasserman McMann retires to the confines of his study to enjoy his rare art collection. Although the number of pieces he owns is small, it will be enough to keep him busy for the evening.

After securing the door to the study, he settles in behind his desk and opens the drawers; everything he needs is at his fingertips. He pushes a button and a polished teak wall panel retracts to reveal a 100-gallon cylindrical aquarium. The flip of a switch illuminates the liquid; one look confirms it isn't quite water. Inside resides his collection.

"Oh yes," he purrs, sliding his pants down to his ankles. Already the song is rumbling in his chest, building steam, begging for release.

"You don't think of them as human/You don't think of them at all." He continues singing as he pops the bright red pimples along his inner thighs.

His eyes are locked on the contents of the tank: two legs, *human* legs.

"You keep your mind on the money, keeping your eyes on the wall..."

The flesh contained inside is saturated and slightly puffy. Tiny bits of tissue threaten to fall loose around the incision points, the meat alien within the wounds, looking more like that of a reptile than a mammal. The remainder of the legs: perfection.

"She always did have sexy knees...especially that soft part bridging the rear of her thigh and calf..." He shudders and digs his nails in; a cyst afflicting the underside of his thigh weeps thick, dark, stagnant blood. A sigh escapes his lips.

135

It wasn't easy to procure Christina's legs before the surgeon had them burned with the other medical waste. It was even more difficult to smuggle them into his home. He had poured tens of thousands of dollars into his daughter's ballet dreams, but her limbs were never more graceful than when they drifted on formaldehyde tides.

"The Lambada? A forbidden dance, my foot!" McMann pours salt on his thighs, followed by rubbing alcohol. As he massages this mixture into his abused flesh a shudder works its way up his spine. The ends of his daughter's limbs dip in toward each other; her dismembered legs seem to be playing footsie together. His moans intensify. Now, before the alcohol can completely evaporate, he adds lye.

"A dancer for money, I'll do what you want me to do."

His daughter's legs have drifted apart now, feet splayed wide, her thighs leading to a tempting nothing between them.

"Tell me do you wanna see me do the shimmy again!"

Panting, he douses his flaming nerve endings with a quick vinegar rubdown. The act is complete.

* * *

A prematurely balding man in a lab coat and glasses is making his way across the dance floor, headed straight for Gerard and Christina. She watches his approach, then nudges her stepbrother. "There's a couple things you need to know before you meet him."

"Meet who?"

"The guy who did *this*." She caresses her thighs. "Don't mention anything about foreign doctors, foreign medicine, foreign medical school, none of it."

"Um, okay…"

The doctor steps up to them, arms wrapped around a large, ungainly box.

"Ger, meet Doc. He's our resident flesh sculptor. And Doc, meet Ger."

The men shake hands. "So what do they call you, doctor?"

"Just 'Doctor' is safest…for us both." Gerard's eyes narrow, but before he can speak, Christina's inquiries about the contents of the box cut him short.

"New gear in need of a test subject." The doctor looks Gerard up and down like a one-eyed dog in a meat market. "This man of yours, he is very healthy. Strong like bull."

Gerard laughs, eyes the other two suspiciously, but ends up being the doctor's kamikaze gerbil anyway. It sounds harmless enough: a light harness is fitted over bare skin with various sensors, a set of four mechanical arms is attached, and the arms react to the movements of muscle groups throughout the back and shoulders. The entire procedure takes no time at all.

"Wear it around for a few hours is all I ask. We observe malfunctions then we make adjustments. Now, I drop a load on." He wanders off in the direction of the men's room.

They watch him leave. She asks, "And?"

"A real catch. Where'd you find him?"

"The type of surgeon who'll do this kind of procedure, you have to ask around at the ethnic salons if they know any freelance plastic surgeons."

"But I thought you said it was because of, you know, extreme damage and all that?"

She smiles. "Isn't that what amputation *is*?"

Gerard feels as though he should be self-conscious, but even with his shirt off, he's wearing more than most of the club's patrons. Rolling his left shoulder inspires the pair of extra arms sprouting from his back to wave, throwing him off balance with the sudden shift in weight. "I've got no idea how you do it," he says. "I can barely just stand here with these things on, and you're able to tear up the dance floor. Seriously, you've got some crazy moves out there. Your mechanic must give that thing a tune-up every week."

"It's just a chair, not a machine."

"Good for you, since your dad thinks machines are autoerotic or whatever."

He chuckles, but the look on her face tells him he's stepped out of bounds. As the doctor returns, Christina wheels herself back out into the foray of thrashing limbs and ecstasy-laced sweat.

If Christina lived in a shell and oozed slime she'd be so much easier to deal with, Gerard realizes. He didn't just end up in a shack full of mollusks all day by chance, it's because he always puts other people off. He ruminates on the limbless life of the snail, how little entanglement they must experience. And the fact that they're hermaphrodites must make etiquette a lot easier to master.

137

He turns to the doctor. "You ever eat a hermaphrodite?"

"What manner of question is that?"

Gerard doesn't know, so he returns to his drink.

* * *

Gerard stands in a desolate, run-down area of town, staring up at a three-level building. From the outside it's impossible to tell what use it serves. The structure is concrete, windowless with a single door nestled behind security bars. The interior is olive green and gold leaf, red lacquer and ivory, crushed velvet and candelabras. Gaunt, pale men in Victorian dress lead him through the establishment.

They leave him in a large, dimly-lit office, saying the proprietor will be with him shortly. A computer hums on the redwood desk; a life-size marionette collection lines one wall; the lava lamps aren't actually lava lamps—they have fetuses in them, among other even less savory things.

After a few minutes of waiting, Gerard decides to check his e-mail and situates himself behind the computer. On the screen, an olive-complected woman glares through the veil of her burka, clad below the neck in only an ammo belt. Animated banners proclaim this is the Hamas Mamas site, a part of the Terror Tricks network.

"What do you think?" asks a man as he enters. He's on the short side, pale with a light blonde coif and self-satisfied grin. "Our latest online product. We expect it will rake in millions."

"Congrats on your, uh, business venture. Look, you wanted to see me about something? Your men weren't too friendly down at the club. Might wanna have a talk with them."

"A client of ours, you met him earlier, yes? Fisticuffs ensued."

"You mean Norbert? There weren't really fisti…whatever."

"The point is we run an upscale establishment. Thuggery is frowned upon here. It's so low-rent."

Gerard takes another look around the office to make sure they are both talking about the same place. "Dude, you run a freakybone brothel!"

"Flesh gallery, Mr. Ali, we operate a flesh gallery." A faint scream worms in through a crack in the wall. "I'll tell you what, relations need not be hostile between us; you're not a bad looking guy, after all. You could fit in nicely here."

Gerard turns, studying a marionette while contemplating the most insulting fashion in which he can turn down the offer of employment. The marionettes are all the same: preteen boys with eyes sewn shut. "These things, they're way too lifelike." When he touches one, it runs away, and the surprise steals his breath.

The man chuckles. "You ever push one too hard, maybe?"

"Too hard?"

"Yeah, you know what I mean. Then you end up lying on top of them, your nose right in their broken little faces, inhaling their death rattle." Since Gerard fails to offer a response the man continues with, "You drawing sustenance from their dying gasp. It doesn't get any more intimate than that."

"No…I suppose it doesn't. Excuse me." Gerard forces himself to move, and after he makes it out of the man's sight he breaks into a full run.

* * *

Gerard rushes back to the Shangri-La, knowing full well something is very wrong and Christina needs to be warned. However, the doormen won't allow him in without his exoskeleton getup, so he has to return to his car and slip into it, not an easy task for one person. After getting the harness straightened out, he hurries back only to be held up this time by the doormen insisting he pose for photos with them. At first they are simple "Hey look, we're buddies!" photos, but they quickly devolve into six-armed bear hugs, six beers in hand poses, et cetera. Finally they allow him back into the club.

Christina is where he left her. She turns away from her cell phone, saying, "Check you out."

He realizes the beers are still in the grip of his extra hands. "Tell me about it. It's almost like I don't need my arms." He busies himself with removing the beers, realizing he's left a wet trail in his wake. "Listen, Christina, there's something—"

She holds up a finger. "Yes, I'm still here. What was that? Hold on…" She covers her ear in order to make out the speaker more clearly. Her demeanor takes a drastic turn for the worse as the conversation progresses. Gerard makes out very little of it, but hears, "Even though I don't have any legs there's still something

139

else I can offer in exchange. Okay, I'll see you soon." She hangs up.

"What was that about?"

"Nothing. It's all taken care of now." She has tears in her eyes even though she's smiling.

"Well, good, 'cause we gotta get out of here pronto. That boss of yours, he's crazier than a black rat's ass at midnight! He could be sending a bunch of fools here any second, and who knows what'll happen then."

He attempts to steer her away, but she locks her brakes. "Look, Ger, why don't you go on home. I'll give you a call later."

"What? Come on, I'm not messing around—"

"I said get out of my face!"

Gerard takes a deep breath, trying to keep it together, then realizes they are drawing the stares of everyone in the vicinity. "Yo, check it—I got six arms!" He waves them back and forth, eliciting a cheer from the crowd, which then returns its attention to its own affairs. Christina is not so easily placated; her visage is enough to send Gerard to the exit. He hesitates, though, and lurks around the club's periphery, waiting to see what she does—or what is done to her.

His wait is a short one. Several muscle men bear down on her, and she doesn't resist.

Gerard recognizes their gold and olive crushed velvet suits, and charges forward.

In the struggle, his metal fingers catch on a muscle man's eye, and blood sprays everywhere.

The violence is unexpected, so the muscle men quickly gather their injured companion and retreat.

* * *

The operating room hidden in the rear of Club Shangri-La is far more advanced than Gerard guessed when he was first told about it. Why there is an operating room in the building remains a mystery, as does the reason he has been summoned to it.

"Hey doc, thanks for getting Christina out of here on the down low. That was a pretty heavy scene."

The doctor has just finished washing his hands and is toweling them off. He beckons Gerard to come closer, ignoring his lackeys as they set up an operating table.

"Neuro-chips," he says. "You heard of this? Proteins are used to fuse living nerve cells onto silicon microchips. The union of man and machine. Soon, we won't need computers to tell machines what to do, we'll just think it."

"Hey hey, somebody's been watching Dr. Wizard reruns. You got any drinks back here?"

"My young friend...I am merely trying to give you information that will help you afterwards."

"Help me after what?"

"That exoskeleton, for instance. It can be retrofitted with motors, microprocessors...expensive, but not impossible."

Before Gerard can reply, the doctor has signaled for the men to wrestle him to the operating table. They strap him down with heavy-duty plastic, a thick leather harness anchoring his head. His yells of protest undoubtedly fail to penetrate the club's wall of noise. The doctor ignores him, instead snapping surgical gloves on as the henchmen hold molded plastic over Gerard's upper arms and apply C-clamps. The clamps are then fastened to the table.

"The Meat Puppet Cabaret," the doctor says, studying his anesthesia machine, "they are my biggest client. You make my biggest client very unhappy." He turns the anesthesia machine off.

The C-clamps are tightened at a snail's pace, pressing into the molded plastic covering Gerard's biceps. His teeth grind together; he's determined not to scream, to cry, to beg. Knowing how these people think, it's a sure bet doing such things would only fuel their perversion.

Another twist of the technician's wrist and the clamp tightens further, muscle now thick and compressed against the bone. A slight wince at the corner of Gerard's right eye gives him away.

The doctor leans in, the hint of a loving smile behind his mask. "Your humerus should be feeling something special right about now, eh?" The thin layer of latex sheathing his fingers is already warm as it strokes his patient's inner arm.

"Don't touch me. I thought you were cool, man..."

"You should know by now that amputations are only performed in the event of a traumatic fracture, typically accompanied by catastrophic soft tissue damage."

With another twist the C-clamps squeeze the very sweat out of Gerard's skin. An enormous man, heavily muscled and semi-dressed in leather, moves to the head of the table. He wields a

141

sledge hammer. Meanwhile, a tray bearing various saws, scalpels, tubes, and gauze is wheeled in. Bags of blood are being prepped by some malformed person whose features are hidden behind a surgical mask and scrubs.

Somebody bumps against the clamps, causing them to scrape the table's edge, their weight and secure attachment jolting Gerard's spine. Inside his head, something clicks, and he erupts with laughter.

"That's good, that's a good one. You had me there." Then, "The boss man is teaching me a lesson. You want to scare me."

The doctor looks at the others, nodding. "That's right, Ger. We *do* want to scare you." Having said that, he nods to the muscle man, who in turn raises the sledge hammer.

* * *

The teak panel in Wasserman's study has been retracted, exposing the aquarium's cataract-murky waters. Heavy-gauge fishing line dangles from machinery above, trailing down through the water, leading to the abrupt stumps of two thighs and two upper arms. The limbs sway back and forth, occasionally caressing each other. Wasserman massages his thighs.

The machinery used to manipulate the dead flesh and bone is relatively simple; Wasserman designed it himself, and spends hours lovingly massaging oil into its curves, its gears and tubing. Yoriko spends her time stoned out of her mind on hash stolen from Christina's room. This allows Wasserman all the time he needs for art appreciation.

Tonight, however, the song is silent within his chest. Something else entirely is germinating, taking root, poisoning the wellspring of his imagination. Gerard's arms drift wide in the tank, as if imploring him for an embrace.

He will, of course, need to reconsider his stepson's status as a developing young man. *He has not only bloomed*, McMann muses, *but he has been pruned as well*. While digging into the meaty part of his inner thigh, he wonders how Gerard is doing. It could take him a while to acclimate to his new career.

Bearing that in mind, Wasserman stops to dial the Meat Puppet Cabaret.

The owner himself answers. "Mr. McMann. It's always a pleasure to speak with such a committed patron of the arts. You aren't calling to get a wing named after you, are you?"

Wasserman laughs. "We'll burn that bridge when we come to it. No, I was just wondering if Gerard is available."

"Hmm…let me check." A minute later the man returns. "Yes, your boy is free for the time being. Shall I put him on?"

"Do, please." Then, "Gerard?" There is silence on the other end of the line, broken intermittently by stifled sobs. McMann smiles to himself. "I just called to say I love you."

The arms and legs continue their slow-motion dance, tumbling over each other again and again.

SQUEEZING OUT SPARKS

BY STEPHEN COUCH

Owen took the bus because, as far as he knew, his car had been stolen. He had driven through the East Side once before, when the highway was under construction and a short cut seemed like a good idea, and he'd kept pressing the door lock button every time he was caught by a red light. He'd imagined the hard-eyed people on the street corners could hear the steady ka-thunk, ka-thunk as his nervous finger worked the rocker switch.

Then, this part of town terrified him. Now, from the window of the CityTrans, it looked toothless and dusty. No one fixed him with glares as he wandered unwelcome through their territory; there were no people at all, as far as he could see. Buildings stood vacant, the graffiti on them faded with time. As the bus passed a gutted strip mall, a sparrow took flight from a broken window.

The squeal of air brakes brought Owen out of his daze, and he looked out the window to see who was getting on board. There was no bus stop, no sign or shelter. After a moment of confusion, he noticed the driver half-pivoted in his seat, squinting at him.

"We're here," the driver said. "Anyone rides out this far, there's only one place they're going."

Owen focused on the building they'd stopped at and read the hand-painted sign over the door: PRO/GNOSIS GALLERY.

He rose from his seat, feeling a wobble in his hip, and thought for the thousandth time about getting a cane.

Fifty-year-olds don't need canes.

He paused at the door and gripped the handrail. "Do you pick up here, too?"

"You know, I never have. Weird," the driver said, shaking his head. "But if I pass by later and see you waiting, I will."

Owen watched the bus drive away until the sound of its motor had faded into silence, then walked to the gallery door. No sign of life. No cars, unless they were all parked on the far side of the building. The only indicator that the place wasn't abandoned was the brightness of its signage and the lack of dust on the door buzzer.

He paused, his finger poised to push. He fished the want ad from his pocket, pouring over it yet again, trying to tease out any clue that it wasn't legit:

FAILED ARTISTS!

LOST YOUR MUSE? WORLD PASSED YOU BY?

GO OUT IN A FINAL BLAZE OF GLORY WITH US!

Of course, they wouldn't come out and say, "Come get mugged!"

A final blaze of glory.

Owen reached out, blinked twice, and pushed the buzzer. A noise other than his own breath: footsteps echoing on a concrete floor, muffled but getting closer. The chunk of a security bolt, and Owen stepped back as the door swung open. A skinny, floppy-haired, lip-pierced kid stared at him, hand over his eyes to shield the sun.

"Yeah?"

"I, uh, came about the ad? In the paper?" Owen held out the torn newsprint.

The kid looked at the scrap of paper and turned away. "Come on in."

The interior of the building was dark. Owen paused and closed his eyes for a moment, letting his pupils adjust—an old trick he'd learned as a boy going to the movies. He couldn't remember the last time he'd seen a movie.

"You coming?" the kid asked, and Owen opened his eyes, the building revealed. It was a warehouse space, once an office building, now gutted of all but the most necessary support pillars. There was some old office furniture, painting supplies here and there, and a few odd-shaped, tarp-covered objects that stood like monoliths, breaking up any clear footpaths.

The kid stood by a beat-up metal desk covered with scattered papers. A computer hummed alongside the desk.

Owen ventured over, and the kid stuck out his hand. "Reed," he said.

"Owen. Owen Garland." He took a seat as Reed did.

Reed wiggled the mouse, and the monitor flared to life, displaying a Word document. Owen could see people's names and addresses arranged in neat columns. INVITES it read across the top.

Reed closed the document, revealing a wallpaper of a naked tattooed girl, and faced Owen. "Business," he said, chucking a thumb at the monitor. "Always getting in the way of art."

Owen nodded. He felt a twinge in his hands and folded them in his lap, feeling like a schoolboy.

"Let me see that," said Reed. He took the ad and peered at it. "Been so long since I wrote it..."

A fat black cat strolled up and rubbed against Owen's shin. He stared down at it, not sure what it wanted. It stared back, got bored, and walked away.

Reed watched it leave and smirked. "So tell me about yourself, Garland. What made you come here? What about this," he waggled the ad, "*spoke* to you?"

You really speak to me, man, said the hippy girl, staring up from Owen's fringe-jeaned lap. The memory was shabby and faded, and he shook it away.

"I was an artist," he said. "A painter."

"You do any showings?"

"All over the country," Owen said, and almost elaborated, but Reed's sudden sour expression made him stop. Was the kid jealous?

"But you quit," Reed said after a pause, a smug note in his voice.

"Well, I felt like I couldn't—"

"Couldn't compete, right?" Reed jumped in. "Younger, hipper artists came along, and all of a sudden you couldn't get arrested, yeah?"

Owen stared at him. He felt another twinge in his hands and lied to take his mind off it. "...Yeah."

Reed smiled. "It happens, man," he said, with what he probably thought sounded like wisdom. He slapped his hands on his legs, stood, and walked to one of the tarps, Owen following.

"So, do you still keep up with the local scene? Do you know what we're accomplishing here?"

Owen shook his head. He glanced at the tarp, but couldn't tell what it concealed.

"We create an experiential, interactive environment for our audience," he said. "In our way, the viewer *becomes* the art. We force them to confront the inherent hypocrisy in being a passive non-participant. Did you hear about our last installation? It was called 'The Stocks.' A couple of local 'zines did a feature on it, but you could tell they didn't really get it." He frowned. "They're all about surface. Toss out a glib comment or two to keep the cloned sheep happy."

Reed looked at Owen as if expecting a response. "Ah," Owen said.

"But never mind that," said Reed. "They'll never get it. This is about *you*, Garland. This new exhibit will show what it's like to have the world pass you by, to be stepped on by the people who don't understand, the people who are all flash-in-the-pan, who aren't creating work for the ages, like us." He reached out for the tarp, but pulled his hand back. "Wait. I almost forgot." Reed sprinted to the desk and returned with a piece of paper and a pen, which he handed to Owen.

"Non-disclosure agreement," he said.

Owen stared down at the paper: A couple of paragraphs written in what a non-lawyer would think of as legalese, with lots of party-of-the-first-parts and such.

He signed it without reading any further.

"Business, huh?" Reed said. "Always getting in the way of…"

Something crashed on the other side of the area, followed by the sound of running claws making frantic purchase on concrete.

"Yves!" Reed shouted. "God*dammit*, if you don't get that fucking cat under control…!"

"Sorry, baby," said a voice. A shaven-headed girl stepped into view, every bit as skinny and pierced as Reed. She looked at Owen like he was a truant officer.

"Hi," she said, with a quick, choppy wave, and then popped out of sight again. "Kitty, kitty!" Owen heard her call.

"Forget the stupid cat, that's not important. Get out here." Reed stood, arms crossed, as Yves reappeared and slunk towards them.

"I said I was sorry."

Reed rolled his eyes. "Yves, this is Garland. He's going to be helping us with our project."

"Um, Owen." He shook her fragile hand.

"I'm glad you're here, for once," Reed said. "You can help me demonstrate the machine for him."

Yves started to speak, but the noise of the billowing tarp drowned her out as Reed unveiled the object beneath with a flourish.

147

Owen peered at it in the dim light. It looked like a derelict electric chair: rigid back, unpadded seat, unsafe-looking wires coiled around it like tinsel. A skullcap was mounted at the top; ragged leather arm and leg straps adorned the rest.

Reed waited, but impatient at Owen's lack of recognition, said, "It's an old-school electroshock rig."

Owen continued to stare.

"C'mon, babe, hop in," Reed said. Yves gave Owen an uncertain glance, but Reed grabbed her wrist and hauled her over, smiling like a shark. "You know you love it."

Owen watched as Yves was strapped into place. "The chair isn't really part of it," Reed explained. "They demolished an old asylum south of town a few months back, and I rescued a bunch of stuff. I think the chair was some kind of quiet-time restraint."

Yves, reluctant at first, seemed to be getting into it as the straps were tightened and the helmet lowered. She squirmed in her seat, eyes going glassy. "I just threw some stuff together to make it look more artistic," Reed said. He stepped back, crouched, and came up with a Bakelite control box.

"You ready?" he asked.

"Just do it," she said, her voice breathy.

"You want something to bite on?"

"Just *do* it," she said, whining now.

"I'll give you Level One, like always," he said, and Owen watched as he turned the dial from one to five.

"Counting down," Reed said. "Ten, nine, eight, sev—" and he hit the button on the box.

Yves squealed and jerked, teeth chattering and eyes rolling. Reed let off the button, and she slumped in place, slack-jawed.

Owen felt his pulse quicken as he looked at her. Seconds passed before she moved, and he let out a breath.

Yves sighed, and a trickle of blood eked from her mouth.

Reed dialed the box back to one, and beamed at Owen like he'd just performed a magic trick. "You: strapped in here. I fix it so it just gives you a tiny jolt, but you ham it up like you're getting the chair. The audience can shock you if they want, or just pass you by." He leaned against the chair. "What do you think, my man?"

* * *

148

Owen swept the paintbrush up and down the gallery wall. He wanted to whistle, but couldn't think of any songs. Yves had some screaming electro-noise playing on the jam box anyway, drowning out anything else.

The constant movement of the brush seemed to help with the tremors, as long as he didn't try to do anything too precise. Painting an entire wall red was as non-precise as it got.

Yves tapped him on the shoulder, and his brush missed her nose by inches as he turned. She laughed and stepped back.

"Lunch?" she shouted over the music.

Owen nodded. "Lunch" meant saltines and peanut butter.

Yves turned off the CD player. They sat on opposite sides of the desk, him facing her and the nude girl on the monitor.

She dealt out half a dozen crackers to both of them, and unscrewed the jar, sinking a knife into the gummy spread. Owen took it out and slathered his crackers, Yves following suit. The cat appeared and meowed at Yves.

"So," she said, offering it a cracker to smell. "What was it like being homeless?"

Owen worked his way through a mouthful. "Well, I wasn't for very long, just a day or so."

Yves thought about it. "You were lucky. Reed's a really nice guy to let you crash here before the exhibit, huh?"

Owen chewed and said nothing.

"I mean, I know he comes across as a jerk sometimes, but y'know, when it's just me and him, he's the sweetest guy." She sipped a Styrofoam cup of water. "Being an artist is hard, and he's under a lot of pressure."

Owen kept chewing.

"You don't talk a lot, do you?"

Owen swallowed. "Nothing to say, I guess."

Yves nodded. "I bet you think a lot instead. That's what Reed does—he's always thinking. That's how he got us this place. Some deal with this real estate dude, Erickson."

Owen downed another cracker. "How long have you been here?" he asked, his curiosity surprising him.

"About six months," Yves said. "Before that, we were crashing with some friends off of 6th Street. And before that, I lived in a crappy house with my crappy parents." She raised her cup. "Here's to freedom!"

Owen bumped his cup against hers, surprising himself again by smiling.

Done eating, she stood and stretched. Owen looked away. "Well, back to work," she said, and walked over to where she was assembling a signboard. Owen shuffled to his half-finished wall. She turned back to him. "You should do that more often," she said. "Y'know, smile. It makes you look younger."

Owen blinked and went back to his painting as the screaming music returned. He imagined fields and trees and beaches hidden beneath the thick layers of crimson.

A hippy girl, equally obscured, danced through them.

* * *

"Son of a cocksucking *bitch*!"

Owen heard Reed even through the door of the storage room, even through the thick layer of tarps he used as a blanket.

He didn't know what time it was—his watch, like his car, his job and everything else, was long gone—but he felt like he had been asleep for only a short while.

He stayed where he was. Reed had been coming back from these late-night jaunts in worse humor every evening, and Owen didn't like to see him berate Yves.

"Baby, what's wrong?" he heard her say.

"That asshole Erickson, now he wants—" Footsteps stomped, scuffed, and stopped short. "—Goddammit, your stupid fucking cat just *tripped* me! I'm gonna *kill* that piece of shit!"

Owen imagined her standing in front of Reed, gentle palms on his puffed-out chest, holding him back as he raged against a world that so unfairly refused to recognize his genius.

"Just tell me what happened, okay, honey? Just explain it to me. I want to know."

A moment passed. "Erickson, it's always Erickson. You know how he's tried to fuck up everything I do."

"Yeah?"

Owen pictured Reed pacing around, hands thrust in his hair. "Now he's saying we need a medical exam for Garland! We need a doctor to check him out and make sure he won't die during the exhibit. Forms to fill out, money we don't have...Goddamn *business* bullshit!"

"So what can we do?"

150

"I don't know, I don't know…fake it? How do you even do that? What kind of paperwork do you get from a doctor when you get a physical?" The slack sound came of a tarp being slapped in frustration. "He says, Mister Expert says, I'd get charged if Garland died. Manslaughter, if not worse. Fuck!"

"Oh, baby…"

"Oh, and the best part? He wants OSHA or some shit to come examine the shock machine!" More stomping. "What are we going to do? He's ruining everything!"

"It's okay, Reed, it's gonna be okay…"

"I should just wreck this fucking place, you know? Burn it to the ground."

"Baby, baby, it's okay, it's…"

"Just go to bed, Yves. I'll be there in a minute."

"…What about the machine?"

Owen heard steps approach the storage room, but they stopped. "Huh?"

"Well, would it make you feel better if you, y'know, put me in the machine for a while?"

"…Jeezus. You and that fucking machine." The steps came right up to the door. "Just get your ass in bed."

Reed opened the door without knocking, and Owen propped up on an elbow just in time to see Yves sprint by in her underwear.

Reed inclined his head back. "You heard all that?"

"Yes." Owen sat up as Reed crouched down beside him.

Reed scratched at his temple. "I don't know, man. It's not looking good at all. We may not be able to—"

"Fake it," Owen said. "I'll go along with whatever you say."

"You would…?" Reed began, but then stopped and shook his head. "It's not that easy. How the hell do you fake doctor paperwork and shit?"

"I can help," Owen said. "I've been…going to the doctor some lately. I may have some old paperwork we can look at. We can make it on your computer, can't we? And you said you needed safety inspections—we can look up those forms online, at the library or somewhere, right?"

"I don't know…maybe, I guess so, but…" Reed seemed hesitant to accept someone else's idea.

"Look," Owen said. "As far as these forms go, as far as their being real is concerned, you have to ask yourself this, and be honest. This guy you were talking about—"

"Erickson," Reed said, frowning.

"Erickson. I know it's easy to think that people are trying to shut you down, that they're against you," Owen sped up as Reed turned his frown towards him, "but you have to answer this, and be straight up about it, is he trying to screw you, or is he just trying to cover his own ass?"

Reed's frown dissolved as he stared at Owen, and a sly smile faded in to replace it. He slapped Owen on the shoulder.

"You're the man, Garland. You've saved my ass, bro." He gave Owen's shoulder a hard squeeze. "Get some sleep. Lots to do."

He left Owen in the dark nest of old tarps, and sleep came after a few sounds from the adjacent office: a couple of grunts, a half-hearted moan, and some snoring.

* * *

He awoke thinking he heard Yves' voice: "Is that one of yours?"

"*Beach in Wintertime, Number Two*," he mumbled, but realized he wasn't lying in a chain motel somewhere, and she wasn't curled at his side, admiring his artwork on the wall.

Owen pulled on his shirt and pants and walked out into the gallery. He turned to the big industrial sink, but stopped. Yves was there in t-shirt and panties, one long leg cocked up on the rim, lather already shaved away from the far side.

"Hey," she said. "Be done in a minute."

Owen turned away and busied himself with the edge of a nearby tarp.

"Did you sleep all right?" she asked.

"Sure," he told the tarp. "You?"

"Pretty good once I got Reed calmed down." He could hear the smile in her voice. "So what are you up to today? Painting's all done."

"Thought I'd catch the bus to the library. I need to—"

"You can look at me, you know. You won't, like, turn to stone or anything, I promise."

He turned to see her teasing grin. She swiped away the last of the shaving cream with an old towel and straightened up while he did his best to meet her eyes.

"I've got nothing to do, either, and Reed is off wheeling and dealing all day." She leaned against a pillar. "Bored, bored, bored."

"Ah," said Owen. "Well."

The cat wandered by, and Yves knelt and petted it. "I'm used to it by now," she said, looking straight into Owen's eyes. "But sometimes I wish there was more to do here than just play with my kitty."

"Ah," Owen said again. "Well."

She scooped up the cat and looked over her shoulder at Owen as she walked away. "Have a nice day at the library."

* * *

When he reached the YMCA, Owen allowed himself a small jolt of amazement: his room was untouched. Leaving it open to the world as he had a few days ago, with all his remaining possessions piled on the bed, seemed to him like a perfect enticement to robbers, but there his stuff was, still stacked in the middle of the mattress.

He wondered if he should go to Wal-Mart next and see if his car was still there, windows down, keys in the ignition. Whatever happened to people being untrustworthy?

Still, the honesty of the YMCA folks worked out in his favor: his medical records from the neurologist's office were still balanced on top of the stack. He grabbed the folder and walked to the door.

On his way out, he left the door extra-ajar.

At the library, he found the books he needed with the help of a friendly student, and plopped down in a back corner to read.

He browsed a book on 1970s art, but didn't see any work from anyone he knew, let alone himself. For that he'd need a copy of MOTEL PAINTINGS FROM HAS-BEENS.

He shook his head and delved into the other books he'd picked up.

Side effects of electroshock: confusion, memory loss...

He grunted and opened another book.

Mechanisms of death by electrocution...

There. *Much* more interesting.

He read for a while longer, cross-referencing with some home electronics books, then stood with a groan and prepared to leave. On his way, he found the young man who'd helped him. Owen fished the last couple of hundreds from his wallet and laid them on the kid's table.

"Thanks for your help," he said.

The student boggled. "I…sir…I couldn't take…"

Owen walked away before he finished stammering.

* * *

Something stank at PRO/GNOSIS as Owen walked in the door, but he couldn't place the smell. Reed was at the sink washing his hands.

"Garland," he said. He turned and limped to the computer. Owen saw a tear in the knee of his jeans, one not part of the marketable 'distressing' that ripped the fabric elsewhere.

Reed sat and rubbed his knee, grimacing. "Tripped," he said. "Last time, though. I won't be making that mistake again."

Owen dropped his file and some papers on the desk. "There're the medical forms. I printed out some OSHA documents at the library, too."

Reed grinned. "My man." He opened the folder and leafed through the documents. "This is good shit. Erickson should buy it." He fired up the computer.

Owen walked to the red wall, wondering where Yves was.

"What's," Reed began, and his tongue stumbled as he read Owen's file, "Crootz-Felt-Jacob…?"

Owen tensed. "…You know that thing you get when you type too long? That wrist pain?"

"Oh, yeah. We'll take that out," Reed said, and tapped the BACKSPACE key. "Don't want to give that asshole any excuse to shut us down."

Owen unclenched and felt a flutter in his hands and, not for the first time, a wobble in his legs.

Fifty-year-olds don't need canes, he told the doctor, and the doctor just stared at him.

The door banged open, and Yves came in with a grocery bag. "I got the stuff!" she said.

Reed turned in his chair. "You what?"

Yves plopped the bag down on the computer desk and favored Owen with a smile before continuing. "The stuff. I sold the last of the CDs like you asked, and bought all the ingredients for the appetizers."

Reed looked at the bag with a smile that was half-anger, half-smugness. "And when is the show?"

"Saturday, duh."

"And what is today?"

"Thursday."

Reed looked around, hand over his brow like he was in a crow's nest. "And did you buy a refrigerator to keep all the 'stuff' fresh until then?"

Yves huffed. "You told me to get all this!"

"I did?"

"Yes, you did! I think...no, I *know* you did!"

Reed shrugged. "If you say so. If you say I told you to buy a bunch of shit we couldn't store and give it plenty of time to spoil so we could serve our attendees rotten food, well, I guess I did..."

Yves stormed away into the back half of the building, calling for the cat. Reed looked up at Owen and winked. "It won't spoil. Got to keep them on their toes, though, right?" He waved at the bag. "How about a real lunch, for once?"

Owen considered all the possible ways he could spoil his or Reed's plans, but in the end shrugged and started pulling food out of the bag. After a while, a sulky Yves joined them and ate as well. She sat close to Owen.

Reed burped and pushed himself away from an empty plate. "That was great, babe," he said. "I'm glad I told you to get this stuff."

Owen felt Yves flinch beside him, but she stayed quiet.

"Why don't you go ahead and clean up?" Reed said, turning back to his document forgery.

Yves started to stand, but Owen put a hand on her arm. "I'll take care of it," he said.

Reed looked up just as Owen removed his hand, stared at the two of them, and smirked. "Whatever."

Owen bundled the trash into the empty grocery sack and took it to the dumpster out back. The flies were thick. He lifted the lid and grimaced at the stink, reminded of earlier.

Something furry poked out from beneath a bag of garbage.

Flies landed on Owen, their legs tickling, but he felt nothing. He shifted the bag and looked at what lay there.

After a moment, he threw his own bag on top, obscuring everything from view, and went back inside.

* * *

When Owen woke the next day, Yves was in the chair, trying to fasten a buckle around her wrist.

"Good morning...?" he said, and she looked up, sweat glistening on her stubbly head.

They looked at each other for a long moment, and Yves said, in a sad, breathless voice, "Could you help me with this?"

Owen took a step towards her, but stopped. "Please," she said. "I can get one buckle done, but I can't reach the other one, or my feet, or the helmet..."

"Or the controller," Owen said.

She looked at him, quavered, and burst into tears. Owen took another step, and another, and at last leaned over the chair, holding her in an awkward embrace.

"I can't find Kitty," she sobbed. "I looked everywhere, but he's gone."

"Oh..." Owen said.

"Maybe he ran out the door, or got stuck somewhere or..." Yves screwed her eyes shut. "Or did I even have a cat? Sometimes I forget things, I'm so stupid...did I just imagine it?" She looked into his eyes. "Tell me I had a cat," she said. "Please, God, please tell me I had a cat."

"You had a cat," Owen said. He felt a tremor start, but clamped down on it. "He loved you very much."

Yves stared at him again, their faces inches apart. "How much? How much did he love me?"

Owen's voice was a whisper. "More than he thought was possible."

He pulled away and fastened the other strap on her wrist. Yves watched him as he worked, tears streaming down her face. With her fully restrained, he lowered the helmet onto her head, fishing a bit of scorched fur from the rim. He reached out to stroke her face, and his hand began to palsy as soon as he touched her.

Warmth blossomed in her eyes, evaporating the tears. "Don't be afraid," she said.

Owen picked up the box. "One?" When she nodded, he left the dial on one.

Yves jerked in her seat when he pushed the button, more from surprise than current. "Feels...ffff...different..." she managed.

Owen gave her another jolt. "So...gentle," she said, a small trail of drool hanging from her lip.

He turned the dial to two and hit the button. Yves stiffened. "Gaaahhhhhhdddd..."

Three, and she bucked in the seat. "More," she gasped when he finished. "More, more more more..."

He dialed back down to one for a couple of short bursts that left her panting, then up to four for a sustained burst. Yves screamed, and he could see a miniature lightning bolt between her tongue stud and the roof of her mouth.

Down to one, a long two, and one again. Yves shook and shimmied, mouth trying to pronounce the Morse codes he telegraphed into her.

Owen held down the button and turned the dial from one to four and back, over and over, with Yves whooping at the roller coaster. At last, he turned it to five, and carried her away.

Yves slumped in the chair, blood dripping from her nose and mouth. Owen set the box down, unbuckled her, and carried her to the mattress in back.

She looked up at him through rolling eyes, and tried to speak through spent smiles and shallow grunts.

Owen reached out and touched her face again, and his hand was still.

* * *

"I don't want to," he heard her say through the thin wall.

"Tough shit," Reed answered. "I had a hard day."

Bodies shifted. "No. N...oh. Oh. Uhn. Oh. Uhn."

A grunt from Reed, followed by snores.

When the snores tapered off, Owen crept from his room, and moving into a patch of moonlight, worked on the control box for a few minutes, remembering what he'd read at the library.

He thought he heard something move in the dark and pictured Kitty stiff-legging up to him, wanting affection. He imagined petting its back, his hand running over the maggot-packed electrical burns.

His hands stayed still as he worked, and he thought Yves had cured him.

But once back in bed, they shook until morning.

* * *

Saturday night Owen wandered the parking lot. People had arrived in advance, and Reed was shmoozing away inside before Owen's official debut.

Someone had a shitty old VW van, and Owen remembered the one he'd driven once upon a time. ONE NUCLEAR BOMB CAN RUIN YOUR WHOLE DAY, its bumper sticker had read.

He wondered what the 21st century version would be. ONE TAINTED BLOOD TRANSFUSION CAN RUIN YOUR WHOLE LIFE.

"Owen?"

He turned, and there she was. She wore a flimsy peasant dress, and the glow from the safety lights lit her like divine radiance.

He almost told her everything, right then and there.

"Reed's ready," Yves said as she drew closer; he could see in her face he'd done his work on her too well yesterday. There was no memory, no recall of her time in the chair. Nothing was there but a charitable affection.

She reached up and patted his freshly-shaved head. "Hey, we're twins."

They walked back to the building, Yves scuffing gravel with her shoes. "Reed keeps having to shoo people away from the chair," she laughed. "They're trying to test it on themselves."

Owen felt a brief burst of panic. Yves took his arm and he calmed.

Yves waved to a girl who sat at the entrance guarding a cashbox. A fat guy with glasses wrinkled his nose as they passed; Owen wondered if that was Erickson.

"Ladies and gentlemen," Reed called from the other side of the room, "my subject!"

A few people clapped, a few coughed; most were bent over laptops, focused elsewhere. One guy wore a shirt that read I'M BLOGGING THIS.

158

"This," said Reed, reaching out and grabbing Owen's shoulder, "is Garland. Once he was an artist, his work shown in galleries from coast to coast..."

"*I've* never heard of him," Owen heard someone mutter.

"...But now he stands before you a broken man, discarded by society, shunned by the artistic community and reduced to homelessness by a world that has passed him by." He led Owen to the chair and strapped him in. The helmet in place, Reed turned back to the crowd.

"Who here has the guts to do to this man's face what we have all done to him when he was just another nameless drone wandering the streets? Who can externalize their contempt, their urge to dehumanize?"

He knelt down and produced the box with a flourish. "Who among you will *kill* this man?"

A few coughs, an increase in the clicks on keyboards, but no one moved forward.

Reed forced a smile. "Very well. I leave the box here. Do what you will, kind people." He turned to Owen. "Any words you'd care to share with the crowd?" And then, quietly, "Sell it, man. Make them want to push the button. I'm dying here." He turned back to the crowd and gave a big grin.

Owen cleared his throat. "She'll be better off without you, you little shitheel."

Reed turned back to him, grin frozen in place. "What?"

"You heard me."

Reed's furious whisper was almost drowned out by the flurry of keyboards. "Tonight? You wait 'til tonight to bust out your little grandpa crush? *You're ruining this for me!*"

Owen smiled. "Oh. Poor baby."

Reed sneered back. "You think you have a chance with that stupid groupie skank? Be my guest, Garland. But you will *not* spoil this for me. This is too important—*I'm* too important—for some useless wino with the shakes to fuck things up."

"Then why don't you push the button and shut me up?"

Reed smiled the smile he must have worn when he electrocuted Kitty. "Gladly," he said, and jabbed his finger down.

Owen didn't feel pain as much as impact: a sledgehammer striking his skull and compressing his spine flat. But then he rebounded, his spine sprang back to full extension, and the electricity was everywhere, blasting through his eyes, his mouth, his fingers and toes, through every pore on his scalp.

People screamed, locked in place or backing toward the door. Even the typists looked up, faces wracked with shock at something real, something immediate and unstoppable happening in front of them.

Owen convulsed as the ECT payload, set to eleven or twelve or infinity or whatever you would call the raw power from the city's lines, slammed through him, burning out every cell in its path.

Reed clawed at the box, unable to unstick the button or move the knob. With a grunt, he yanked it free, wires trailing behind, and landed flat on his ass among a crowd of horrified spectators.

"Someone call 911! Call the police!"

Two dozen cell phones appeared, all dialing at once.

"No," Reed said, scrambling to his feet. "No!" Owen watched him shoulder his way through the crowd. A couple of people grabbed him and wrestled him, squirming, to the floor.

Owen smelled the steam rising from his body. He couldn't move, and wondered if he'd fused himself to the chair. The room slid out of focus, but snapped into sharp relief when Yves stepped forward. She reached out a hand to touch his cheek, and when it pulled away, he could see the black sludge touching him had left on her fingers.

A tear blurred his vision, and when it cleared, Yves had somehow found time to redecorate the building: lava lamps, bead curtains, and black light posters as far as the eye could see. She had changed out of her dress, too, into bell bottoms and a tank top. She leaned in close, and the rhinestone peace sign on her headband caught the light.

She spoke, but Owen couldn't hear her.

"Here's to freedom," he said, and his words sounded like music.

And the music sounded like silence.

YOU COME WHEN I CALL

BY TREVER PALMER

The cock felt as thick as a baby's arm as it roughly jammed into his asshole.

Dugan Farris wanted to scream, but he couldn't. Jessie's dirty panties were stuffed in his mouth, and he'd be damned if the fishy stink of the crotch wasn't about enough to make him throw up.

He choked back the hot vomit that threatened to scream up his throat.

"Now, now," Jessie said, "does that hurt, little man?"

Dugan flashed his eyes at her. Pain was masking his face like a cheap Halloween mask. Tears, flooding from his red-rimmed eyes, coursed down his cheeks.

"Hurry up and come, Jason," said Jessie. "I think it's about time I milked Mr. Dugan, again."

Jessie reached down between Dugan's thighs. She grabbed his cock, hard as a fucking rock, and began to stroke it. She used her index finger to wipe away the pre-come that glistened on the purple head.

"Oh yes," said Jessie. "You're going to do just fine."

As she let go of his cock, Jason threw back his head. He grabbed a hold of Dugan's hips, thrust himself deeper into the tight asshole, and with a loud grunt that made Dugan's hair stand up, Jason let loose with a geyser of thick come that flooded Dugan's anal cavity.

As he felt Jason pull out of him, itching with the flow of blood that leaked from his asshole, Dugan was almost proud he had been sodomized. He'd already been forced to suck off the mongoloid brother, and he couldn't take another dollop of come that was as thick as egg-drop soup shooting down his throat. He swore that he could feel the little fish swimming around in his stomach.

"That's a good boy, Jason," said Jessie. "Now run along. I have more work to do with Mr. Farris."

Jason unfolded himself from his knees. He stood 6'3" and weighed a solid 300 pounds.

But the poor boy was retarded.

And he was oh so disfigured. His face was so gruesome even Jessie made him hide it. Jason concealed his awful features behind a Frankenstein mask. He had worn it for so long that he now considered it his true features.

"Go on now," Jessie told him. "Go play with your toys."

Jason pulled up his overalls, shook his head, and violently slapped it. Then he did as he was told. He took one final look at Dugan and left the room.

"Now," Jessie said, "we can get to work."

She walked across the room, which was void of furniture. A large window allowed the crisp autumn sun to peek inside.

Jessie picked up a large canvas and returned to Dugan.

He strained against the ropes. Blood ran in rivers down his wrists and ankles, he was pulling so hard with no way of getting free. The retarded fuck had tied him too damned well.

"You really shouldn't have turned me down for your artsy fartsy show, Mr. Farris. The paintings I brought to you were my life's work."

Dugan struggled against the panties in his mouth. The best he could manage were Neanderthal grunts.

"You took my life and trashed it," Jessie said. "You said my work was juvenile and an embarrassment. Do you remember saying that?"

Dugan spat out against the panties. Jessie grabbed him by the hair and furiously nodded his head.

"Of course you do," she told him. "You remember as if it were only yesterday." She put a hand to her mouth and giggled. "Oh, that's right! It *was* only yesterday."

* * *

After closing the gallery, he'd gone outside to the parking lot. He'd slipped the keys into his BMW, and that's when he was attacked. Jason had grabbed him by the neck with such force that Dugan thought his skull was going to pop right off his shoulders.

But he couldn't be that lucky.

As the monster held him tightly, Jessie had emerged from the shadows beneath the sodium lights. And dear God, besides a pair of ratty flip-flops, she was naked.

Dugan Farris had stared at her, feeling himself grow hard at the sight of her fat nipples and the deep, dark shadows between her thighs. As she'd come closer, Dugan could see she was sporting a full, thick patch of black pubic hair.

"Get him inside the car."

The monster had shoveled Dugan into the backseat and crawled in after him. Jessie slid behind the wheel.

Still in a headlock, and smelling the fresh onion stink that attacked him from beneath Jason's armpits, Dugan had watched as they drove him to a farmhouse on the outer limits of the Pikes Field county line.

He'd been pulled from the car and hustled into the house where he was stripped naked by Jason. The retard had been rough as he tore away Dugan's clothes.

Naked, Dugan had whimpered as Jason forced him to the floor and brought out the ropes.

Trussed up like a hog, Dugan had begun to scream.

And that's when Jason had slipped his cock inside Dugan's mouth. The monster bucked its hips back-and-forth, grabbing hold of Dugan's head and forcing him down deeper onto his meat-pole. Finally, after he'd come down Dugan's throat, Jessie had called Jason off and shoved her dirty panties inside his mouth.

"I bet you like that, don't you?" she'd asked him. "I could tell the way you were looking at me when I strolled into your gallery. You were practically popping a hard-on." Jessie threw back her head and laughed. "So tell me, big shot, how does my pussy taste?"

Dugan grunted, straining his eyes to see her as she circled around behind him.

"That good, you say?" She slapped him hard on his bare ass and laughed again. "Now, let's see what kind of art we can create."

* * *

When she came back, Dugan could see she was carrying a bowl of something in her hands, a broom tucked beneath her arm.

"Before we get to the main attraction," Jessie said, "let's have a little bit of fun. What do you say?"

Dugan managed a mumble.

"This is smashed pumpkin paste," she said, gesturing toward the bowl, "and we're going to use it to lube you up just right."

163

Dugan could feel her naked flesh as she knelt down behind him. Even in that state, scared for his life, he couldn't help but get a hard-on.

Jessie smeared the pumpkin paste between his ass cheeks. It was slimy, and Dugan did his best to keep his cheeks closed. But Jessie just slapped him again, and he fell forward a little bit, losing his balance.

"Now," she said, "for the final piece."

And that's when she shoved the broom handle inside his ass. Dugan screamed against the panty gag. Tears mixed with greenish snot as they ran down his face.

Jessie stood back and admired her work.

"It looks like you have a tail," she giggled. "You look a mess."

Fighting against the pain wrecking his body, Dugan watched her return to the canvas. She took out a brush and waved it around the room like a wand, before unscrewing the top on a tube of paint.

"We're going to do this just right," she told him. "I think you'll like what's coming up."

Dugan watched her as she began to paint the canvas. She used long strokes to cover the white space with black. In the darkness she was painting, Dugan could feel his life slipping away with it.

There was no way he was getting out of this madhouse alive.

Slowly, Jessie finished painting the canvas. She leaned back, smiling.

"How does that look?" she asked him. "Do you think it's good enough to hang in your fucking gallery?"

Dugan couldn't help himself. He shook his head back and forth violently.

Jessie laughed.

"I don't think so, either." She shrugged. "But that's okay. It's not finished, yet."

* * *

Dugan watched her.

Jessie, sitting cross-legged on the floor, began to paint herself. She swathed the brush over her nipples, circling each one with crude black strokes, and then an arrow on her flat belly, pointing down towards her crotch.

"You can't help but stare at me." She winked at him. "You know you want to fuck me." She stood up, fingering aside the long hair that flooded her face. "Tell me," she said. "Let me know that you want to fuck me."

Feverishly, Dugan nodded his head. He really *did* want to fuck her. The fact he was tied to the floor and had been sodomized both by a retarded lunatic and a broomstick seemed to slip his mind. Jessie was one hot piece of pussy.

"I thought you'd say that," she said. "But I'm sorry. I wouldn't touch you with a ten-foot pole…a broomstick, however…"

She strode to where Dugan was tied up, kneeling and sliding the canvas beneath him.

"You destroyed my life's work when you turned me away. Now, I'm going to return the favor."

Jessie reached down, fingering the curly pubic hair in Dugan's crotch and pulling on his balls.

"These things nearly touch the floor," she said.

Slowly, she reached out and grabbed his cock, starting to stroke it back-and-forth. It amused her that he was already hard.

"I love uncircumcised men," she told him. "You get those extra inches that the doctors don't cut off when you're born."

Dugan sighed against the panties.

"This is the plan," Jessie said. "I'm going to jerk you off so many times that I'm not going to leave anything but a bloody little stump. You're going to spill your seed all over that canvas, and I'm going to destroy your life like you've done mine."

Dugan stared at her.

She laughed.

He could feel her soft fingers wrapped around his cock.

"Ready?" she asked him.

And that's when he came, shooting great gobs of come down onto the canvas, milky white droplets drowning into the wet black paint. His entire body shook with the orgasm.

"You're a fast one. I barely touched you."

Dugan limped down against the restraints. Even though he was no longer struggling, vainly attempting to escape, they still bit into his naked flesh. But now, gasping for air after he'd come, he completely forgot about their restrictive pain.

"Don't go thinking you're out of the woods just yet," Jessie said. "You and me and your cock still have a long way to go."

Jessie reached down. Dugan's cock was hanging limply between his thighs. She grabbed it again and began to pump. She ran a finger through the wet paint, scooping up some of Dugan's come, and slipped it between her lips and sucked on it.

"We're going to make art, baby," she said. "But I have to ask you, does art imitate life? Or does life imitate art?"

And she jerked on Dugan's limp cock.

He screamed into the dirty crotch of her panties.

* * *

Sheriff Green turned down the volume on his radio. The twangy sounds of Buck Owens singing "Tiger by the Tail" slowly diminished.

Slowly, he ground his car to a halt.

From the road, he could see Dugan Farris's car parked outside the old Myers house.

"What the hell?"

That morning, he'd spoken with Patty over to the Sack of Suds restaurant. She'd mentioned Dugan hadn't come into work. It was a strange occurrence for him not to show up, and he hadn't called, either. Green could tell that she was worried about the little pissant Dugan Farris.

"I'll see if I can't turn him up," he'd told her. That seemed to relax Patty. Besides, it wasn't like he had anything else to do today.

Green turned his car onto the muddy road leading up to the Myers house.

He pulled up next to Dugan's car, shut off the ignition, and stepped out, hitching up his belt. The sheriff pulled a pack of Red Man chew from his pants pocket, took out a plug, and stuck it into his cheek. Without thinking, he spat a large piece of chaw down into the mud.

Green walked over to Dugan's car, putting a hand over his eyes and peering inside. There didn't seem to be any signs of foul-play.

And that suddenly made him think.

Why would he suspect any foul-play to start with? Maybe Dugan was out on a social call. Or maybe he'd taken the day off

166

and just hadn't called into work. He did own the damned gallery, after all.

Because the Myers family was weirder than shit, that's why.

He'd only seen the daughter once and that was at the town hall Halloween party. She'd come dressed as a whore she told everyone, and Green couldn't deny the authenticity of her costume. She'd been fixed up in a halter-top so tight you could see her nipples poking through, jean shorts that crawled straight up into her twat, and torn fishnet stockings. He also remembered those high-heels she'd been wearing. They'd been blood red and shiny beneath the town hall lights.

The son, on the other hand, was a totally different story. He'd never seen the boy before, but he'd heard plenty of stories and knew he supposedly hid his disfigured face behind some kind of mask. He never left the Myers' old farmhouse.

Green felt a chill run down his spine.

The Myers' parents had been dead going on ten years, now. Green, and most of the townspeople, had never liked the old cocksucker and his prude wife. There wasn't a great turn-out for either one of their funerals, and as he remembered it, neither kid had come to the funerals, either.

Overhead, the heavens opened up, rain beginning to fall in steady buckets.

Green hunched down in his coat. He didn't like the idea of bothering the Myers, but he wanted to make sure that Dugan Farris was doing okay.

He walked steadily through the front yard, avoiding mud puddles, and took a step up onto the front porch.

And that's when Jason attacked.

Green heard the monster coming. He heard Jason's boots as they sloshed through the mud, and he turned, grabbing for his revolver.

As he turned around, Jason's pitchfork stabbed through his coat. Green could feel the tines as they grazed his skin, drawing hot blood and torn meat. He pushed himself back with the attack, flattening himself out on the muddy ground.

Jason lofted the pitchfork over his head, and was about to bring it down on Green, when the first pistol shot took him in the chest. Jason was thrown back by the blast, landing hard on the mucky earth.

"You son of a bitch," Green muttered.

As he began to stumble towards his feet, he noticed Jason was doing the same. The monster seemed to be shrugging off the wound, still intent on killing Green.

But this time the sheriff was ready.

He let loose with two shots that tore into Jason's body. The blasts knocked him down, beating him to the earth with deadly lead.

Green wasn't surprised when Jason started to get back up. Yet he didn't fire. The monster was wounded very badly, with wisps of steam issuing from the hot bullet holes. Then, as he made it to his feet, Jason immediately toppled over: dead.

"Jesus Christ," muttered Green. "What a morning."

He shrugged off his jacket and began to make his way back up the front steps.

Green looked at Jason lying on the ground. He couldn't help but wonder what was hidden beneath that Frankenstein mask. He stepped over to the monster and knelt down beside him, gingerly feeling for a pulse just to make sure Jason was dead. But there wasn't one, so he holstered his weapon and slipped his fingers beneath the mask and gave it a tug...

"Oh my God," he whispered.

Green stared down at Jason's disfigured face.

The skull was lop-sided and sporting wisps of graying hair. One of the eyes was round as a marble, while the other was squinted tight together. The nose was crudely broken, and a row of badly decayed fangs peeked out from the twisted lips.

Green dropped the Frankenstein mask back down on the ground.

Now what's that little tramp up to inside?

He made his way back onto the front porch, pulling his revolver from its holster as he climbed the steps. Gently, he put his hand on the front door handle. It opened easily as he turned.

Green fought back the urge to call out "Anyone home?" Even in such a tight mess, expecting Jessie to jump out with a pick-axe or hatchet at any moment, he couldn't help but giggle at the thought.

The smell of hot sex, dust, and rotted pumpkins filled his nostrils. He twitched his moustache.

Green searched the downstairs, but like he figured, found nothing. Jessie either had Dugan trussed up down in the cellar or upstairs. *Or, they might have eaten him for lunch.* Green wasn't about to put anything past the Myers children.

Slowly, he began to make his way up the stairs, waiting for a floorboard to creek or any noise that would give his position away, but it never came. He already knew that Jessie would know he was here. The pistol blasts he'd poured into Jason took care of that. Now he was the fly in her spider's web.

Green made his way to the top of the landing, his fingers sweaty as they rested on the pistol's trigger.

"Dugan Farris," he said. "Are you here?"

He listened for a long moment, and that's when he heard the muffled sounds coming from the room at the far end of the hall.

Green began to make his way towards the room. There was still no sign of Jessie. He reached out and gingerly opened the door. What he saw on the other side made his jaw drop.

Dugan was trussed up like a hog on the floor, and the broomstick still stuck out of his bloody ass like a mangy tail.

Dugan grunted against the dirty panties in his mouth.

Green strode across the room. He knelt beside Dugan, feeling his bones creak, and pulled the panties from his mouth.

"Dear God, man," the sheriff said. "What have you gone and got yourself into?"

Dugan gasped for air, staring at the room's open door.

"Look out!" he cried.

The shotgun blast nearly took Green's head off. Thankfully, he dove on the floor as quickly as the words had left Dugan's mouth. Standing in the door, Jessie stood with the smoking weapon.

"I'm going to blow your fucking head off!" she screamed.

But Green was just a bit too fast for her. He lowered his revolver and pumped two quick shots into Jessie's guts. Hot blood painted the walls as the girl fell backwards, squeezing the shotgun's trigger and releasing a final round into the ceiling.

"Kill that bitch!" Dugan roared.

Green ignored Dugan and walked to where Jessie was sprawled on the floor. He could see that death was ready to take her, and he kneeled beside her.

"Why?" he asked.

"He shit on my life's work," she said, spitting up frothy blood bubbles. "I wanted to do the same to him." She flashed a red-toothed grin. "I turned him into my greatest masterpiece."

Green stole a glance over his shoulder and grimaced at the sight of the broomstick.

Jessie spit up again.

"I guess you're going to arrest me," she managed to say. "I want to hear my rights."

Green grunted and watched as Jessie's eyes rolled into her head. The grim reaper had come for her, and he figured Satan had set a place for her at his table. He reached out and closed her eyelids.

"Untie me!" Dugan screamed. He was in a frenzy; spit erupted from his mouth with every word. "And get this damned broomstick out of my ass!"

Green got to his feet, ignoring the pop of his aging bones.

"This is probably going to hurt," he said.

Green grabbed hold of the broomstick and slowly pulled. The splintered wood came out of Dugan's asshole with a loud slurping sound, and tried not to gag at the shit on the handle.

"Oh dear God," Dugan let out a strained sigh.

Green tossed the broomstick aside.

"Now untie me," Dugan commanded.

"You just wait a second, boy," the sheriff said. "I'm not finished, yet."

"What the hell do you mean?"

Sheriff Green walked around until he was facing Dugan. He took out his pistol and unbuckled his gun belt, letting it, and his trousers, fall to the floor. His small cock, springing out from a nest of gray pubic hair, poked at the air.

"What are you doing?" Dugan asked. The sound of fear cracked his voice.

"I'm going to get myself a piece of boy pussy is what I'm doing," Green told him. He walked around to Dugan's rear and dropped to his knees. Putting the pistol up to Dugan's temple, he slipped his cock into what was left of his asshole.

Dugan grunted from the force of the rape. Between his legs, his penis, worn red from the dozens of times that Jessie had jerked him off, shrank back into his stomach. He had to admit that the pain coursing through his cock was ten times worse than Sheriff Green plowing into his rectum.

Suddenly, Green reached around and grabbed Dugan's cock and started to jerk him off. Blood, from the spots where it'd been rubbed raw, squeezed through his fingers.

"Don't worry, boy," Green said. "I'm not the kind to fuck you and not give you a reach around."

CHEF OF THE GODS

BY ANDREW WOLTER

John meticulously inserted the bloodstained knife into David's anus. Although he felt rushed by his guest's nearing arrival, he reminded himself to take his time. This had to be perfect.

John could tell that the walls of David's rectum were tender and generously lubricated with fecal residue. He could feel the tension of the handle slacken as the tip tore into the interior membrane with the slightest bend of the knife. He had to be certain to keep a steady hand and drive the blade in approximately eight inches. Only then could he make the necessary lacerations to ensure an easy extraction of the large intestine.

It wasn't like the last one, no. What was his name? Jared? Jason? Whatever he called himself, his anus was tight and dry like petrified wood. John recalled how he had to dig into the rectum with his carving knife. At one point, John strategically positioned the tool at a forty-five degree angle and used the palm of his hand to forcefully hit the hilt of the knife. Of course, after tearing and thrusting into the cavity for so long, John found himself with a wasted corpse and a ruined recipe.

And wasn't that what they all were—regardless of the pretty faces and forgotten names—an effortless recipe that was part of a colossal menu? Yes, they were but one facet of a piece of the grand scheme that was within reach of John Gallagher's hopeful longing. *You'll come back to me soon, Alan.* Always this encouraging thought, as he fed his special meals to the young men with whom he had invited to dinner. Never a doubt in his mind, as they feasted upon human flesh prepared to the likeness of luxurious cuisine. Yet they never reciprocated. There was never a piece of Alan in any of them. Instead, John Gallagher had been greeted by grimaced features and faces twisted in terrifying bewilderment. And would it be that John understood rejection; would it be that he had never harnessed the skill of a culinary artist; would it be that he'd never fallen in love with the one man he could never have? He would have never continued in his endeavors. In fact, it

172

was because of these circumstances that John Gallagher had become an expert in his learned trade.

John paused as David's innards easily engulfed the blade. His hand halted and his body tingled with a giddiness that all too soon made his cock stiff. Oh, how he imagined it was *he* inside of *Alan*! His lustful reverie was abandoned by the sound of three succinct knocks upon the front door.

John released his grip of the knife and languidly stood to his feet, gazing down at the scene on the floor. Upon a blanket of black tarp, the bloodied corpse of the young man named David appeared as statuesque art. His arms were upturned and exposed the soft pale meat of his flesh. The young man's neck exposed a single red line that symmetrically reached from one ear to the other. His smooth stomach was concave, like a bowl welcoming a fresh salad. His legs lay limp and randomly bent, highlighted by the hilt of a carving knife that was accented by the rust-colored juices of blood and shit that seeped from his ass.

Taking in the delectable scene, John raced his bloodied fingers through his dark chocolate hair. With his digits midway through the gesture, he immediately stopped. He heedlessly walked toward the adjoining bathroom and began rinsing the red stains from his hands.

I could have been a sculptor.

John was welcomed by Caden's tall and lanky form when he opened the door to his condo. For a moment, John's thoughts were put on pause by the similar features of Alan. Caden's blonde hair was gelled forward and spiked into highlighted shocks that crowned his forehead. His azure irises were huge and sparkled like the most picturesque of oceans. The young man's sharp chin and hollow cheeks displayed a man blessed with the genes of a model or the curse of a sickly disease, John knew not which.

Yes, John was sure that Caden was the one! He reveled in the delicious thoughts of Alan—dreamily running his fingers through Alan's soft locks of hair, down his neck, and over the carved torso that he so wanted to touch, had Alan allowed him to.

"You added some color to your hair," Caden announced.

John jerked from his reverie. "Uh, what?"

"Your hair—I didn't notice the red highlights at the coffee house the other night."

John smirked and wondered if the "highlights" Caden pointed out would begin to drip their blood red color. "I thought it was time for a change. Won't you come in?"

"The red on black looks great. Besides, it's in right now." Caden walked past John.

John closed the door, turned the lock on the knob, and secured the deadbolt.

Caden took notice and joked, "What, are you planning to hold me hostage?"

"Something like that." John's snicker was joined by Caden's obnoxious, high-pitched laughter. *Jesus*, John thought, *why are all the guys I pick up so damn flamboyant?*

Alan never acted that way. Alan was a *real* man—football games, sports bars, and the talk of the latest woman-on-woman porn. Perhaps that was why he became overcome by the facade that he wasn't into men. Yes, that was it! John knew Alan was attracted to him, regardless of what he said. John could feel it when Alan's sapphire eyes burrowed into him from across the other side of the dining table. That overexcitement was inexplicable, and the way with which Alan hugged him was undeniable. Alan had loved him. If not for the brainwashing of society, he would have come through. Both he and Alan would have been fine. If not for those rash decisions, John wouldn't have had done what he had.

"Whatcha thinkin' about?" Caden asked as he took a seat on the plush sofa.

John observed the mischievous grin that etched Caden's plump lips. *So much like Alan.* The young man provocatively rested his hand on his own crotch. "I'm thinking of all the things I'm going to do to you," John playfully reciprocated.

"Wow," Caden exclaimed. "Well, let me know when you're ready for the games to begin."

Shying away from Caden's overt remark, John turned toward the kitchen. "I'm going to get you a glass of wine. Dinner's going to be a while."

From the living room, Caden called to John. "Hey, I'm not that big of a wine drinker."

John returned with a glass in hand. "Well, perhaps you need to enjoy the finer things in life." He offered the glass to Caden.

Caden held the wine glass up to his eye, observing the red liquid within it. "That's dark, almost black."

"It's a red."

The young man took a sip and swallowed hard as if it were a shot of cheap bourbon.

"How do you like it?"

"It's bitter, but it has a sweet aftertaste."

"It's a Pinot Noir. Imported," John lied. He entertained the thought of persuading Caden that the concoction the young man continued to sip was a fine wine.

John fancied the recollection of slicing open David's throat, using the same knife that was now deeply buried in his ass, and letting the man's blood drain into a small mixing bowl. He was delighted by his ability to mix the proper portions to create a perfect, potable wine. Caden's wine consisted of one part Pinot Grigio and three parts blood from David. Of course, David's blood wasn't untainted. There was a part of Jared or Jason—whatever his name was—in the blood. And of the young man whose name John couldn't recall, there was a part of Brian. Within Brian, a part of Kevin. In Kevin, a part of Alan. Thus, there was always a part of Alan, regardless of how diluted it might have become, within the recipes served to John's guests.

"This is pretty good," Caden remarked as he slurped the last drop of his wine. "Can I have another glass?"

"Yes, you may. It will go well with dinner."

"What's on the menu?" Caden asked.

"Italian."

"I love Italian. What kind?"

"Manicotti," John answered as he handed the full wine glass to Caden.

It was always Italian. Whether the thick veins of a young man cooked al dente and smothered by a marinara sauce, the soft-boiled penne produced from an evenly severed small intestine and tossed with a pesto paste, or hat-shaped tortellini cut from the edges of the stomach and covered with a creamy, garlic alfredo sauce—John loved preparing Italian food. There was so much diversity in the menu. There were many different sauces to compliment the numerous types and shapes of pasta.

"I need to finish a couple of reports and start prepping dinner. I'll be in my office for a bit."

"No problem, I can kick it out here," Caden assured John.

As John returned to the scene of mutilation that would provide the ingredients for the night's dinner, he locked the door behind him.

Tonight will be the night you come back to me, Alan.

* * *

There was a time, once, when he believed he was in love. It was the only instant that mattered. Perhaps it had been two months previous, perhaps five. The months didn't make a difference. In John Gallagher's mind, time wasn't measured by months, weeks or even days. Instead, time was calculated by a violent body count and an undying passion for cooking.

The bodies of those young men—how many were there now? Three? Five? Six?—were nothing more than John's hopeful conduits through which Alan would return. To John's disappointment, when they proved to be nothing more than lustful wanderers awaiting a midnight rendezvous, when there came a time in which their responses to his queries weren't satisfying enough, they became food. But their smooth flesh and warm viscera didn't act as John's meal; he could never be that selfish. Instead, the carnage would become the delicacies of each new guest with whom he believed he could exhale Alan's essence.

"Come into my kitchen," said the chef to the vagabond. Have this exquisite meal, for you will never taste anything like it. That's right, eat...stuff yourself. Ah, don't choke. You have to swallow it; you have to have a piece of him in you. You have to become him.

* * *

The knife felt sticky as John returned his grip to the hilt and gave it a slight push forward. It was tough at first, like using a butter knife to cut a piece from a well-done ribeye. However, as he skillfully retracted the blade a couple inches and re-inserted it, a new flow of blood soaked the parched tissue.

John grabbed David's left leg and slung it over his shoulder. A soft crunch emitted as he mimicked the same gesture with the right leg. For a moment, the sexual position excited John—David's ankles resting on his shoulders and the butcher knife buried halfway into the hole beneath the man's prostate. *Could fuck you like a beast, and treat you like the whore you are.* However, John's thoughts ceased as he reminded himself that David didn't embody Alan. Not to mention, he didn't want to ruin dinner.

With his right hand, John delicately pressed the blade further into David's ass and nimbly twisted his wrist upward to create a curved incision. John traced back the slit, pulling the knife down into its original position. He did this several times as he deepened the starfish lines of David's sphincter, making it wider and easier to access the large intestine.

After ten minutes of the same routine, John easily pulled the blade of the butcher knife from out of David's insides. The blade was stained deep gray, almost black, from the accumulated blood, shit, and viscera. Reaching his hand into the gaping wound, John began feeling for the end of the large intestine. John reached in further, his arm being swallowed by David's hole, and tightly gripped the moist entrails of the young man. He gave a brisk tug, pulling back with one quick jerk.

From out of the victim's ass slid the long, ribbed, wormlike organ. John observed David's stomach sink as he continued pulling. A sour stench ignited the air, the smell of rot and shit. John exhaled. The large intestine effortlessly slithered out like a pale blue snake escaping its cool desert nest.

After he had extracted a foot and a half of David's innards, John halted and began squeezing the purple-colored gore from the organ and into the silver bowl he'd earlier used to drain David's blood. John reached for the cutting board to his left and grabbed the meat cleaver beside it. After positioning the corrugated organ on the cutting board, he began chopping off five-inch segments.

John was certain tonight's dinner would be his best yet.

* * *

There was once a place. It could've been anywhere in the world; worship knows no borders. However, the location was in a second-story condominium in the heart of a heated metropolis. It was just off Central Avenue, in an area where whores, Goths, and teenage runaways co-existed and fucked in drug-induced dazes. This was the place where John Gallagher resided.

John studied Alan as he cut into the grilled chicken parmesan. Juices wept as the knife effortlessly glided through the meat. Alan brought the portion to his mouth, breathed in the

177

aroma of tomatoes and basil, and used his tongue to lap at the surface of the meat before inserting the piece into his mouth. The end of it brushed against his fleshy lower lip. Alan chewed and closed his eyes, savoring the accentuating flavors of the marinara and parmesan cheese. He followed it with a sip of Pinot Noir.

John was mesmerized by Alan's mannerisms. It was as if Alan were a delectable meal. Everything about Alan was so perfect. Everything about tonight was more than perfect. It was the right time to tell Alan how he felt.

"I love you."

Alan almost choked on the meat he was in the process of swallowing. He took a gulp of wine from his glass and his body went rigid from the three words just spoken by his friend and dinner host. Alan cleared his throat.

John accepted Alan's dead-on gaze. It was as if oceans swallowed him. He smirked in anticipation of Alan's response.

"What?"

"I said, 'I love you'."

Alan chuckled slightly. "I'm your friend, John, but I'm not...like you. I'm not..."

"Gay?" John finished. "It has nothing to do with gay or straight. It has to do with love."

"No. No. Stop." Alan's fist hit the table. The silverware clanked against the plates.

John's heart dropped into his stomach and tears welled in his eyes as he took a deep breath. *No, no, no,* his mind raced. This was the worst case scenario. This was what he'd feared. Rejection. No, he knew the way Alan felt about him. It showed in their embracing hugs when they would talk late into the night. It was displayed by Alan's light pat on the small of his back when he would enter John's condo before they went out for drinks. It wasn't playfulness; it was sincere! It had to be.

Ejecting from his chair, John raced alongside the table toward Alan and dropped to his knees to look up toward Alan. "But the times we shared. The talks we had. You said you cared about me."

"Yes," Alan agreed. "I care about you, John, but as a friend. Don't do this."

Alan reached for the wine glass and John grabbed his hand. "Friends can become lovers, Alan."

Alan briskly retracted his hand as if he'd been jolted by an electrical shock. "Get the fuck away from me, or I'm going to leave!" His voice was monotone, emotionless, and empty.

John recoiled from Alan's threat. With each step he made toward the kitchen, it felt as if a piece of him had flaked from his body. His exterior was chipping away with each footfall. It began with the numbness in his legs, a result of the adrenaline frantically coursing through his veins. His hands tingled, and he flexed his fingers to his palms in rapid succession. John's head throbbed. He could feel the heat brimming toward his scalp, aware of the thudding in his temples.

He could end it all.

No, no, no, his mind screamed against Alan's rejection. *Just fucking end it!*

John grabbed the meat cleaver from the cutting board on the counter. Just hack at your goddamned wrists with that fucking blade and watch the blood flow all over the linoleum. Let it happen in this room, where you cooked his last fucking meal.

No, no, no, John wrestled with his aching thoughts. *He has to love me. That fucker!*

John returned to the dining room, standing behind the chair in which Alan sat.

Alan continued slurping his chicken parmesan and swallowing the wine to accent the flavor, unaware that John stood behind him.

"I said I loved you," John whispered.

Alan jumped in his chair, but he refused to face John. Instead, he picked up his fork and shoveled another piece of meat into his mouth. "And *I said* fuck off."

With that, John lunged from behind, the raised cleaver in hand. He brought it down and planted it into Alan's chest. As he released the handle, John watched Alan's whole body began to convulse. He tried using his shaky hands to unbury the cleaver.

John came around to face Alan and pushed Alan's fretful arms aside as he clutched the handle of the cleaver. He tugged it from his chest and a crackle emitted like that of a blazing log in a fireplace. John raised the blood-soaked blade high in the air and droplets of crimson softly pelted his face. Ah, Alan's blood on his flesh. *Let it soak into my pores.*

"I know you will be with me, Alan. I know how to prepare you for our union."

John plunged the cleaver between the tender flesh of Alan's right shoulder blade and his neck. The blood spitting from the wound stifled the beginning of Alan's scream, and John knelt down and held onto Alan's weakening arms. He opened his mouth to the blood that shot from Alan's neck. It spurted into his mouth and over his lips like a lazy lover.

Later that week, another man would arrive as John's dinner guest. He would have the same physical characteristics as Alan. The main course would be ravioli prepared from Alan's innards. The sauce would have to be just right.

* * *

"It looks delicious," Caden remarked, as the plate of manicotti was set before him.

John left for a moment and returned with the almost-empty bottle of Pinot. He filled Caden's glass. "This will go well with the cuisine."

Once the prep work of extracting David's intestines had been complete, it was simply a matter of boiling the ridged, wormy shells to kill all the bacteria. Not to mention it softened the tough exterior. After eleven minutes at a rigorous boil, the color of the innards had become pale gray. However, the marinara sauce that smothered the meal could easily hide the odd color. But before that, John carefully loaded the tubes with ricotta, mozzarella and Parmigianino cheeses. After placing them in a non-stick baking pan, he poured a tomato basil marinara over the half dozen stuffed tubes. Twenty minutes later, he topped off the dish with fresh grated parmesan and accented the red sauce with a hint of parsley.

John sat across from Caden and waited for the young man take his first bite. After Caden had packed his mouth full of manicotti—pieces of David and, more importantly, Alan—John satiated his own appetite. He bit in to the tender intestine of David, savoring the cheeses and the bitterness of the human organ that encased them. As he chewed, he took a sip of wine. An orgasm of flavors burst in his mouth—sour, faintly sweet, and richly creamy. Ah, he could have chewed that one piece forever, never allowing his taste buds to be accosted by any other flavors.

John finally gazed from his plate to his guest. "How is it?"

"It's a bit tough," Caden analyzed.

"It's cooked *al dente*."

"Oh."

John watched Caden take another piece of dinner into his mouth. After two chews, the young man quickly grabbed the linen napkin beside his plate and expelled the food into it. Caden placed his fork beside the plate and took a sip of wine.

"You can't be finished yet, Alan." John's stare became intense, squinted.

"Caden."

"What?"

"My name is Caden. I don't know who the fuck Alan is." Caden pushed his chair back from the dining table and stretched his legs forward.

John rose from his own cushioned chair, slowly approaching the opposite side of the table and passing his visitor. "What about David? Do you know who David is?" John grabbed a braided rope from the desk behind Caden.

"I have a friend named David," Caden called back as he took another sip of his blood wine.

"Is he alive?" John took slow and careful steps toward the back of the chair in which Caden sat.

The young man laughed. "I hope so; I just talked to him earlier."

"Of course," John joined the playful amusement. "Then I guess he's not the same David lying in a pool of blood on my bedroom floor."

Before Caden had a chance to turn his head, confused by his host's comment, John grabbed the young man's arms and pulled them behind the back of the chair. Although Caden had bucked up from his seat—pelvis thrusting upward and legs kicking—John casually confined him to the dining chair. First, he wound the rope around Caden's wrists so that the young man was unable to move his arms from behind him. In quick succession, John wrapped the rope around Caden's chest, waist, and legs, making the man immobile. All the while, Caden's screams repeated, "What the fuck are you doing?"

John's nonchalant reply was "Stop resisting."

John walked around the chair to face Caden, and he screeched like a girl. "What the fuck, man?" John pulled back his fist and launched it forward, landing a flat knuckle on Caden's mouth. Caden's cries were immediately silenced as blood erupted from his plump lips.

181

"There, now that we have an understanding Alan..."

"My name is Ca—"

Another right jab plowed into his left eye.

"Your name is Alan," John reiterated.

Caden stared at the harsh lines that made up John's determined face. His host's brow was contorted, lowered in fortitude, and the man's eyes were narrow and cold, as if his stare were piercing right through him. Caden could feel the blood pulse beneath his swollen eye and the warm fluid run over his lower lip. His sniffles echoed through the intimidating silence as he attempted to rationalize with the man named John. "What do you want?"

"I want you, of course. I've always wanted you, Alan."

Caden began to open his mouth to speak, but John immediately cut off his words.

"I know, you say your name is not Alan, but you've been drinking his blood. You've feasted on his insides. You see, there's a bit of Alan in the cuisine. I think if you eat some more, you may begin to feel him inside of you. Only then will you become him. Then, we will be together. I'm bringing you back, Alan."

"You're fucking crazy," Caden cried.

John landed a heavy backhand against Caden's cheek. He grabbed a stuffed manicotti from the young man's plate and rammed it into his mouth. John shoved it in as far as he could as Caden began choking and gasping. "Chew it! Eat it you fucking baby!"

Caden spit out the food and coughed. John slapped him and his tears spilled down his reddened face.

John shoveled more manicotti into Caden's mouth, forcing it down his throat with his fingers. His gag reflex created a hollow gulping thud, and John retracted his hand and observed the mashed food projecting from Caden's mouth. A rush of ruby-colored vomit poured out, and Caden took in a deep breath and began sobbing. "Why? Why won't you stop?"

Like a child throwing a fit, John stomped away.

Caden began screaming like a girl. "Stop! Please?" His squealing sobs cut off every other word.

John placed his hands over his ears. *Why aren't you here with me? I need you now. I thought he could be you. He looks just like you, Alan. Why won't you come back to me?*

Caden's shrieks overpowered John's thoughts, and he gritted his teeth in frustration and raced to the kitchen. He returned behind Caden with a pair of meat-cutting scissors in hand. Caden continued to wail like a banshee as he wrestled with the ropes that restrained him. "Why? Why? Why?!"

John grabbed Caden's blonde locks of hair and pulled his head back. He locked eyes with Caden as he stared directly down at the young man's face. "You aren't good enough to be *him*!" John pushed the scissors down and gouged the blades into his throat. The beginning of a yelp was cut short by a gurgle as a red fountain of gore jutted from Caden's throat. John extracted the scissors and repeated the stabs into the torn flesh of his dinner guest's throat several more times before he stopped.

"Fucking, whiny bitch!" John yelled at Caden's lifeless body.

It doesn't matter. You'll come back to me eventually, Alan.

That, John always knew. After all, there were many more meals left on the menu.

THE MAKER OF FINE INSTRUMENTS

BY BRENDAN CONNELL

A smile appeared on Willi's lean face. He considered his friend's remark to be absurdly naïve.

"Smile if you want," Kurt continued, "but trust me—you really do need to get out into the world more. You're becoming a hermit."

"When I'm playing professionally I'll be out in the world plenty."

"And when you're in a madhouse?" Kurt asked sarcastically. He looked at Willi's small head crowned with longish brown hair and highlighted by a pair of cerulean eyes set in the two dark, gouged-out caverns above his cheeks. "Yes, I could see you going mad. You are the type."

"I won't offer you another beer, Kurt; you're intoxicated."

Kurt drained the last drops of bitter fluid from the glass in front of him. "I don't want one here," he said rising to his feet. "I'll get one at the club. Still don't want to come?"

"No, thanks. I really do have to practice."

Kurt twisted his lips in obvious disdain. "Ok," he said, waving his hand. "*Auf Wiedersehen.*"

Willi, when finally alone, opened a fresh bottle of Franziskaner for himself and lost no time in setting to work. He took his cello out of its case, stroked its neck and then, sitting down, proceeded to go over his scales. The bow danced easily over the strings and Willi's somewhat cadaverous face took on a beatific look, not unlike that of a martyred saint. He played well, with clean tones, his fingers going down in such a way as to hide their unequal strength. He went through a number of pieces, sipping on beer the whole while and certainly enjoying himself much more than if he'd been amongst people at a bar or club.

It grew late; his fingers somewhat clumsy; his eyes began to close as he played. He leaned his instrument against the chair, staggered to the couch and lay down, flicking off the light as he did so. Several hours later (it was still totally dark) he awoke, disoriented, his throat parched. He stumbled to his feet and proceeded to make his way to the kitchen. He tripped and fell, feeling his knee crack through something.

"*Verdammt!*" he cried.

When he got up and turned on the light, he saw his violoncello lying on the floor with a great hole through its belly. He stared at the wounded instrument, which lay before him like the expiring corpse of a woman with whom he'd had a deep and intimate physical relationship.

It was a genuine disaster. The cello, an excellent old Giuseppe Pedrazzini, had been given to Willi for his eighteenth birthday by his grandparents, who had undoubtedly paid an exorbitant sum for the instrument, it being hardly one of those run of the mill items turned out of the factories by the hundreds or even thousands.

* * *

The next day found him on the street, the broken cello in its case. He had not slept at all the night before and had spent the morning on the telephone, calling everyone he knew for advice on where he might get the instrument repaired. A fellow student, whom he very much respected, suggested he might try the shop of Charles Martens, who was described to him as 'a complete eccentric, but certainly the best luthier in Zurich'.

Willi thought it was curious he had never heard of the man.

"It's not really so curious," his friend had said. "He's one of those maverick geniuses who are more or less hostile to public scrutiny; the last thing in the world he would want is to have a reputation."

The place was an expansive old structure on a small street called Zollikerstrasse, which Willi reached by taking the tram to Dufourplatz and walking up a steep path in the rain.

He rang the bell, and a minute or two later, the sound of a gruff voice came through the door:

"Who is it?"

"A customer!"

"What nature of customer?"

"I am a cellist!"

The door was opened by a rather short, broad-chested man of about fifty or sixty years of age, a semi-circle of iron grey hair wreathing his bald head. He stared acutely at Willi for a moment, glanced at his cello case and said, "Fine. Come in and we can talk."

Willi followed the man inside, through a very dark vestibule and into a spacious apartment. The place was set up more like the residence of some fin-de-siècle poet than a shop. Beautiful antique furniture was tastefully dispersed. Several valuable quadros hung from the walls. A prayer rug from Ladakh sat in the center of the room. A beautiful English spinet was set against one wall, an extremely antique looking oboe mounted above it, next to which protruded the head of a reindeer stag, a magnificent twenty-pointer. A stuffed quail and a mole sat atop a fifteenth century Florentine armadio; while on a pedestal of its own was a kingfisher. There was an odd but not unpleasant aroma in the room, as if someone had recently been using turpentine and burning joss sticks—a vague fragrance that carried with it something of the opium den, something of the artist's atelier, a touch of the surgical theater.

"So how can I help you?" Martens asked, sitting down and motioning for his guest to do the same.

Willi sat uneasily on the edge of an extremely extravagant Venetian rococo chair. "I—I was hoping you could repair my cello," he began. "It—it's damaged, and I understand that you're something of an expert."

"Let me see it."

Willi rose from his seat and, with trembling hands, took out the damaged cello. Martens investigated the instrument briefly, and said in a rather haughty tone, "I don't have time. I simply don't have time for these sorts of ordinary repairs. Generally I only repair and restore beautiful Italian instruments, or exotic items that are either mine or which I'm very interested in. Your cello here simply does not interest me."

"No?"

"No. And, to be frank, I'm not really sure if you'll find anyone else really able to do the work adequately. It's one thing to repair the body of an instrument, but it is a very different thing, a very difficult thing, to repair its sound. If this one even ever had a sound worth preserving."

"It has—it *had* a wonderful sound! To me it is absolutely worth preserving, and I'll pay for the work."

"You are young. This is probably your first instrument, which is something like a first lover. You cannot bear to let her go.

But in the end, should you follow through with your caprice and have it repaired, you will most likely end up with some patched, regraduated, retrofitted old bass-fiddle, a sort of slatternly whore of a cello. Cigarette?" he offered, opening a case of Egyptians that sat on the little table before him.

Willi abstractedly accepted a cigarette; he inhaled the rich Nilotic smoke, let it surround him like a curling python.

Martens asked him about himself, his musical studies and aspirations. Willi at first responded to the questions somewhat sullenly, but soon grew enthusiastic, as it was impossible for him to be otherwise with a subject that concerned him so deeply. They talked until their cigarettes were smoked down to butts and sat crushed in the ashtray.

"Well," the older man said, "you seem to suffer from audiophilia as I very much do myself. Come, I will show you my workshop."

Willi followed him back, along a hall and into a vast, open room with objects ranged thickly on all sides. A great leather apron hung from a hook. On two workbenches were arranged the usual woodworker's tools—chisels, planes, rasps, awls, etc.—and portions of several instruments in various states of repair. He showed Willi beautiful pieces of Brazilian rosewood, granadilla, and Caribbean mahogany. He had marvellous pieces of elephant ivory, sea-turtle shell, and whalebone; exotic feathers, ungulate horns, coral, and certain reptile and mammal skins used for drum and chordophone membranes.

Instruments were everywhere: English horns, sitars, clarinets, bassoons, a few pianos, trombones, bells, drums, gongs, a balalaika, a glockenspiel—even a Jewish ram's-horn trumpet called a shofar.

Willi looked around with interest. He examined an ngombi, a bow-harp used by the Bakalai tribe of West Africa, constructed of thin wood covered with gazelle-skin; it had eight strings made of dried tree roots; its head was apparently the skull of a human, or possibly an ape, a bizarre and misshapen cranium with bulging glass eyes. Then there was a pair of antique Indian cymbals in massive beaten bronze. And a meijiwiz, a double idioglott reedpipe from Old Palestine made from the wing-bones of an eagle and exquisitely decorated around its finger-holes with concentric circles and insect motifs.

Willi gazed at all this with increasing interest, now examining one item, now another. He tested the tone of a variety of Egyptian violoncello called a kemangeh-a'gouz and caressed the nipple of a Javanese gamelan gong.

"And what is this?" he asked, pointing to an object which hung from the wall, the white and graceful neck of a swan, its open-billed head crowning one end.

"That, my young friend, is a swan's horn. It is my own invention—one I made keeping in mind only the most hardened laws of science."

"Is it real?—I mean, it really does look like an actual swan!"

"It *is* an actual swan. The head and neck and a bit of the breast of an actual swan, preserved, even somewhat beautified, with glass-like enamel." He reached up and took it down from the wall. "The unusual conformation of the wind pipe of the bird makes it ideal to be transformed into a horn. These properties were first observed by Aldrovandus, though due to today's rather lame level of education, I cannot expect you to have heard of the man. In any case, the length of the swan's neck far exceeds that of its gullet. It has also in its chest a sinuous revolution; that is, when wind rises from its lungs, it ascends not directly into the throat, but first descends into the capsulary receptacle of the breast bone; by a serpentine recurvation it ascends again into the neck; and so by the length thereof, a musical modulation is affected. As you can see, I've had to add a few accoutrements, but what I have added does for the most part follow the bird's natural structure, though my creation here is of course better formed for music."

So saying, he put his lips to a mouthpiece fitted to the lower end of the object and began to play. The sound was incredibly strange, superbly sweet. Martens stood with his legs slightly apart, eyes closed, a look of supreme concentration on his face as he blew forth wind into the outlandish instrument he had created. Music filled the room, almost melancholic, thoroughly mystical, great cries of angst interwoven with splinters of pitch, exceedingly sharp, as precious as diamonds. Feathery high notes flew up, seemed to melt in the air, and were suddenly juxtaposed with resonating bass, klaxons of most thrilling, almost impudent flourish. The hair on the back of Willi's neck stood on end. The complex orgy of intonations that poured forth from that twisted white neck thoroughly affected his nature, one which was rather absurdly sensitive to the grace of fine music.

"As you can see," Martens said when he had finished, "it is not your run-of-the-mill wind instrument, but a rare item reserved for the true epicure of melody." He twisted his lips into something resembling a smile. "Of course the 'swan's horn' is not your instrument; you are a player of the cello. You might look at this piece here; it is quite decent, certainly better than the item you brought in for repair."

Willi looked at the cello Martens had produced, though in his abstracted state, he knew not from where. The instrument was a beautiful 1701 Stradivari with a two-piece back of maple of medium curl, ascending from the joint. The cello was perfectly in tune, and had obviously been played only a short time before.

"Don't just dabble with the strings, let me hear something!" Martens demanded.

Willi, though unaccountably nervous, proceeded to play a piece by Luigi Boccherini. The instrument itself was precious, delivering a peculiar nectarine-like sound which had the solidity of stone, a rich, powerful bass, yet was full of light and air in its vibrant upper register. Feeling the fine tool respond easily to his touch, the young man was inspired, forgot his discomfort, and executed the piece exceptionally well.

"You play not at all badly," Martens said, though neither his face nor voice betrayed enthusiasm. "Your tone is clean and even, and though I would certainly not call your phrasing impeccable, it is quite decent for a tyro. My opinion is that you hold promise."

"If one day I could play half so well as Rostropovich or Yo Yo Ma, I would be more than content."

"Rostropovich and Yo Yo Ma!" Martens growled, showing his teeth. "They are mediocrities—mere mediocrities—scum an ambitious schoolboy like you should easily be able to surpass."

Willi hardly believed what he was hearing. The man before him, though he undoubtedly knew music quite well, was also most certainly a bit of a madman. To insult two of the world's greatest virtuosi of the cello! If that was not raging madness Willi did not know what was.

Martens looked at the young man with piercing eyes. "Do you think I am a fool?" he asked.

"I never said anything of the kind!" Willi protested.

"A face like yours is easy enough to read. Here, give me that instrument!"

So saying, he literally yanked the cello out of Willi's hands. A moment later, the older man was seated on the edge of a work bench, the cello between his knees, the bow flying over the strings. He played Popper's *Spinning Song*. The lightness of his cross-string bowing at the top of the instrument was genuinely awe-inspiring; his technique was wonderfully fluid, near to arrogant. The man exuded the supreme knowledge and blunt confidence of a master. Notes were paraded forth in astonishingly quick succession, yet each one was endowed with an amazing degree of clarity, as distinct and expressive as human speech.

When Martens had finished, Willi stood silent. He had certainly never seen playing of this caliber before, playing so sharp it could very nearly be termed dangerous, and he was in something of a state of shock.

"Your playing is . . ." he murmured, without finishing the sentence.

"My playing is good," Martens said. "It is quite good—actually marvellous—certainly better than those heroes of yours. The only man who ever played the *Spinning Song* as well as myself was Arnold Földesy, Popper's pupil."

"I have recordings of him at home."

"Then, if the mechanism of your ears is in order, you can see that my views are not so extravagant."

"Then your own recordings . . ."

"I have none."

"But . . ."

"Young man, one truly interested in the musical arts has better things to do than imprint their genius on circles of vinyl or little digital disks, so the parade of maggots that inhabit this earth can have their ears massaged while they go about their mundane little tasks!"

Willi was silent for a moment, humbled. "Your cello is wonderful," he said, "but I'm sure I could not afford to buy it. So, I suppose I should not take up any more of your time."

Martens gave a short laugh. "You shall take up more of my time; I can see quite clearly that that is your destiny. Come back tomorrow, at two in the afternoon, and I will give you a few pointers on your playing. A lesson. You're obviously in sore need of a bit of proper instruction."

"Tomorrow?"

"Yes. And here, put away this violoncello and take it with you. I insist that you practice on it tonight."

"But—But don't you need it?"

"Need it? Look around you. Does it seem that I lack instruments? Besides, this is just a loan, for a few weeks, or months, maybe more, I don't know; it all depends on your comportment."

Willi left the place with his head almost spinning. He could not believe the instrument he had in his hands. The whole thing seemed a little surreal. He could not really say that he liked Martens, but he certainly was attracted by him. The man's haughty fervour was undoubtedly not unlike that of other great musicians and composers of the past—like Gluck, like Beethoven, like Schönberg, who would smilingly bow to the sounds of ignorant hisses as if he were being applauded.

* * *

Willi began to take frequent lessons from Martens, who was a demanding, often aggressive teacher. Occasionally he hit the student with his bow. Sometimes he burst out into peals of grating laughter at Willi's efforts. Yet the young man was thoroughly content. It seemed to him that he was passing through a barrier, finally learning the subtle secrets of music that had long escaped him while studying under normal teachers. Martens, with his air of authority and genius, his assertive excellence in any instrument he approached, made all others seem like slothful fools in comparison.

He was something of the ideal interpreter, being fully capable of grasping the period, style, taste, and intention of all the compositions he played. He showed Willi much about the necessary relaxation of certain muscles and tendons and, at the same time, the stretching of others.

And gradually, the student was shown things, the things Martens valued highly, his most treasured instruments, both those he collected and the items he himself had made. Several back rooms on the ground floor were set up like those of a museum, with everything arranged tidily, many of the smaller objects set in cases. There was a six-key bassoon of the Jeanet school, as well as a fine square piano by Erard Frères. With unsuppressed excitement Martens showed Willi his collection of exotic

191

instruments which included many strange and valuable pieces. There was a slit drum from the Camaroons, and then a rather gruesome specimen, a human thigh-bone trumpet from Tibet, a portion of the bone sawed cleanly through to form embouchure.

Along with all this were the instruments Martens himself had designed and made: a wind instrument he had created from the cured proboscis of an African elephant—a giant blackened S-shaped tube, one end fitted with a mouth piece made from an ivory tusk—and another from the neck of a giraffe. There was a drum he'd made from a camel's hump, and a kind of dulali, a nose flute, he had constructed from a marmot, a funny little item which, when played, sounded not unlike the frail weeping of a human child.

Martens showed Willi a shepherd's shawm constructed, in part, from the entire body of a duck-billed platypus, and then a most curious stringed instrument made from an Australian bat, a delicate miniature harp which he claimed sounded especially charming when played in the stillness of an evening.

"What in the world is that?" Willi cried, pointing to an intimidating and coarse mass of fur, sharply divided horizontally in two contrasting colors, the top half made up of a broad head with a short and square muzzle, upper neck, and back being silvery-grey while the limbs, belly, lower cheeks, and muzzle were jet black.

Martens picked the object up and turned it in his hands. "This is my redefinition of a honey-badger," he said. "It's a large mustelid which I have taken the liberty of converting into a most rare melodic apparatus. Notice the bottom end of the belly, where it widens, enclosing a decorative serpentine panel of mammoth ivory and baleen. And the strings, see how they pass through this moveable piece of bone, which is quite simply the creature's femur; it's used for altering pitch, very much like a capotasto."

"But who in God's name would want such a thing?"

"The Crown Prince of Kuwait for one. He purchased a piece from me very similar to this some years back and paid a pretty sum for it."

"I never knew that such strange instruments existed," Willi said. "Some of these are truly fantastical."

"Oh, one can make musical instruments out of all sorts of things. The ancients were much more flexible than us moderns and had not such a narrow range. These days, however, people are hardly interested in music as an art, and much less so the manufacture of the fine apparatuses necessary to produce it properly. When I was younger, and living in Munich, I made a great drum out of a hippopotamus. The large, thick-skinned African river animal filled an entire side of my studio. In the morning, I would beat it, that great piece of parchment, and make the hemisphere within resound most beautifully. But oh, how the neighbors complained!"

* * *

Willi kept his appointments with Martens religiously. There was no question that the man, aside from being a truly great musician himself, was also endowed with the qualities of a great teacher. He made Willi feel thoroughly dissatisfied with himself, and in turn made the young man focus all the more, striving after the ideal of which Martens was continually talking, the perfection which he indicated as only accessible to a few select souls.

"If you listen to me," Martens said, "and if you are a truly obedient student, one day you might make music the like of which the world has never heard before—music approximating the collisions of planets and suns, of universes belching out new galaxies where the last tonal frontiers are left behind as sounds issued from you like clusters of stars! There is an alchemy to all this, an alchemy of mind and flesh!"

These words were spoken on the sixth week of their acquaintance. Four days later, after the older man had given Willi some valuable hints on the placement of the bow between the bridge and fingerboard, he asked, "Would you like to see something of interest?"

Willi said that he would, and Martens led his student to a set of chambers on the second floor that he had never been in before.

"I do not even allow the cleaning woman in here," Martens said as he unlocked a door. "This is where my most precious instruments are kept—it is where I conduct the most brilliant of my musical experiments."

Willi became very grave as he followed his teacher. He felt as if he were entering a religious sanctuary and was about to be initiated into the rights of some sort of peculiar cult by its high priest.

The first room they walked through was completely bare. Not a single rug or piece of furniture sat on the parquet floor over which their footsteps echoed. They entered a second chamber, a room that was almost completely dark and the windows were covered with thick red drapes. Martens flicked a switch and the place flooded with a soft and powerful luminosity, like that in the workroom of a dentist. One wall was neatly lined with bows and various utensils, tools of all sorts, scalpels and odd shaped pieces of steel that, while being obviously antique, veritably had the appearance of abstract sculpture, the whole array clean and glittering like jewellery. Toward the back of the room was a great blue curtain that hung wall to wall from a single rod.

"This is where I give my private concerts," Martens said with a wry smile.

Willi stood silent and anxiously ran his tongue over the texture of his teeth. He thought he heard a faint noise, issuing from behind the curtain.

"Is someone back there?" he asked with unease.

"Not someone," the maestro replied, approaching the curtain and pulling it aside. "Not someone, but objects, articles whose nature should be clear to you from their context." He took a step back and stood with his posterior towards Willi, the surface of his body from there to his neck arched triumphantly. "What is it you see? What is it you think you see?"

"I don't know."

Willi perceived several sets of eyes, blinking, staring from behind a framework of metal drawn out into threads. Odd things were there, things which he could almost guess at, but did not dare because they were animate. Martens stood erect, dominant, like some deity or giant, some being to be worshipped as having control over life-forms and mystical spheres.

"Every item of nature is endowed with its own individual voice. Imagine the infinite songs of the cosmos, of the force controlling all phenomena of the physical world—no more human voices—the cosmos is not especially human—it is often quite as savage as chaos!"

He opened the door of one of the mesh cages, and the next moment a great band of distorted flesh rested in his arms.

Willi involuntarily retreated a step.

"You need not be afraid of her," Martens said coolly. "She is quite harmless, very nearly domesticated, thoroughly de-toothed and de-clawed and simply waiting for skilled hands to caress her strings. You still hesitate? Watch!"

He snatched a great bow from the wall, hooked his foot around the leg of a chair, pulled it towards him, sat down and leaned the strange living apparatus up against one knee. The creature's eyes darted fitfully around the room, thoroughly pathetic. Then the bow touched the fibers that stretched across the gut of that wild dog-like animal, the bweha, that poor scavenger plucked from the savannahs for most outlandish musical experiments—the bow touched those fibres, danced over them, rending forth sounds thoroughly peculiar, a piece of music that could very well have been composed in the murky world of the intermediate state. The tone was large, ripe and breathy; grave and patently troubling. The eerie melody seemed as ridges of water curling over, crashing on the remote and desolate shores of the underworld; as clouds of *Fledermäuse*, wings beating, might swirl rapturously upward to feed on other clouds of gnats; a strange, spooky piece it was, intoxicating as opium, violent as a homicide. Dismally dark passages collided with stormy orgasms of sound as Martens ran his fingers over the strings, slashed away with the bow as if he were decapitating some host of helpless enemies; now stabbed solemnly, as if he were sinking it in the breast of a betrayer.

"The ancient Egyptians," he said in a sonorous voice, spacing his words out like a poem. "The ancient Egyptians...those most mysterious...most brilliant...dwellers of the past...believed a jackal-headed god...Anubis...guided the dead...to those who judged their souls."

Here his thumb and forefinger pinched the creature violently around the neck. It let out a siren-like wail; the sound of delicate china shattering into a thousand luminous fragments; a welter of tonalities to make ears bleed, eyes water, and the blood go sour in veins. And then the tempo changed, became more rapid, the music described a wild chase through a phonically dangerous fairyland; every note sounded with immense importance, as if thousands of lives and destinies rested on the power of Martens' bow. And then a final disarming breath of lyrical innocence, artfully superficial, imbued with a complete and obvious lack of candour, a sweet but deceitful ambrosia, a strange and concluding strain tempting the listener to balance on the lips of this modest melodious nepenthes, only to fall inside and be consumed by its digestive enzymes.

Martens was finished; his eyes glowed, radiant as from some inner inferno.

Willi was shaken to his soul; he remained rooted to the spot, lips parted.

"So you enjoyed it?" Martens asked.

"In," Willi's voice cracked. "Yes, in a shocking sort of way."

"Shocking? One of the functions of great music is to shock!"

"But this animal . . . The cruelty!"

"Cruelty!" the maestro cried, his face growing red. "Did I invite you into my inner sanctum to hear such banalities? I am not some kind of simpleton who makes mice sing by hitting them on the head with a mallet; I am an artist, a man who practices his talent with both skill and good taste. I see you quiver. You think you know what good taste is, but you do not, you know very nearly nothing young whelp!" A swollen vein appeared on Martens' forehead. He continued, angry and excited, "You have your choice between being an artist and some kind of worm or insect; you can either reach the stars, or creep on the ground like some gnawing worm my foot should crush!"

Willi felt his head begin to swim. His vision became blurry; he felt humiliated, sickened—upset with Martens, but even more upset with himself, for his own inadequacy. He turned towards the door.

"If you wish to leave, then please do so," Martens said coldly. "I will not stop you. You might return when you feel able to humble yourself, when you feel able to see and hear great things, feel capable of taking instruction."

* * *

When Willi reached his own apartment on Eidmattstrasse he could not relax, practice or sit still. His mind was full of the strange things he'd seen and heard, of Martens. There was something so mysteriously exciting about this man, so utterly magnetic. To be pushed out of his presence made Willi feel horribly depressed. He lit a cigarette, took a puff, extinguished it in the ashtray, and walked out the door and down the stairs.

Outside it was overcast, early in the evening; dark grey clouds smirched the sky. He shambled along the street, his small head sunk to his chest and eyes fastened on the ground. It was clear he had to make a decision. Martens frightened him, but the man also enthralled. Willi wanted very much to learn from him, to be his disciple—but he was uncertain what it would cost, for there was something about the maestro that was unaccountably dark, possibly dangerous.

He walked along the Bahnhofstrasse, and without really thinking what he was doing, entered the Carlton Bar, a place he would normally never go—even if he was up for venturing out into the world. Severe bankers sipped glasses of beer and knots of younger people chatted around tables over cigarettes and coffee.

Willi sat down at an empty table by the window and ordered a small lager. He took a sip and stared blankly at the table in front of him. In his mind he still saw those fitful eyes, that wild-dog-like apparatus, and heard its cadences. It was a monstrosity, yet he could not deny that he was enriched for having heard it. The making of such a device was certainly a great accomplishment, yet could he trust to put himself in the hands of the maker?

"So you have ventured out into the world at last!"

Willi looked up. It was Kurt, standing over him.

"I was passing by and saw your face in the window," his friend continued. "At first I thought it couldn't be you."

"It's me. I am drinking a lager."

"Perfect. Then you can buy me one as well."

Kurt sat down and lit a cigarette, exhaling two jets of bluish smoke through flaring nostrils. The waitress came and he ordered.

"So," he said when his beer had arrived and he had wet his lips, "you're taking the day off from practice for once?"

Willi shrugged his shoulders and took a swallow of his own beer.

Kurt laughed shortly. "My god!" he said. "You look even more depressed than usual. So, maybe you've finally lost your mind, just like I said!"

"And you?"

"Me! I am doing what any man under the age of thirty should—looking at the young ladies, drinking, enjoying myself. Even if you are mad you surely know what I mean. That is what sitting here and paying six francs for a beer is all about anyhow, isn't it—to be in the company of humans? Come, drink up; we will go to the Oliver Twist—the women are more in our category there."

"No, I can't," Willi said getting up from his seat, though his glass was still half full. "I—I have an appointment. Sorry, goodbye."

Without waiting for a reply he rushed up to the counter, paid for the drinks and exited the bar. It was nearly dark outside and beginning to rain. Kurt's commonplace words were still crawling in his ears. Young ladies, drinking, enjoying oneself—these were surely the occupations of the non-entity. Such a creature truly was an insect in comparison to the sublime Martens.

Between the two evils, he thought, Martens is the lesser—or maybe I should really say the greater. If he is evil, at least he is great in his wickedness. Kurt is simply sordid. To lead such a commonplace, physical life as his would make me miserable. It would be impossible; it is much too late for me to turn back.

He now walked with determined, long strides, his eyes keen and head uplifted. Back at the apartment he practised vigorously, until past two in the morning.

* * *

Willi returned to Martens, thoroughly repentant, thoroughly humbled. He offered his most sincere apologies for his lack of insight, and the teacher haughtily accepted them.

"If you listen to me, you will one day play like a god. As it is, when I listen to you, I feel as if you were trying to chip frozen notes out of blocks of ice. There is no personality; you treat the instrument as an object separate from yourself; you really need to be one with it, your every fiber attuned to that other scene of existence, that of the clef, the minim, quavers, bars, and slurs—a parallel universe to that of ordinary man, where countless births and deaths happen with the stroke of a bow. But sometimes I think that maybe you lack sincerity, maybe you do not really care for the music as I do."

"I am prepared to do whatever it takes to be a great player," Willi said with feeling. "Show me the path, and I will follow."

"Ah, if you only meant it! You could be far greater than I if you were only able to make the necessary sacrifices. My own aspirations have always been put in check because of my inability to treat myself as an object. The seer cannot pretend to be the unattached seen. Yet an object is what I sorely need—a human being, a young fellow like you to mold."

198

"But that is what I am here for—to be molded!"

The disgust Willi initially felt for the strange living instruments of Martens was reversed into a dynamic enthusiasm. He investigated these creatures with interest. There was an instrument made from a living vulture, stripped of feathers, its body covered with a marquetry of ivory and abalone shell, sound holes short and perfunctory hollowed from its chest-cavity, a remarkable piece which, to play, required iron-clad control. Then there was a deer with three legs severed from its body, and the fourth, the right hind, left in place with the meat between the skin and bone extracted, disintegrated with a delicate application of diluted hydrochloric acid; and then the hard substance, that *osso*, hollowed out into a pipe; a musical instrument to be played by blowing in at one end while the wind was directed through the animal's hind quarters and croup, along its back and withers, and then out its mouth, into which a bell was fastened.

Willi himself began to enjoy strumming on a cat, shaved of fur and turned into a kind of thumb piano, its back fitted with seven iron tongues decorated with bronze studs at both ends with iron and brass fittings, a portion of its body skilfully hollowed out, yet without mortal consequence, without destroying the inner workings of the organs, a pretty zigzag pattern incised on the creature's flesh; an instrument expertly made, with a sonorous tone.

Willi's favorite, however, was a flamingo which had been divested of those parts of itself used for walking; its beautiful long neck had been stiffened with strips of pine and then inlaid with a finger-board bearing twenty metal frets; thirteen tuning-pegs were mounted down one side, two large pegs for a pair of *cikari* strings and eleven small pegs for sympathetic strings. It was a gorgeous pink chordophone with a tone delicate and ornamental as gold filigree. Martens was able to play this with an almost x-ray clarity of articulation and an exceptionally wide range of touch and tone that filled Willi with wonder.

"It is the most beautiful instrument I have ever seen," he said.

"Oh, I will make better—you for instance and something else for myself."

Willi looked at him inquiringly.

Martens showed him his latest acquisition, the large flightless double-wattled cassowary, a colorful creature with a brilliant blue

199

and purple head bearing a kind of keel-shaped helmet, red flesh hanging down from its throat, and a body covered with long black feathers. The great brute strutted back and forth along the narrow limitations of the cage, an odd and atrabilious look in its eyes.

"In evolutionary terms," Martens said, "the flightless birds are some of the earliest types to have developed. I am highly interested in this creature's throat, and am quite certain something really magnificent can be done with it."

* * *

"You, of course, understand you'll never be the same?"

"I don't want to be the same. You have shown me other worlds, other landscapes, and those are the sort of places I want to live. I feel this is the most decisive moment of my life, and I'm determined to go forward!"

Martens looked at the young man intently; he lit one of his strong Egyptian cigarettes and proceeded to explain about the first phase:

"Normally, the intestines are pulled from the animal immediately after its slaughter, while the gut is still hot. This ensures the blood vessels that run into the casing will be broken off close to the gut wall. To allow the organs to cool is to risk having these veins break off as much as five centimeters away from the casing wall. This creates 'whiskers' that lower the quality of the gut for musical string use. To ensure the best quality, the gut must be removed immediately, separated from the fat, and put into cool water. Traditionally, the string makers were located very close to slaughterhouses, so they could get the guts as hot and fresh as possible. My method is of course a thousand times superior. I do not even have the guts leave their source. By letting them remain, more or less, in their natural setting, I can make strings of truly distinguished excellence, instruments thoroughly individual."

"But how will I be able to eat?"

"Oh, you don't need to feel any anxiety regarding that. I'm not going to use it in its entirety, just a good bit of the second cut of the intestine, where the muscular fibers are longer, but far less necessary to your anatomy. You will still be able to take foods into the mouth and swallow them. Though, of course, I would have to recommend you stay away from tough things, red meat and the like. But that is a small sacrifice after all. Soups can be quite nourishing."

"I've always liked soups."

All the old fashioned equipage appeared, objects sharp of tooth and edge, a trephine, canulas—all the outdated tools which served him better than the precision gear of the modern specialist. The air became dense with the smell of carbolic acid and chloroform. An incision was made; Martens immersed Willi's guts, the 'second cut' as he had said, in cold water for several hours to make them pliable, then gave them a nice hot soak for about forty-five minutes before machining; using a metal-bladed scraper he stripped off the outer serosa from the muscle layers, pulling away the long white thread of tissue, while at the same time crushing the inside mucosa membrane, so soft, thin, and pliable. He worked with vigor until the mucosa was a veritable liquid and could be squeezed down and out the opening he had created in the casing tube. Using a splitting horn, he divided the gut into four ribbons, long, white and beautiful, thoroughly chaste. Continuing his strategy, that of procedure and design, he changed the exterior contours of Willi, gave his back a high and full arch so as to give lateral push to the strings, which ran over the fingerboard of his thorax, and to distribute that push evenly over the plate.

"Done?" Willi murmured, feeling himself drift up from his anaesthetised state.

"Not quite, but we are not too far away. I still have to fit you up—shape the pegs, fingerboard, nut, and saddle to match the particular behavior of your body. That is, of course, after I give you a soul!"

Using a Mennell's patented endo-tracheal apparatus, Martens re-anaesthetised Willi. The maestro felt his creative energy greatly stirred and determined while finishing the work on his pupil. He removed the cassowary from its cage, anaesthetised it, and when the creature was fully insensible, dragged it with great effort to a work bench, its weight being a good deal more than he'd expected.

Willi's abdomen, divested of some of its interior bulk, was a much changed article; a sound post was inserted to reinforce it on the treble side, to affect the vibration behavior of the plates and counteract the forces acting on it from the strings—naturally to affect the timber of sound and the playability of Willi considerably. The Italian name for the sound post is '*anima*' or 'soul' because of its changeable influence on the sound of an instrument.

201

"This is no good at all," Martens said to himself upon examining the quality of his nearly completed work. "The sound post must not be fitting quite properly to the inside surfaces. *Verflixt!* I'm going to have to go into him again!"

He turned to his selection of gleaming jewels, blades, and gathered a particularly vicious one into the nimble fingers of his right hand. And then, looking around, he was suddenly confronted by the cassowary. The long legs of the bird whipped up in the air; it thrust them forward, against Martens' chest, and the man was hurled to the floor. It was indeed heavier than he had thought, weighing a good one-hundred and forty pounds, far too much for the quantity of anaesthetic he had given it.

"You bastard!" he screamed, and made an attempt to stab at one of the bird's legs with the scalpel in his hand.

The cassowary was obviously frightened, disoriented from the anaesthetic and angry to begin with. By nature it was a creature easily provoked. The loud human cry, along with a slight prick it received to its leg, made it even more alarmed. It darted its long neck forward; a sixtieth part of a minute later, it had Martens' left eyeball lodged in its sharp beak, having plucked out the organ of sight with a single and swift jerking motion. Martens, enraged and somewhat shocked, called out to Willi, but the young man was still fully anaesthetised and could offer no assistance. The cassowary, having seen blood, grew tremendously excited and proceeded to attack in earnest with the sharply pointed nails of its three-toed feet, digging deep into the man's neck with the dagger-like middle claw, which was a good five inches in length and as dangerous as the blade of a stiletto. The carotid artery was ruptured and Martens could do nothing more than gaze on with a single bleary eye while the blood flowed fast and freely from him, with a gurgling sound somewhat reminiscent of the Indian dholak drum when rubbed with certain slight motions of the wrist.

* * *

It was a beautiful and warm day. The outdoor tables in front of the cafés were practically full. Colorful beds of flowers, of zinnias, scabiosas, and daisies touched the air with their perfume. Children played in the streets; young women wore skirts and walked with bare legs.

Kurt had not seen Willi for some time, since the day at the Carlton Bar, and as he was walking along Eidmattstrasse, decided to drop in and pay him a visit. As he entered the large old building, he heard screams, some sort of disturbance coming from above, as if an argument were occurring in one of the flats. A woman with a pinched face drooping with folds of yellowish skin accosted him on his way up. Her eyes were dull and bilious; she opened the grim wound of her mouth and spat out her words:

"You going to see your friend are you—the freak musician up there?"

"If you mean Willi," Kurt replied, "then yes, I'm visiting him. What business is it of yours?"

"He has been up there rocking away pretty much constantly. Playing terrible stuff, much more trying than it used to be. Before, I did not mind it so much, but now, I feel like I was listening to something nasty—nasty and sinful! If you could tell him to cool it off it would be very much appreciated. If he doesn't, I will just have to call the police!"

Kurt turned and trudged up the stairs without replying; the woman continued to talk behind him; as her voice receded into the background, the resonance from Willi's apartment became prominent. Kurt stopped at the door and listened, shuddered, bunched his fingers into fists; he felt as if needles were being inserted into his ears, his auditory nerves pierced, as they gathered in bizarre accents, a plaintive twanging, like the effects of phrenitis, confused strider that made him think of brutal torture, of men being whipped with fronds of thorns and couples compelled to sport naked upon beds of shattered glass. Certainly if ever there was a music composed out of the torments of hell, this would be it, the music of the damned soul, of the hungry ghost lost and condemned to wander throughout eternity over dead plains in search of some morsel of food for its great swollen but empty belly; of women plummeting into lakes of pitch, blood, and mire and men made to wallow in tubs of gore and filth. This was music rank as the obnoxious odors of an unbearable place of punishment, music without any true melodic or harmonic line, wherein the architecture was destroyed as if with a bomb; music suffused with agony, without even an instant's relief from most excruciating physical and mental pain.

Kurt flung one fist forward and beat against the wood; without waiting for a reply, he gripped the handle and threw the door open.

Willi sat on a wooden chair in the center of the room, shirtless, wearing nothing but a pair of dark blue shorts. He strummed away on the thick strings made from his own guts, which were secured below his belly to a ring slotted over a large ivory pin stemming from his single garment. He was a phonocidal maniac, no longer quite human but rather a variety of strange monster, the quasi-quintessential dark fantasy instrument; his back was perforated with charismatically flame-shaped sound holes, his abdomen inlaid with graceful ebony fleur-de-lis and pierced with carved Gothic rosettes, and his neck stretched out grossly, into a kind of cylindrical rod, with four ebony pegs set with lozenges of pearl. Yet the sound he gave forth, soulless, was offensively off-kilter, searing the ears in its shrieking intensity as if living beings were being lowered into pits of boiling fire, hung by their tongues, skewered with white hot irons, made to commit obscene acts with reptilian devils and then tenderised, pounded to pulp with blunt mallets.

Kurt stood transfixed in horror. He felt as if he'd just walked, from the clear and joyful light of day, into the casings of a nightmare. Willi appeared stretched, elongated, and twisted in some strange, unspeakable fashion, made into an incredible, eccentric creature that might have been plucked from a horrid comic strip—a surreal and frightening being, a gross caricature of humanity spliced with violoncello.

A voice cried from downstairs, the sour, shrieking voice of the yellow woman, "Enough of this; I'm calling the police!"

Kurt turned to his friend and called out his name. But Willi did not stop; he merely looked up with a set of wild, dewy eyes and continued to play, the fingers of his right hand, lithe as snakes, dancing frantically over those strings of his own guts, while his left, metamorphosed into a bow, sawed dextrously away, intensifying the galloping serenade of torment. The sound grew horrendous; a belching massacre of stammered and contorted notes; extreme abstraction and violence mixed together, like a frenzied wolf tearing apart a painting by De Kooning with its jaws; a witch's Sabbath of distortion and dissonance; like some naked and helpless creature being hounded, harried by pursuing fangs through a forest of living blades.

"Willi!" Kurt shouted. "For God's sake, Willi!"

But the tune in no way faltered; on the contrary, Willi, hearing his own name shouted, responded by becoming higher octane than ever. There was a blur of frenetic limbs; his lips were open, vacillating, and his teeth bit down sporadically on his blood-leaking tongue.

Kurt, horrified, stepped backward across the threshold, then turned and ran, practically threw himself down the stairs. In panicked speculation, he wondered what sort of help was possible for that mad and mutated friend of his, and whether he should fetch a psychiatrist, plastic surgeon or priest—or simply flee from all responsibility, pursued as he was by that mad flurry of painfully exotic notes which were like a swarm of toxic, stinging things.

THE AUTHORS

INANNA GABRIEL lives in Columbus, Ohio. Her work has appeared in several online horror and sci-fi magazines including *Midnight in Hell* and *Dark Fire Fiction*, as well as in print in the anthology *The Creative Minds Collection* from Misanthrope Press. Visit her website at www.inannagabriel.com.

BRANDON FORD is the author of the novels *Crystal Bay* and *Splattered Beauty*. He has also contributed to the anthologies *Abaculus 2007* and *Sinister Landscapes*. Visit him at myspace.com/writerbrandonford.

FRANK ROGER was born in 1957 in Ghent, Belgium. His first story appeared in 1975. Since then his stories have appeared in an increasing number of languages in a variety of magazines, anthologies, and other venues, and since 2000, his story collections have been published in various languages. Apart from fiction, he also produces collages and graphic work in a surrealist and satirical tradition. He has more than 700 short story publications (including a few short novels) in 29 languages. Find out more at www.frankroger.be.

STEVEN SHREWSBURY, author of the novel *Hawg*, *Godforsaken* and the forthcoming *Tormentor*, lives in central Illinois. Over 350 of his tales have appeared online or in print in such places as *Apex Magazine*, *Tales of the Mountain State 2*, *Hardboiled Cthulu* and *Deathgrip 2*. Aside from other solo projects, he is hard at work on collaborations with Maurice Broaddus, Nate Southard and Brian Keene. His website is www.stevenshrewsbury.com.

R.J. CAVENDER is the founder of the +Terrible Twelve+ authors group and Editor-in-Chief of the +Horror Library+ series of anthologies. His work has appeared in *NFG Magazine*, *Dark Recesses Press*, *Haunted Attractions*, and the *Our Shadows Speak* anthology. He resides in Tucson, Arizona and is currently working on compiling his next yearly anthology for Cutting Block Press (www.cuttingblock.net).

L. L. SOARES's fiction has appeared in such magazines as *Cemetery Dance*, *Horror Garage*, *Bare Bone*, *Gothic.net* and *Lullaby Hearse*, as well as the anthologies *The Best of Horrorfind 2*, *Right House on the Left* and *Traps*. He is also the current co-chair of the New England Horror Writers (NEHW). He lives with his wife and fellow author Laura Cooney, and their iguana, Pippi Greenstockings. Check out his website at www.llsoares.com, if you dare.

KEVIN LUCIA's short fiction has appeared in *Coach's Midnight Diner*, Shroud Publishing's *Abominations* and *Northern Haunts* anthologies, *Dark Horizons*, *Issues 3 & 4*, and *NextGen Pulp Magazine*, *Issues 1 & 4*. He recently finished his first novel for Shroud Publishing's upcoming dark fantasy series, *The Hiram Grange Chronicles*, entitled, *Hiram Grange & The Chosen One*. Visit him at www.kevinlucia.net.

JESSICA LYNNE GARDNER is a horror writer, business writer, journalist, and poet published in over a dozen anthologies and magazines including *Shroud Magazine*, *Phobia*, *Twisted Tongue*, and *Sinister Landscapes*. She can be found at myspace.com/JessicaLynneGardner and her website www.JessicaLynneGardner.webs.com.

ERIC ENCK is the author of five novels, including *Snuff* (with Adam Huber) and *Tell Me Your Name*. Eric is about as trustworthy as two cannibals giving each other blowjobs. He lives in Delaware.

JAMES ROY DALEY is the author of *The Dead Parade*, released in 2008 by Permuted Press/Swarm Press. He is a professional musician that studied scriptwriting and film making at the Toronto film school. Visit him at jamesroydaley.com.

JOHN EDWARD LAWSON is a Maryland author and editor with nine books published. You can spy on him at www.johnlawson.org.

STEPHEN COUCH is a computer programmer, a cover band vocalist, and a lifelong Texan. His fiction has sold to such markets as *Horror Library Vol.* 3, *Something Wicked*, and *Talebones*. Visit him online and poke him with virtual sticks at www.stephencouch.com.

TREVER PALMER's mother was watching *Creature From The Black Lagoon* when she gave birth to him on April Fool's Day. Since then he's held various jobs which include doing time in a slaughterhouse, a mental hospital, and a porn theater. He now lives with thirteen cats, which tell him what to write. He can be contacted at treverpalmer@hotmail.com.

ANDREW WOLTER is the author of *Nightfall* and *The Rules of Temptation*. He lives and creates within the metropolitan area of Phoenix, Arizona, amidst the stucco and glass that surround his environment. While his writing blurs genre boundaries, Andrew feels there is always a place for darkness in any work of art. He is currently working on a number of new projects, including his first short story collection and a new novel. Visit Andrew Wolter on the web at www.AndrewWolter.com.

BRENDAN CONNELL was born in Santa Fe, New Mexico, in 1970. He has had fiction published in numerous magazines, literary journals and anthologies, including *McSweeney's, Adbusters*, *Leviathan 3* (The Ministry of Whimsy 2002), *Strange Tales* (Tartarus Press 2003) and *Fast Ships, Black Sails* (Nightshade Books 2008). His first novel, *The Translation of Father Torturo*, was published by Prime Books in 2005; his novella *Dr. Black and the Guerrillia* was published by Grafitisk Press the same year.